Being raised in a strict, humorless household
did nothing to dampen Lady Lily Langdon's
romantic nature—nor cool her lifelong affection for Edward Wallis, Earl of Whitby, her
elder brother's oldest, dearest friend. But Edward cannot see the lovely woman she's become for the wild schoolgirl she once was. So
with lessons in flirtation from her American
sister-in-law, Duchess Sophia, Lily means to
open Edward's eyes and win his heart.

But just when her seduction begins to take
hold, tragedy strikes. Edward has lived a rakish life, believing he would never grow old—
and a terrible twist of fate threatens to prove
him right. Yet adversity only strengthens Lily's
resolve to find the ecstasy she knows is waiting in Edward's arms—and to prove to the
handsome, haunted earl that it is *never* too
late to fall desperately in love.

By Julianne MacLean

LOVE ACCORDING TO LILY
MY OWN PRIVATE HERO
AN AFFAIR MOST WICKED
TO MARRY THE DUKE

*If You've Enjoyed This Book,
Be Sure to Read These Other*
AVON ROMANTIC TREASURES

AS AN EARL DESIRES *by Lorraine Heath*
JUST ONE TOUCH *by Debra Mullins*
THE MARRIAGE BED *by Laura Lee Guhrke*
MARRY THE MAN TODAY *by Linda Needham*
TILL NEXT WE MEET *by Karen Ranney*

Coming Soon

TAMING THE BARBARIAN *by Lois Greiman*

Julianne MacLean

Love According to Lily

An Avon Romantic Treasure

AVON BOOKS
An Imprint of HarperCollinsPublishers

This is a work of fiction. Names, characters, places, and incidents are products of the author's imagination or are used fictitiously and are not to be construed as real. Any resemblance to actual events, locales, organizations, or persons, living or dead, is entirely coincidental.

AVON BOOKS
An Imprint of HarperCollins*Publishers*
10 East 53rd Street
New York, New York 10022-5299

Copyright © 2005 by Julianne MacLean
ISBN: 0-06-059729-1
www.avonromance.com

First Avon Books paperback printing: August 2005

Avon Trademark Reg. U.S. Pat. Off. and in Other Countries, Marca Registrada, Hecho en U.S.A.
HarperCollins® is a registered trademark of HarperCollins Publishers Inc.

Printed in the U.S.A.

10 9 8 7 6 5 4 3 2 1

For Stephen and Laura—the two people who make up my happy home.

And a special thank you to Kelly Harms, for your intelligent, insightful editorial guidance, and for the true heart and dedication you show in your work. On top of that, you are organized, efficient, and just plain good at your job. You constantly impress me.

Thank you also Paige Wheeler, my agent, who I adore. Seven years and counting!

Finally, thank you Michelle Phillips, my cousin, my best friend and critique partner—for all the laughter, stimulating conversation, late-night brainstorming and deep, heartfelt friendship.

To live is like to love—all reason is against it, and all healthy instinct for it.

Samuel Butler, 1835–1902

Prologue

Wentworth Castle, Yorkshire
Summer 1872

It was at the youthful age of twenty-one that Edward Peter Wallis, Earl of Whitby, raised a coffee cup to his lips and made the conscious decision that he did not want to die. Or rather, he did not want to grow old—for being young was far more entertaining.

"Here comes your little sister, dashing up the hill," Whitby said to his friend James, the Duke of Wentworth, who sat across from him at the breakfast table.

They'd had the table brought outside onto the

1

sunny stone veranda, having decided they needed fresh air to ward off the disagreeable effects of their excessive consumption of brandy the night before. Although now it seemed a rather idiotic idea, as the sun was casting a blinding reflection off the sterling silver coffeepot in the center of the table, making it necessary to squint. And squinting was never advisable when one was nursing a pounding headache.

"Look at her run," Whitby said, lounging back in his chair as he watched Lily, her blue-and-white skirts flying everywhere. "You don't suppose she's going to ask me to play hide-and-seek, do you? Good Lord."

"Maybe tag," James replied irritably, resting his forehead on a finger.

Whitby was still wearing the same clothes he'd worn the night before, and his face was prickly with stubble. He felt grimy and quite honestly disgusting, yet he couldn't help smiling at Lily, who was racing toward him with a fresh smile on her face, her bright dress clean and crisp. She had just turned nine.

He leaned toward James. "When do you think she'll be old enough to realize we're still half pickled when she comes running up the hill to our breakfast table? I swear it goes completely unnoticed to her innocent eyes when we stagger our way to find her behind the rosebushes or wherever she takes herself off to hide." He lowered his voice to a near whisper. "And she giggles, James. She doesn't know we find her because we can *hear* her." He chuckled and took another sip of his coffee.

"Speak for yourself, Whitby. You may still be pickled, but I am sober enough to feel the throbbing in my brain, and if Lily asks me to chase her . . ."

"You'll tell her to go play with her dolls."

Lily came to a slow stop on the veranda, breathing hard and smiling. She wore her shiny black hair in two braids with blue ribbons that matched the broad ribbon sash on her dress. "Lord Whitby! I knew you'd be here this morning!"

"And how did you know, Lily?" he asked, leaning forward in his chair and resting his elbows on his knees, ignoring the pounding in his head. "Did a little bird tell you? Or perhaps it was that spider on your shoulder." He pointed.

Lily jumped and brushed at herself. "Where?"

Whitby laughed, though it hurt to do so.

Lily shook her head at him. "You are a tease, Lord Whitby. And you need to take a bath. You both do. You smell like cigar smoke."

Whitby raised an eyebrow at James. "From the mouths of babes."

"I'm not a baby," she said. "And for that, you shall have to be the seeker. Close your eyes."

Amused—and as always, quite unable to refuse darling Lily anything—Whitby did as he was told and closed his eyes.

Lily's boots tapped quickly along the flat stones toward the left. "Come and find me!" she called out a few seconds later.

The thought of getting up out of the chair gave Whitby pause. He didn't really want to move. "Damn, James, why don't you go." Whitby tipped his head onto the back of the chair. "She's *your* sister."

"But she asked *you*," James said.

"She always asks me."

"That's because I never play with her. You have much to learn about discouraging unwelcome female attentions, my friend."

Knowing he'd never convince James to play with Lily, Whitby forced himself to stand, though it cost him much. "There is no such thing as unwelcome female attentions, James. Even if they *are* from a nine-year-old."

Whitby heaved a deep sigh and grudgingly crossed the veranda. "Here I come!" he called out.

He descended the steps and immediately saw the bright, white hem of Lily's dress behind the birdbath, which was nowhere near wide enough to hide her. Yet she thought she was invisible.

Smiling and chuckling, he shook his head. "Perhaps you're behind the azaleas!" He walked softly toward the birdbath. "Or here, under the bench!"

Lily giggled.

"What's that I hear?" Whitby said, stopping only a few feet away, seeing her as plain as day. "You must be hiding in the hedge!"

She giggled again, and he lunged around the birdbath. "Found you!"

Lily screamed and took off, and Whitby ran after

her, throwing his arms around her and tickling her ribs until she bent over, clutching her side. She laughed and screeched until he stopped and slapped his hands over his ears. "Great Scott, Lily. My head."

She straightened. "You're getting too old for this, aren't you, Lord Whitby? One of these days, you won't want to play with me, and you'll be very dull like James. Very *old*."

"James isn't old."

"Well, he's certainly dull," Lily said spitefully.

Whitby felt honor-bound to defend his friend. Or perhaps he was inclined to help Lily understand that her brother was a complicated man. If he was reserved, he had his reasons. "He's dull because he doesn't play hide and seek? Surely he's interesting in other ways." Whitby could certainly think of a few.

"He doesn't play anything. Like I said, he's practically an old man. As bad as my father."

Whitby narrowed his eyes at her. His tone became serious with a gentle reprimand. "I doubt that, Lily."

She shrugged casually, and he could see she regretted the remark, for her father had been a cold, cruel man. To compare anyone to him was beyond exaggeration.

Whitby bent forward to speak to her at eye level. "I promise I will never stop playing with you, Lily, because I have no intention of ever growing old."

"Everyone grows old."

"Not me." He straightened and rested his fists on his hips. "I will stay young forever. Young at heart at least."

Lily smiled. "Then I shall grow up and catch up with you in years, and then we can get married. I should like that."

"Married! Good God, Lily, what are you thinking? I'm the worst rake in the world, and you, darling, are a child."

He tugged at one of her braids and turned to walk back to the veranda for more coffee, which he sorely needed. After running around just now, his headache had returned with a vengeance.

He rubbed the back of his neck as he walked, and thought nothing of the fact that Lily had run off without a word in the other direction.

Chapter 1

Wentworth Castle, Yorkshire
October 1884

With the late-afternoon sun beaming in through the lace curtains and bathing her room in bright, shiny light, Lily Langdon sat at her desk, tapping her foot impatiently on the floor while she tapped her pen in a similar rhythm upon the letter she was trying to write. She gazed at the clock on the mantel, ticking away in the silence, while the sunlight reflected off the silver-and-gold plated face.

She was anxious and edgy today. She couldn't pretend not to know why. She knew enough about her own emotions to understand it. It was the first day of her brother James's annual shooting party. The guests had been arriving all day, and in a very short time, she would have to begin preparing for dinner—dressing in one of her elegant gowns and donning heavy jewels.

She'd already chosen the gown for this evening— her dark blue satin Worth with the black velvet roses emblazoned on the hem. She need only select the right earrings to go with her sapphire necklace. Then she would be ready to venture downstairs and meet all the guests in the drawing room.

Lily continued to tap her pen upon her desk, still feeling frustratingly anxious. It was not something she enjoyed, mingling in a room full of strangers. Of course, they wouldn't all be strangers. Her family would be there, and friends of her family, some of whom she had known forever . . .

Perhaps *that* was why she was anxious.

A knock sounded. She rose from her desk chair, crossed the room and opened the door. "Mother . . ."

Her mother, Marion, the dowager duchess, stood in the corridor with her hands clasped in front of her. She wore a long-sleeved black day dress, buttoned stiffly around her neck. Her dark gray hair was pulled into a tight bun at the back of her head. "Lily, I must have a word with you."

Lily stepped back and invited her into the room.

While her mother gazed around at everything— the pile of unfinished letters on the desk, the modern novel lying open on the bed—a sense of inadequacy swept through Lily.

She quickly moved to close the book and turn it over, face down, wondering if she would ever be able to disregard the enduring weight of her mother's disappointment in her. Lily's mother had never understood Lily's romantic nature, in particular when it made Lily take exception to her duties, for Marion was a strict, humorless woman, and she would never even consider questioning her duties.

Marion sat down on a chair, while Lily sat on the sofa opposite. They gazed at each other uncomfortably for a few seconds before Marion spoke.

"Lily, as you know, the guests have been arriving throughout the day."

Lily nodded.

"As it happens, there is a particular gentleman who arrived not more than an hour ago—a young man I encouraged Sophia to invite, as I believe he is a charming and respectable young man. He is Lord Richard, the Earl of Stellerton's youngest son."

A youngest son. Lily squeezed her hands together in her lap. There was a time when her mother would only consider an eldest son as husband material—for Lily was after all the daughter of a duke. But Lily was twenty-one now, and not exactly without her share of knocks and scratches. She suspected her mother was becoming desperate.

"How old is he?" Lily asked, grasping frantically for calm, intelligent questions when all she really wanted to do was leap out of her chair and say, "I don't want to be shepherded!"

But she didn't leap out of her chair because she

supposed she did want guidance. She was afraid of trusting her own judgment when it came to men. She knew how foolish one could become when blinded by passion, for she had become infatuated with someone once—Pierre, a charming Frenchman with an enchanting accent. That man had unfortunately turned out to be something very different from what she had believed him to be. Yet for a brief week or two, she had fancied herself in love with him.

And then there was Whitby. Always Whitby. But he did not see Lily as a woman. He saw her as a child or sister. To hope for something more where he was concerned was unrealistic and foolish.

So yes, she needed guidance, because she wanted to get on with her life.

"Lord Richard is twenty-six," her mother replied. "I met him when he arrived, and I can assure you, he's very handsome."

Lily lowered her gaze. "You know I don't consider that the most important quality in a husband."

"Well, you did at one time," her mother said flatly, revealing the embers of resentment that still smoldered over Lily's recklessness with Pierre.

Lily wondered if she would ever be able to make up for that misstep.

"Is he expecting to meet me tonight?" she asked. "Is that why he came?"

"Yes. Like you, he doesn't enjoy London during the Season, and he is looking for a quiet country girl."

That sounded promising.

"What do you plan to wear this evening?" her mother asked.

"My blue Worth with the black velvet roses."

Her mother's gaze drifted toward Lily's dressing room. "The blue Worth . . ." She pondered it for a moment. "Perhaps something more traditional. What about the green gown you wear with your cameo?"

The green gown was certainly more traditional. It had long sleeves and a lace neckline that was far less daring than the blue gown. "If you think it would be more appropriate . . ."

"I do. Lord Richard is a highly regarded young man, and he has just taken the chaplain's position on his father's estate. His father seems to think he has a bright future with the church and might one day become a bishop."

"He sounds perfectly ideal." Lily crossed her ankles and squeezed her hands together on her lap. "But what if he finds out about what happened with . . . ?"

It was difficult to say Pierre's name. She didn't like to think about how foolish she had been. "Lord Richard might not want me," she said. "I might hurt his chances of becoming a bishop."

Her mother frowned and spoke in a firm voice. "That is water under the bridge, Lily. No one knows but the members of this family—"

"Whitby knows."

Her mother said nothing for a moment. It was no

secret that she had always detested Lord Whitby, ever since the first moment she'd laid eyes on him. He was the one who had befriended James at an early age, and had exerted more influence upon him than she'd ever been able to do.

When she did speak, her voice was strained. "Yes, unfortunately he does, and I wish that were not the case. If I had had any say in the matter three years ago . . ." She stopped herself. "I suppose that is neither here nor there. The point is, Lily, you must move on. You were young and you made a mistake, but thankfully there were no lingering effects from it."

Her mother was of course referring to the matter of Lily's virginity. She still possessed it.

"But what if Lord Richard approves of me and wants to marry me? Would I tell him what I did?" An image of Pierre's dingy boardinghouse room flashed in her mind. She thrust it away. "I can't imagine keeping something like that a secret from my husband."

Her mother's brow furrowed. "Why ever not?"

Lily experienced the confusing mixture of frustration and sympathy she always felt when her mother said things like that, for she had never loved Lily's father. She had probably kept many things about herself secret from him.

But since James had married Sophia, Lily had seen for herself what was possible in a marriage. There were no secrets between them. They loved and trusted each other completely—something she never could have imagined when she was growing up. And now she wasn't sure she would want to jeopardize such a future for herself. She wanted openness and honesty in her marriage, just like James and Sophia had in theirs.

Oh, and passion, of course.

Yet, if Lord Richard or any other prospective groom knew about her reckless behavior with a Frenchman at eighteen, there might never be a marriage . . .

Lily flinched. She sometimes felt as if she were teetering on a narrow precipice, and one day soon, she would fall to one side. But which side would it be? Would she end up closed off like her mother, or open and loving like Sophia?

She felt her chest constricting under the pressure to choose the right side, before she merely lost her balance and toppled whichever way the wind blew.

"Wear the green dress tonight," her mother said. "And the cameo. It is so becoming on you."

"Thank you, Mother." Lily stood and walked Marion to the door.

Later, however, while she sat at her vanity watching her maid, Aline, do her hair, she found herself wondering what *another* man would think of the green dress and cameo. She suspected that man would prefer the blue one with the more daring neckline.

But as she considered it more, she reconciled herself to the fact that Whitby would probably not even notice what Lily was wearing. He would be noticing the other women, as he always did. Which was why she had to forget him.

If she had a farthing for every time she said that . . .

She gazed fixedly at herself in the mirror for a long moment. She thought of her childhood suddenly, and heard the distant sound of her own laughter as she dashed about the garden, playing tag with Whitby. His visits had always been a bright, shining light in an otherwise dark existence, when she'd lived in a house without laughter.

Her heart ached suddenly with grief and a painful longing for those singular moments from the past. She laid a hand over her breast.

"Are you all right, my lady?" Aline asked.

"Yes, I'm fine," she replied.

But she was not fine. Not really. She hadn't been fine for a very long time.

She wished she could travel back in time and find the girl she'd once been. The girl who'd known how to skirt the shadows. The girl who was not afraid to act upon her passions. Was that girl gone? Lily wondered curiously. Or was there still a part of her alive somewhere, deep down inside? She leaned close to the mirror and looked carefully into the blue of her eyes.

Chapter 2

$\sim$ $\circ$ $\circ$ $\sim$

At quarter past four in the afternoon, a liveried footman with clean white stockings and
shiny buckled shoes hurried down the steps of
Wentworth Castle to open the coach door for one
final guest—the Earl of Whitby, the duke's oldest
friend.

Wearing an impressive dark brown wool over-
coat and matching hat, Lord Whitby stepped out of
the coach and smiled up at James, who had just
emerged from the house with Sophia at his side.

Whitby walked up the steps, pulling off his
gloves as he approached. He stopped before James
and Sophia, his shoulders rising and falling with a
deep sigh.

15

"Well. Another year gone by, another shooting party upon us. Where does the time go?" He reached for Sophia's hand and kissed it. "Duchess, you look stunning as always."

She smiled at him. "Oh, Edward, give me a hug." She pulled him close and wrapped her arms around his shoulders. But when she stepped away, she glanced with concern at James.

Whitby had expected such a reaction from her. He was unshaven, exhausted, and he knew he'd lost some weight since they'd last seen him.

Whitby turned to James and shook his hand. "You look well, too, James."

James eyed Whitby curiously. "But *you* look like hell, my friend. What the devil were you up to last night?"

With one booted foot raised on a higher step, Whitby tapped his gloves on his thigh and looked toward the moors in the distance. "The usual, I'm afraid. Colchester had one of his theater parties at his country house last night. Went a little late." Whitby returned his gaze to James and smiled. "So I just decided to stay up to catch the train this morning, rather than try to sleep. I'm tired, that's all."

"You slept on the way, I hope," Sophia said.

"Yes, I did manage to get some rest."

Which was not entirely true. Whitby had in fact sat awake all day, worrying about his sister. Annabelle.

But he did not want them to know that. They

would ask why, and then he would have to tell them. And he was not ready to talk about it.

Sophia linked her arm through Whitby's and led him up the rest of the stairs to the front door. "Well, there will be no such wild, late night parties here. We will all retire at a decent hour like the mature, responsible adults that we are. Lights will be extinguished at precisely ten o'clock."

Whitby laughed and glanced over his shoulder at James, who was following behind them. "Who is this impostor leading me into the house? Or has your wife finally given up her American ways?"

Smiling, they entered the grand hall, their laughter now echoing off the gray stone walls and the high cathedral ceiling.

"And how are the boys—little Liam and John?" Whitby asked. "Getting into trouble yet?"

"Gracious, yes, and growing faster than weeds," James replied. "Just the other day, Liam rode the pony without either of us holding onto him."

"Rode the pony on his own. Good gracious, James. He's only two, and the heir to a dukedom, might I remind you? Your mother couldn't have been pleased."

James smiled. "We didn't tell her. Thought we'd spare her the anxiety."

They walked past a shiny suit of armor on display at the bottom of the stairs.

"Well, now that the pleasantries are taken care of, let's skip to more important matters," Whitby said. "Is Lady Stanton here?"

Sophia stopped and slapped his arm. "Lady Stanton is a married woman, Whitby. Shame on you for asking."

"We are *friends*, Eleanor and I." He grinned. When Sophia smirked at him, he surrendered to her proper influence. "All right," he said. "Tell me who the unmarried ladies are. I suppose they and their mothers are waiting to wrestle me to the ground."

Sophia shook her head at him while James looked on, amused and unsurprised. She listed off the names while they climbed the stairs, escorting Whitby to his room in the east wing.

"I promise I will dance with each of them," he said as he entered the Van Dekker room—the guest chamber they always reserved for him when he visited. The green velvet curtains were pulled open, held back by gold braided tassels. His trunks were already waiting for him, stacked in the center of the room, as his valet had taken an earlier train.

Whitby shrugged out of his coat and tossed it onto the canopied bed—a massive structure made of old English oak, with a headboard that duplicated the turrets of the castle itself and bed curtains tied back at the posts. "There will be dancing, won't there?"

"Of course," Sophia said. "Tomorrow night. Tonight we'll gather in the drawing room at seven and dine at eight, then we'll play some cards afterward."

She and James paused in the doorway.

"We'll leave you to get settled," James said.

As soon as they were gone, Whitby sank onto the cushioned bench at the foot of the bed and pinched the bridge of his nose. He inhaled deeply a few times, feeling shaky and winded after climbing the stairs. He probably should have eaten something today.

He reached into his breast pocket, retrieved his flask, and quickly unscrewed the cap. He took a sip and forced himself to swallow.

His valet walked in just then and saw his pained grimace. The man stopped suddenly in the doorway.

Whitby held up a hand. "Don't say anything, Jenson."

Jenson, who had been Whitby's valet for more than twenty years, walked to the bed and picked up Whitby's coat. "I had no intention of speaking, my lord."

Whitby watched Jenson hang the coat in the corner wardrobe.

"It's a sore throat," he explained, not knowing why he felt he needed to explain himself to his valet. But what could he say? He'd lost his father at the age of eight. Jenson, now sixty-one, had occasionally filled that role.

"*Another* sore throat, my lord?" Jenson said with evident disbelief.

Whitby shook his head at him and downed the rest of the contents in the flask, finally feeling the welcome, numbing heat it offered.

It was close to seven-thirty when Lily stopped in the doorway of the crimson and gold drawing room. Inside, the heavy drapes were drawn and the room was lit invitingly by dim lamps and candles. A few young ladies were seated on the sofa with their mothers in nearby chairs, while some of the gentlemen stood next to the piano. They were laughing over something. Another group of guests, including Sophia and James, stood before a crackling fire in the hearth.

Lily wondered if Lord Richard had arrived yet. She would be glad to get the introductions out of the way.

At that moment, she felt someone approach from behind, and before she had a chance to turn, a large hand wrapped around her elbow. "Lily. Thank God, you're late, too."

She turned and found herself staring up at Lord Whitby, dressed in formal black and white dinner attire, his golden hair thick and wavy. He was smiling down at her, waiting for a response. She noticed he looked thin.

Tongue-tied as usual, she gazed up at him and felt instantly lost in the deep blue of his eyes and the playful allure of his smile. He was so beautiful.

She wished she didn't feel that way about him every time she saw him. She wished her stomach wouldn't erupt into a wild flock of frenzied butterflies. She wished she could just see him as a brother.

"What do you say we sneak in together," he said, leaning close, "and no one will be the wiser? Come on."

He placed his hand at the small of her back and guided her into the room.

She went, more than a little aware of the fact that she'd not yet spoken a single word. She cursed this effect he had on her. The same thing had happened to her the last time she'd seen him—a few months ago at one of the London balls. He had been flirting with someone else that night, as he always was. That particular night it had been Miss Violet Scott, who had been sure Whitby was going to propose to her. Lily had not enjoyed herself that night.

"There," he said. "No one even noticed us." He nodded at the footman who immediately approached carrying a tray of champagne. Whitby took two glasses and handed one to Lily. "Cheers," he said, then he took a few deep gulps.

Once that was done, he gave her his full attention. "So how are you, Lily? You look well."

She swallowed hard and tried to smile, but a nervous shiver was scuttling through her, and she felt her lip quiver. "I'm fine . . . thank you. Fine today. Are you fine?"

Good God. Someone just smother me with a pillow . . .

His eyes glimmered with amusement as he leaned forward ever so slightly—charming and handsome and full of life and exuberance. His lips were moist; it was intoxicating just to look at him. Lily became filled with the old familiar longing that never gave her a reprieve.

"Fine, thank you," he whispered in reply.

He was making fun of her. She should have laughed along with him. She should have tossed her head back and slapped his arm. But she couldn't. Her stomach was wrenching into a knot. She felt as if she'd just been dropped onto her behind on the cold, hard floor.

At that instant, James and Sophia appeared beside them.

"I thought you might have forgotten about us," James said.

Whitby turned away from Lily. "Heavens no. I simply wanted to look my best and thought I should take my time." He glanced over James's shoulder. "I see Spencer is here. I heard he has a new rifle he wants to show off."

"Indeed he does," James replied. "Come and say hello to him. He'll tell you all about it."

Without so much as a glance back in Lily's direction, Whitby followed James across the room.

Lily watched him for a few seconds while the butterflies in her tummy continued to swarm, then she took a sip of her champagne. When she looked up again, Sophia was staring at her.

"Are you all right?" Sophia asked.

Lily pasted on a smile. "Yes, of course. Why wouldn't I be?"

Sophia shrugged. "No reason. Your face just looks a little flushed."

Wishing she didn't feel completely mortified, Lily raised a hand to her cheek. "I was late. I had to hurry to get here. And perhaps Aline tied my laces a little too tight."

"Lily, my dear," her mother said, joining them.

"Come and meet the other guests. There are a few you don't know."

Lily followed her mother to the other side of the room, privately humiliated over the fact that she was still shaken from her brief and utterly insignificant encounter with Whitby. She had promised herself she would forget him. She had wanted to feel nothing, but that had not been the case. Unfortunately, whenever she saw him, she felt everything—every nerve in her body, every emotion in her heart, every impossible wish and every agonizing desire.

Her mother led her across the room to the gentlemen who were gathered by the piano. There were a few familiar faces, but some new ones, too. One in particular stood out—a young, dark-haired man who was not unattractive. He was staring at Lily with apparent interest.

Lily's mother made the introductions, and sure enough, the young man was Lord Richard—her potential future husband if her mother had her druthers.

Lily smiled politely, then listened to the conversation rather than joining in, while at the same time stealing discreet glances at Lord Richard. A few times their eyes met, and he gave her a smile. She began to feel more at ease. Her pulse slowly returned to its normal pace.

A short time later, the conversation was clipping along and Lily was smiling brightly at all the people in the group. She forgot about her flushed cheeks. She forgot about Whitby. She did not look across the room, perhaps because she was very aware of Lord Richard's interest in her, watching her and evaluating her. She did her best to be charming and friendly, laughing at witty remarks that were made, gazing with interest at whoever was speaking at any given moment. Then, when the dinner gong rang out and the time had arrived to proceed into the dining room, she smiled candidly at Lord Richard before taking the arm of her elderly neighbor, Mr. Horton, for they were to line up two-by-two according to precedence.

They entered the vast, formal dining room, lit by dozens of candles set in silver candelabras, spaced evenly down the long length of the white-clothed table that was set for thirty. Colorful bouquets of flowers trimmed each place-setting and filled the room with the delightful fragrance of a summer garden. Before long, everyone was seated and the extravagant service began.

Lily sat at a diagonal across from Lord Richard, so they were unable to speak to each other directly, but it was a fine opportunity to observe him and see how he behaved with the others around him. He seemed very polite. Occasionally he smiled at Lily, and she smiled back.

On other occasions, she found herself gazing up at the other end of the table where James, Sophia and Whitby were laughing and engaging in more animated conversation. Whitby was seated next to Lady Stanton, who was very beautiful and evidently very amusing. Everyone laughed at the things she said.

Lily forced her gaze back to her plate and resolved to keep her attention on the people sitting beside her and across from her.

After dinner, the ladies returned to the drawing room for coffee, while the gentlemen went to the library for claret and cigars.

"It's nice to see Lord Richard here," Lady Stanton said to Lily's mother, while the coffee was being poured. She leaned forward to pick up her cup. "He has become quite handsome of late. Indeed, I believe he would be a very good match for the right young woman—a woman who enjoys country life." She directed her smiling gaze at Lily, who said nothing as she picked up her coffee cup and stirred it with a spoon.

"He is indeed an upright young man," Lily's mother said. "Any young lady would be fortunate to catch his interest. Very fortunate indeed."

Lily glanced across at Sophia, who was watching her. Sophia smiled warmly.

Later, after the gentlemen had joined the ladies in the drawing room, Sophia approached Lily who was sitting alone on the settee by the window.

"You look lonely over here," Sophia said, sitting down and touching Lily's knee.

Lily raised her eyebrows. "No, not at all. I was enjoying watching everyone else talk."

With a quiet, gentle voice, Sophia said, "You know, Lily, there was a time when you enjoyed social gatherings like this. You used to long for excitement and a new face now and then. A *handsome* face." She gave Lily a knowing, sidelong glance.

Lily managed to reach the edges of a smile, though she felt little joy to go along with it. "That was when I was young and innocent and knew nothing of the wicked ways of the world." She spoke with mocking humor, though there was more than a little truth to it, and they both knew it.

"So what do you think of Lord Richard?" Sophia asked, thankfully changing the subject. "Your mother thinks he would be a very good match for you."

"I'm sure he would be," Lily replied. "I'll look forward to getting to know him over the next few days."

Sophia stared intently into Lily's eyes. "Will you?" The skepticism in her voice was unmistakable. Sophia had always been direct. "Or would you prefer to get to know someone else?"

A thick cloud of uneasiness descended upon Lily as she sat speechless on the settee.

Sophia knew.

How long she had known, Lily had no idea. She remembered telling Sophia three years ago that she had once fancied Whitby when she was a girl. Lily had thought she was over him at that time. She had sincerely believed she was. In fact, she had thought of him very little over the year prior to that.

But something had changed lately. Lily had gone to London in May and thrown herself back into the scorching crush of the Season. She'd seen Whitby over and over at balls and assemblies after not having seen him for almost two full years—the years after Pierre, when she had retreated from society in general. She had skipped the London Season altogether in those years.

But when she saw Whitby again last May, she'd remembered all too clearly the day he had come with James and Sophia to fetch her out of that boardinghouse and bring her home and save her from certain doom. He had carried her down a flight of stairs and taken her into the safety of a private coach. He had not judged her—like she'd felt the others had, especially her mother after she'd arrived home. But she couldn't blame them. Even Lily had judged herself and continued to judge and condemn herself. But Whitby never had, nor did he seem to judge her now. It was all forgotten. He never mentioned it. Though he never talked to her about anything of consequence . . .

Sophia took Lily's hand. "You know you can trust me, Lily, don't you?"

Lily nodded.

Sophia squeezed Lily's hand a little tighter. "I like to think that we are close, and I believe that we are, but there is something you have been keeping from me—and everyone else, for that matter—for a very long time. I believe you care for Lord Whitby, but you haven't wanted anyone to know."

Lily looked down at Sophia's hand upon hers and said nothing for what seemed like an eternity. At last, she sighed. "You are very intuitive."

Sophia's shoulders relaxed, as if she'd been preparing to coax it out of Lily with a large conversational pump.

"How long have you known?" Lily asked.

Sophia glanced around the room to make sure no one was listening, then spoke quietly. "I've known since the day you told me three years ago, when I was first married to James. But since then, I thought you were over him. I continued to believe that, until you left London unexpectedly in June when everyone thought he was going to propose to Miss Scott. But when James and I returned home, you never mentioned him or asked about him, so I thought perhaps I was wrong. Until tonight."

Feeling exposed all of a sudden, Lily asked, "Am I that transparent?"

"No. If you were, your mother would know and Whitby would know, too. He has a very keen awareness when it comes to women expressing their interest."

Yes. Lily knew how clever he was with women. She had been watching him for years. "Does James know?" she asked.

Sophia shook her head. "No. I've mentioned my suspicions to him a few times, but he has never believed it could be true. Perhaps because you're his sister, he has a hard time imagining you being in love—with Whitby, at any rate, since you've known him forever. James most likely sees the two of you like a brother and sister."

"But we're not."

"No, you are not, which is very clear to me."

Lily couldn't begin to express the elation that came from knowing that someone saw her as something other than a sister to Whitby.

"I think you're the only one who sees it that way," she said, still finding it impossible to imagine anything coming of it.

Sophia grinned with gentle compassion. "Only for the moment."

Lily's heart bounced a little in her chest. "What are you saying, Sophia?"

"I'm saying what you think I'm saying. Perhaps the time has come to see if there can be more between you."

Lily stared dumbfounded at Sophia. She had been talking herself out of loving Whitby for so long, she couldn't even begin to comprehend the possibility of any other fate.

Her thoughts went immediately to all the reasons why. "But mother despises him."

"James doesn't."

"But Whitby's so much older than I am."

"Twelve years," Sophia replied. "A mere obstacle, easily circumvented."

Lily felt her eyebrows lift. "Easily circumvented?"

"Yes." Sophia glanced discreetly around the room again. "Life is too short, Lily. You've cared for Whitby for a long time, and you haven't seemed able to care for anyone else, even though you've tried. If you want him, you should pursue him and see what comes of it. Then at least you'll know whether or not the two of you are meant to be together."

Lily laughed out loud, then put her hand over her mouth, afraid she'd attracted the attention of the other guests. "Just like that? *Pursue* him?"

"Why, yes." Sophia was looking at Lily as if she couldn't understand what the problem was, which was very typical of Sophia. She had a tenacious will, and every Englishman knew that Americans had hard noses for getting what they wanted. Lily supposed she could do with a few lessons in diligence from her sister-in-law.

Lily dropped her gaze to her hands again. "But James is right in one respect. Whitby does see me as a child and a sister. If he sees me at all."

"You don't know that."

"Yes, I do. He barely notices me when there are other women around—women who know how to flirt with him. In fact, he barely notices me even when there *aren't* other women around. Just tonight, he was far more interested in hearing about Lord Spencer's new rifle than he was in talking to me. Whenever we're in the same room together, it's like I'm invisible."

"Have you ever tried to make him see you?"

Lily scoffed at the suggestion. "By doing what? Jumping up and down and waving my arms over my head?"

"No, silly," Sophia replied quietly. "He's a man.

You're a woman, and a very pretty one. All you need to do is flirt with him, but don't be too available. Don't chase after him. A good flirt will manipulate the man into thinking he's chasing after *her*. And perhaps wear a more daring gown. Surprise him, so that he has no choice but to finally see that you've grown up."

Lily gazed pensively at her mother sitting before the fire. "I was going to wear my blue Worth tonight, but Mother thought I should wear this. She thought it would be more suitable to meet Lord Richard."

"Ah, yes," Sophia said, glancing over at him. "Lord Richard."

Lily looked over at him, too. He was talking to his father and a few others. "He seems very nice. I certainly wouldn't want to discount him."

"Neither would I, if I were in your shoes. But you know, if Whitby sees that you have captured the interest of another man, it might be just the thing to make him notice you."

Lily began to feel uncomfortable. "I wouldn't want to use Lord Richard, or mislead him in any way."

"No, no, of course you wouldn't do that," Sophia said. "What I'm saying is that you are young and unattached, and this is the time to test the waters with different men. I think you should try to get to know the both of them over the next few days. Do you think you can do that?"

Lily's lifetime dream came to her mind—the vision of Whitby leaning down to kiss her, his lips touching hers lightly at first, before he pulled her into his arms for a more passionate kiss.

Her heart began to race with excitement. "Do you really think it's possible?"

"I wouldn't be having this conversation if I didn't."

The blood stirred in Lily's veins, sending a burst of excitement from the top of her head down to her toes. Sophia was confident. She believed it could be done. Could Lily believe it, too? Gooseflesh tingled on her thighs.

"I don't have a daring gown," she said. "Even the blue Worth has a conservative neckline compared to what some of the other women are wearing."

Sophia smiled wickedly. "I have a few. And my maid knows how to use the sewing machine. We could easily alter one to fit you for the dancing to-morrow night."

"But what about Lord Richard?" Lily said. "I don't want to do anything that might spoil my chances with him. If I am to be realistic, I must remember that the chances of Whitby actually falling in love with me are slim."

Sophia patted Lily's knee and smiled. "Don't worry, Lily. I suspect if Lord Richard is like most men, he'll approve of your new look. They both will."

On the other side of the drawing room, Marion set down her coffee cup and realized she was only half listening to the conversation around her, for she was distracted. She did not like the look of things over by the window, where Sophia and Lily were speaking privately and keeping their voices noticeably low. It was not proper. They should be here with the other ladies, conversing politely.

She glanced over at them again, and saw a look in her daughter's eye that she had not seen in quite some time. Lily looked rather eager and animated.

It was a look that caused Marion some concern, and she was most agitated by the involuntary clenching of her jaw.

Chapter 3

❦❧

"**D**id you enjoy yourself last night?" James asked Whitby, who was sprawled out in a chair in James's dressing room. James slipped his arms into the gray tweed hunting jacket his valet held out for him.

Whitby, already dressed in his hunting attire, flipped his hat over in his hands. "Yes, it was a fine time. Sophia seemed to enjoy herself."

"She always does. She likes entertaining." James turned away from the cheval mirror and faced Whitby. He stared at him for a moment. "Pardon my candor, but you look like hell again this morning, Whitby. Tell me you ate breakfast."

Whitby continued to flip his hat. "I'm quite sure I did."

"You're quite sure? When someone asks if you ate and you did, you don't say you're *quite sure* you did. You say you *did*. Unless you're trying to hide the fact that you weren't hungry because your head was still swimming in brandy from the night before."

Whitby leaned back in the chair. He wasn't in the mood to defend himself. He had far too much on his mind.

He tilted his head at James. "What's gotten into you all of a sudden? I remember a time when you avoided breakfast, too, after a so-called late night in the drawing room."

James faced the mirror again while his valet tugged at his sleeves. "Yes, but I've matured, thank God. I don't take this body for granted anymore."

Whitby did not take his body for granted either. Not by a long shot.

"You, on the other hand," James continued tersely, "act like you're still nineteen."

Whitby stared astonished at James. "And why not? What's wrong with enjoying myself? I'm not dead . . . at least not yet." He tried to sound playful.

James turned again, leaned down and reached into Whitby's breast pocket. He pulled out the flask and stared at it, then tossed it into the trash basket. "You will be if you keep this up."

Whitby stared in stunned silence at the flask in the bottom of the basket. An ominous silence ensued. James waved his valet away, and the man walked out of the room.

As soon as the door closed behind him, James said, "You're my oldest friend, Whitby, so I consider it my duty to ask. When was the last time you were sober for more than a day?"

Whitby, slouching in the chair, narrowed his gaze at James. He couldn't believe he was having this conversation. He'd come here because he'd wanted to have a good time. He *needed* to have a good time. He did not come to be lectured.

For a long moment he sat there, and when he finally spoke, the irritation was clear in his voice. "I'm not a drunk, if that's what you're asking."

"Then explain this change in your appearance."

Whitby glared at James. "What is this? For God's sake, you're beginning to sound like your father."

James's eyes narrowed with displeasure at hearing such a thing. His voice was low and controlled when he finally spoke. "And you're sounding like yours."

It was no great secret that Whitby's father had been constantly inebriated during the final years of his life, before dying at the age of forty-two.

Whitby dropped his hand to the armrest. Normally, he would have stood up and faced James directly, jabbed a finger on his chest and challenged him to make such an accusation a second time. But today, Whitby just couldn't. For one thing, he *was* still soused and he didn't entirely trust himself to get out of the chair and stand steady.

Secondly, he was finding this whole conversation unsettling. It was reminding him of his failures regarding his duty to his family, in particular to Annabelle, who was the most vulnerable to Magnus. His cousin. His enemy, who was finally going to get what he wanted if Whitby's health did not improve.

So Whitby simply rolled his eyes at James.

"Jesus. You're way off course. I've had a sore throat lately, that's all. Bloody hell."

"A sore throat," James said doubtfully.

"Yes, and the brandy numbs it."

"Have you seen a doctor?"

Whitby glared at James, annoyed with him for asking these intrusive questions. He did not want to talk about this. "Yes, I've seen a doctor," he lied, and that lie gave birth to another. "And for your information, he's the one who suggested the brandy."

James eyed his friend with careful scrutiny, then reached into the trash basket for the discarded flask and handed it back to Whitby. "Why didn't you tell me?"

"You were enjoying yourself too much, acting old and self-righteous. Now I know how Martin must feel, in the unenviable position of being your younger brother. Perhaps he and I should compare notes."

Hearing the faint humor in Whitby's voice, James appeared to relax slightly. He took a deep breath. "The doctor said it will pass?"

"The sore throat?"

"Yes, the sore throat," James said, growing visibly frustrated with Whitby's apparent lack of concern, and not appearing to be entirely convinced he was being honest.

Whitby nodded. "Yes, of course it will pass. I probably should have stayed home and nursed it, but I've never missed one of your shooting parties and damned if I'm going to start now."

James turned to the mirror again and placed his hat on his head. "Well, let's just hope you'll be able to shoot straight."

That evening, Lily entered the dimly lit drawing room at seven o'clock sharp. She paused at the door, glancing over all the guests and feeling self-conscious in Sophia's deep crimson evening gown with a shockingly low off-the-shoulder neckline.

She raised a hand to touch the ruby necklace she wore. The sensation of the cool air touching Lily's collarbone and cleavage was most unnerving, for she hadn't worn a gown like this in years, not since she was eighteen and full of courage and confidence. She had tried very hard to look beautiful then. But she was no longer that girl.

Lily swallowed over her nervousness and entered the room. A hot fire roared in the grate. The gold chandelier overhead gleamed with a dozen flickering candles.

Her mother had not yet arrived. Lily was glad, because she wasn't looking forward to explaining the way she looked.

Whitby had not arrived, either, she noticed. Nor had Lord Richard. Sophia was standing by the piano, talking to a few of the ladies. She spotted Lily immediately and excused herself from the others, crossing the room with an eager look in her eye.

"You look exquisite," Sophia whispered, when she reached Lily. "He will most definitely notice you tonight—especially in that color."

"But what then?" Lily asked. "He'll tell me I look nice and move on."

"No, you will surprise him and capture his interest, like we talked about."

Lily was doubtful. "I don't know if I'll be able to pull it off."

"Of course you will," Sophia said. "Just remember, it's all about pretending to be confident, even if you're not."

Lily smoothed her hands over the front of her skirt. "No man has ever chased me before. Well, one did. In this very drawing room. And you know how that turned out."

Sophia led her fully into the room and lowered her voice to a whisper. "Yes, but you mustn't think of that. All you have to think about is Whitby, and how you're going to let him know you want to be caught."

Lily felt her cheeks flood with color. She didn't think she had what it took to be coquettish, not with Whitby, for he had become like a character in a fairy story to her. She idolized him.

It was ridiculous, she knew, because he was just a

man—a man she'd known her entire life.

At that moment, her eyes turned toward the
door, and there he was, in all his handsome, heavenly splendor, walking into the drawing room and
picking up a glass of champagne from the footman.
Oh, he was spectacular. More than spectacular.

Over the years, he'd matured and become even
more manly, if that was possible. More confident in
the way he carried himself. The bones of his face
were strong and well defined, and tonight, his
golden hair was unruly in the most deliciously rakish way.

She glanced at his big hand holding the delicate,
stemmed champagne glass. His emerald ring
gleamed in the evening light. Lily nervously
sucked in a breath and wet her lips.

Dressed in black and white formal attire, he
moved to the other side of the room and stopped
beside the window. He struck up a conversation
with a few of the other gentlemen.

Sophia signaled to a footman who immediately
came toward them with a tray of champagne.
Sophia and Lily each took a glass, then Sophia
touched Lily's arm and redirected the way she
stood. "Turn your back to Whitby."

Lily did as Sophia suggested, and slowly sipped
her drink while they chatted.

"He just looked at you," Sophia said.

"Who? Whitby?"

"Yes. He looked you up and down from head to
foot. My word, he has no shame."

"He looked *me* up and down?" Lily said, astonished. "Surely not. He must have been looking at you."

"No, he wasn't. Well, that does it. I'm convinced. A red dress works every time."

They continued to chat and sip champagne, and Lily finally got up the courage to look over her shoulder at him the way Sophia had told her to do.

He immediately met her gaze, and before she had a chance to look away, he raised his glass to her.

Shocked, she faced Sophia again. "Did you see that?"

"Yes," Sophia replied, smiling. Not a minute later, the corner of her mouth turned up in a satisfied grin. "What a surprise. He's coming over here."

"Are you sure?" Lily asked, still not quite ready to believe he wanted to talk to *her*. Surely, he was coming to talk to Sophia. "What about my flirting with him and making him think he's chasing after me? I had expected that to take all night."

Sophia shrugged and chuckled. "I guess Whitby doesn't need to be manipulated."

Lily felt her face flushing red.

"Relax," Sophia said, "and don't turn around until he speaks first. Act unsurprised to see him, then after a few minutes of aloofness, say something witty and smile at him with your eyes. Men like that."

At that moment, Lily felt Whitby nearing like a great tidal wave about to crash, then he stopped beside her. Her stomach did a wild, out-of-control flip. She strove to ignore it and do as Sophia suggested. She would act aloof.

"Good evening, ladies." Whitby bowed slightly. "I must say you both look stunning tonight."

He turned his attention to Lily and stared at her briefly. For a panic-filled instant, she was certain she was going to fail miserably at this, because she had no idea where her voice was or how to use it. But then thank God, words suddenly, somehow, spilled out of her mouth.

And they weren't ridiculous.

"Thank you, Whitby. How was the shooting today?"

He didn't respond right away, but rather took a second or two to study her face. He did indeed look surprised. It was as if he were looking at her for the first time. Was it the dress?

He looked at her eyes, then her nose and lips, then down at her ruby necklace. Then he quickly returned to his usual self and the moment passed. He had evidently glanced at her, thought she looked different, and that was that.

He made his reply to both Sophia and Lily. "Quite dismal, actually. No one seemed able to hit anything. Shouldn't be too difficult to do better tomorrow. We certainly couldn't do any worse."

Lily should have said something in response. She wanted to, but butterflies had invaded her stomach again and they had found a direct path to her brain.

Sophia quickly took up the reins of the conversation. "Was it the weather?"

"It was windy," he said, "and I suppose it was just one of those days when everyone had a run of bad luck."

He went on to describe how many pheasants and woodcock were bagged and by whom, then he and Sophia continued to carry the conversation, while Lily was all but a casual observer.

Suddenly, she found her hopefulness and excitement beginning to fade. Perhaps she had been fooling herself, latching on to Sophia's optimism, when in reality, Lily was simply not the right woman for Whitby. She didn't know how to talk to him.

Another guest joined them. It was Lord Richard. "Good evening, ladies. Whitby."

Whitby nodded at him.

"Lady Lily," Richard said, turning toward her. "Your mother tells me you are reading *The Pilgrim's Progress*. It is one of my favorite works. I read it for the first time when I was just a lad."

All eyes turned to Lily. She glanced up at Whitby, who was watching her over the rim of his champagne glass as he took a sip, waiting for her reply.

She smiled at Lord Richard and managed to put on a confident air. "How interesting," she said. "I haven't finished it yet, but it is indeed a fascinating story."

They discussed the lengthy religious allegory in some depth, but as soon as there was a break in their conversation, Whitby bowed slightly and said, "If you will excuse me . . ."

With that he turned and left their group, crossing to join Lady Stanton on the other side of the room. Lady Stanton saw him coming and met him halfway, smiling and raising a bare shoulder as she greeted him.

Lily tried to keep her attention focused on Lord Richard, who was still talking about Bunyan's Slough of Despond and the Burning Mount. Richard then began describing something in the second part of the book, which Lily hadn't read yet.

In truth, she was finding it difficult to listen to him, because she was too busy trying to fight off the heavy ache of her disappointment. Again she had bored Lord Whitby. Again he had found another woman far more intriguing than she. Perhaps it was time to give up her childish dreams and start acting sensibly. Whitby was obviously beyond her reach. She'd always known that.

But she also knew that her hopes would not be easy to shed, for they had lived for too long in her heart.

"Please don't give up yet," Sophia said after dinner, when the men were still in the dining room.

"He's not interested in me, Sophia. There is no point trying to pretend otherwise."

"But you can't give up because of one small failure on your first attempt. No one ever accomplished anything by giving up. You must try again."

"I don't think so. My chances for happiness are better with Lord Richard."

Sophia lowered her voice. "But are you attracted to him?"

"I could grow to be."

Sophia's expression softened. "I suppose I can't force you, can I?"

Lily smiled and shook her head. "I think it would be best if I got over Whitby once and for all. I can't keep dreaming about the impossible, not when it stops me from really living."

Sophia leaned forward and kissed Lily on the cheek. "If that's what you want, I will support you. I only want you to be happy." She stood. "I'm going upstairs to check on the boys and make sure they're sleeping, but I'll be back shortly. You'll be all right?"

Lily nodded and watched Sophia leave.

A few minutes later, the doors opened and the gentlemen walked into the room. James and Whitby came in first. Lily watched Whitby for a moment, feeling sad, for she was about to give up on something that had been a part of her whole being forever. She had known Whitby since she was barely able to walk. He had always been there in her life, extraordinary in her eyes.

He looked her way, and his gleaming gaze gripped her with its usual mesmerizing force. Lily's body grew warm with the familiar desire that had simmered within her for too long, unfulfilled. Lately it had begun to burn, and its tenacity in the face of her opposition frustrated her beyond any imagining.

He smiled at her—a slow, lazy smile that shone mostly in his eyes—and excused himself from James. He began to make his way across the room toward Lily.

She shifted uneasily on the sofa and sat up a little straighter. She cleared her throat and looked around, wondering suddenly if Whitby was in fact on his way to talk to someone else. Lady Stanton perhaps? No, Lady Stanton was on the other side of the room.

All at once, Whitby was standing before her—tall and sumptuous, muscled and magnetic . . .

Her pulse quickened, and she had to fight hard to remember what she had just vowed about wanting the impossible.

Chapter 4

When Lily was a little girl, she had adored Whitby's playfulness. Now, as a woman, she adored something else entirely—the spellbinding seduction in those mature blue eyes, the size and strength of his hands, and the divine perfection of his mouth and nose and cheeks.

She saw his body now, when she hadn't as a girl. She wanted to lay her hand on his chest or taste the flavor of his lips. He was the most beautiful man she had ever known, and even now, certain that he could never fulfill the painfully mystifying lust she felt for him, she could not bring herself to look away. He was a dazzling, captivating undertow of desire, and he would always pull her under.

Damn him for stoking her lustful fires when she had just resolved, yet again, to forget him.

Lily swallowed hard, and struggled to contain her fascination with him, so she would at least be able to speak.

"May I?" he asked, gesturing to the empty space on the sofa beside her.

"Of course," she replied, sliding over a little.

He sat down and leaned back, resting his arm along the back of the sofa and crossing one long leg over the other toward her. She tried to breathe normally, but it was a challenge when she was so intensely aware of his hand only inches from her ear.

He sat for a few seconds, staring at her with a rakish smirk. What in God's name was he smiling about?

Finally he spoke. "Tell me you're not actually enjoying *The Pilgrim's Progress*. If you are, I'll stand up right here and do a jig."

Lily gazed at him, feeling dumbstruck. "Well . . ."

He inclined his head at her, almost as if he were threatening to scold her if she didn't tell him the truth.

Lily smiled. Her stomach whirled with an exhilarating thrill. "I haven't exactly finished it yet."

He leaned toward her, only slightly, a small movement she would not have noticed had it been anyone else sitting beside her. But it wasn't anyone else. It was Whitby—Whitby!—and all her senses were alert to even the slightest move on his part or the slightest change in his expression. She was even aware of his delectably masculine scent.

He lowered his voice. "You haven't finished it because you fall asleep at the bottom of each page. Am I right?"

She smiled again and nodded, releasing some of her pent-up tension with a laugh. "All right, I confess. I can't seem to remember what I've read from one moment to the next, because I find my mind wandering to more interesting things. Like the coal dust in the fireplace."

Whitby chuckled. So did Lily. Then she realized with no small measure of amazement that she was actually sitting on a sofa with him and they were having a conversation. A real conversation. He was looking into her eyes and she was looking into his.

"Every time I've ever seen you reading," he said, "you've always had the very latest novel in your hands. Or something gothic. I remember once seeing you reading *Melmoth the Wanderer*. I read it, too, shortly after that."

Lily recalled reading that book about four years ago. It was a frightening story of a man who had made a pact with the devil to prolong his life.

She was surprised Whitby remembered what she'd been reading. Or had even noticed, for that matter.

"That book terrified me," she said. "I used to read it at night in the library, and once I had to dash up the stairs to get to my room because the wind had been howling and my heart was in my throat."

Whitby tipped his head back. "Ah, yes, that was a compelling book. I couldn't put down. I had to sleep with the lamp on one particular night, if I recall."

He rubbed a finger behind his ear and stared at Lily for a moment. He blinked slowly, and she thought he looked tired. She wondered if he'd been ill recently.

"I hear Lord Richard has been paying you particular attention since he arrived," Whitby said. "You appear to have made an impression."

She lowered her gaze. "Yes. Mother invited him. She thinks he would be a good match for me."

Whitby glanced over at Lord Richard. "And what do *you* think?"

She considered the question very carefully. If she were being honest, she would tell Whitby that she wasn't keen on the idea because she was in love with *him*, and had been in love with him all her life.

But she remembered what Sophia had told her about attracting gentlemen—that she mustn't make herself too available. And knowing Whitby, if she told him that, he would leap off the sofa and dash for the door.

Instead, she said pensively, "I am certainly considering him. He's quite handsome."

Lily watched Whitby's hooded eyes as he peered at Lord Richard, and wanted desperately to know what he was thinking. Was there any trace of jealousy in his mind? Was he finally grasping the concept that she was a woman now, ready to be loved by a man?

When he returned his attention to her, she resolved to put some of Sophia's advice into practice. She could do this. She could.

Lily smiled teasingly at him and decided to say something daring, like Lady Stanton would say. "I suppose what I really want, Whitby, is to be seduced. What woman doesn't want that?"

Good God. She had never said anything so scandalous in her entire life, and she had to swallow clumsily over her own shock.

Whitby said nothing for a few seconds, then the corner of his mouth curled up. He was surprised. Lily had surprised him, just like Sophia had told her to do. And he appeared to be . . .

Dare she say impressed?

He tilted his head to the side. "And do you think Richard has what it takes?"

She raised an eyebrow. Coquettishly. It was all a great act, yet it was exciting and thrilling and made all the hairs on her arms stand up and tingle.

She found herself getting caught up in this charade, actually believing that she could be flirtatious and interesting, and maybe even witty if she made the right effort. She struggled to keep her mind sharp.

"That remains to be seen," she said with a playful lilt to her voice. "What do you think? Seeing as you are a man of experience."

They both looked at Lord Richard. Lily was still

poundingly aware of Whitby's arm along the back of the sofa, his hand relaxed and bent at the wrist, almost touching her shoulder. She couldn't believe she was having this conversation with him. Did he find it strange, too? Did he find it as invigorating as she did?

"I agree," Whitby said, "that it remains to be seen. He is certainly very polite. Almost too polite to be daring."

"Can a polite man not be daring?" she asked. "Are *you* not polite, Whitby? You seem very well mannered at this moment. Perhaps there is another side of *you* that remains to be seen."

A sensuous current of electricity passed between them. "Perhaps there is."

They stared knowingly at each other. Lily's heart thundered within her breast. Her palms were growing clammy, her head spinning. She wanted to jump up and down and squeal!

She resisted the urge, of course. After a few heated seconds, she grinned at him with an intentional confidence and looked away.

"Perhaps I will go and talk to Lord Richard now," she said. "I suddenly feel very curious." She gracefully stood.

"You're leaving?" Whitby asked.

Triumph sang in her veins. He didn't want her to go. All the more reason that she should. She would leave him wanting more.

"Not leaving," she replied. "I'm only crossing

the room." But she was leaving their *tête-à-tête*. "Perhaps later we can find each other on the dance floor and I'll tell you whether or not Lord Richard was . . . *polite*."

He smiled at her, as if they were secret allies. "I'll look forward to it."

With that, Lily turned and walked away from him, feeling exuberant and excited and full of glee, having finally tasted the sweet flavor of success.

She had done it. She had attracted Whitby's attention and kept it fixed on her. There had even been a sexual energy between them—a teasing allure that promised something more. There had been temptation. Desire. He was intrigued now. She knew he was. She wanted to laugh out loud.

She also knew that he was still watching her as she walked across the room. She did not look back.

Good God, had he just flirted with Lily? Whitby asked himself with stupefying shock and more than a little unease.

Jesus, he had! And he'd bloody well enjoyed it, too.

Whitby watched her walk off and noticed for the first time the slender length of her neck and the delicate curve of her shoulders. And those hips . . .

She looked exquisite tonight, by God. He'd never seen her look that way before. The red gown was stunning on her, and her bosom was . . .

Well, he had certainly never noticed that before. He'd known for a long time that she was growing into a woman, but he'd thought nothing of it. She simply wasn't the type to catch his eye, and she was of course James's baby sister, the little girl in braids.

But tonight she was different, and not just in the way she was dressed. Everything about her was different. What in God's name had she done to herself?

Whitby watched her casually approach Lord Richard, who was standing with a group of guests, including Sophia and James. She joined in the conversation, while Whitby continued to watch her. Lord Richard said something to her and she laughed.

Whitby wondered if he was talking about that dreadfully dull book again. No, he couldn't be. It wouldn't have made Lily laugh.

He was suddenly unnerved by the fact that he had to fight the urge to go over there and charm circles around that pup, Richard. He could if he wanted to. Maybe if he had more energy and didn't need to sit here and rest, he would do it. He could easily put a spell on Lily and be the victor in winning her attention tonight.

But that was his competitive nature talking, he told himself. If there was a beautiful woman in the room, he couldn't help but flirt with her, which is what had just happened with Lily. He had merely gotten swept up in the game and had forgotten who she was.

He supposed he didn't really know who Lily was any more. He had known once, of course. He'd played with her for years when she was a girl. He'd enjoyed those games. But when she grew too old for pony rides on his back, there wasn't much left between them. What did a twenty-six-year-old man say to a fourteen-year-old girl, after all? They'd simply stopped talking to each other, and except for the brief day he'd spent in her company when they took her away from Pierre, this present shooting party was the first time they'd actually had a conversation.

And it had been very different. She was a woman now, and she had been flirting with him.

Still trying to ignore the fatigue that seemed slightly more relentless tonight, he ran a hand through his hair and promised himself he would be more careful next time and try not to be distracted by the way Lily looked. She was still "little Lily," and she was not someone he could toy with. If he did, James would likely slice him up into cubes and feed him to the dogs for breakfast.

At least that would bring a swift end to things.

Chapter 5

❝I don't understand it," Lily said to Sophia later that evening after the dancing had begun. "He flirted with me earlier. He implied he was going to dance with me, but he's been ignoring me completely. This is even worse than it was before. He's never outright avoided me before. Maybe I was too forward."

Lily and Sophia walked around the perimeter of the green saloon, where the guests were dancing informally to a polka. There were no dance cards this evening. It was an intimate party and all the guests knew each other too well for such formalities.

Whitby wasn't dancing, however. He was lean-

ing against the wall in the corner, talking to some
of the gentlemen.

"Perhaps," Sophia said, "he's avoiding you because he did feel something and he's uncomfortable with it. Think of his friendship with James,
after all. Whitby would surely have some reservations about flirting with his best friend's younger
sister."

Lily sighed heavily. "Then why am I even bother-
ing? If he could never do that to James, then I—"

"Oh, Lily, don't give up yet. You were so happy
and excited earlier. Something obviously sparked
between the two of you. He just needs to get used to
the idea and come around to see that it doesn't have
to be impossible. If he wants you badly enough, he
can make it happen. James would not be unreason-
able. Remember, you have me on your side."

"Whitby doesn't look like he wants me very badly
right now. Look at him. He hasn't even glanced in
this direction. He looks completely bored."

Sophia looked at Whitby. She had no answer.

Just then, Lord Richard approached. "Lady Lily,
would you care to take to the floor?"

Lily had to shift her thinking and force herself to
forget her disappointment. She smiled warmly. "I'd
be delighted."

He led her into the middle of the room and they
skipped off into the bouncing insanity of the polka.
Everyone was laughing and howling, as it was past
midnight and significant amounts of wine and
brandy had been consumed.

The dance ended and Lily laughed with Richard, both of them out of breath. "We almost knocked your father over just now," she said. "I thought we were surely going to collide."

"Me, too. What a night. I can't say I've ever had so much fun. The duchess certainly knows how to entertain."

"There was a time," Lily replied, "when our shooting parties were frightfully dull. That was before James married Sophia. When Mother was in charge."

They both looked over at Marion, who was watching from the corner with the other ladies her age.

"Does she mind how things have changed?" Richard asked.

"She did at one time, but she's accepted it now. Although she might not be completely comfortable with it. The ladies look rather displeased, don't they?"

Lord Richard smiled and turned his back on them. "Your mother looks like she's got a cramp in her side. They're tolerating it at best."

Mrs. Carrington—their neighbor who was playing the polka on the piano—began playing again, but this time a country dance. Richard led Lily back onto the floor. The ladies lined up on the left, facing the gentlemen.

The dance began, and they moved around each other in the proper formations. "May I say, Lady Lily, that you look stunning this evening?"

"Thank you," she replied.

"I can't imagine your mother approved of *that* dress."

There was a hint of vulgarity in his tone, and it made Lily feel suddenly self-conscious, especially of her low *décolletage*. "Did you prefer the one I wore last night?" she asked.

"Oh, no, not me. I definitely prefer this one. I hate it when women dress like their grandmothers."

Lily tried to smile at what she wouldn't exactly call a compliment.

They joined hands and walked in a circle around each other. Richard smiled presumptuously at her. "You wore it for me, didn't you?"

They separated and came back together again, going through the steps side by side. "I wore it because I liked it," she replied.

"I like it, too. I was actually quite surprised when I saw you tonight. I must confess, last night when we were introduced, I had taken you for a bit of a prude."

Lily snapped her mouth shut, stunned by his uncouth manner. "Why would you think that?"

"Because of the way you acted—like a scared mouse. I'm guessing now that it was because your mother was so close by. But tonight I see there is something bold about you. I quite like it."

He crossed behind her, and she could feel his gaze on her bare neck and shoulders. When they came around to face each other, she felt almost as if he was leering at her. Lily felt her skin prickle, and worried that perhaps she had gone too far with her flirting.

"Thank God I don't have to be in that rank church tomorrow," he said offhandedly.

"I can't say that I've ever heard a chaplain say such a thing before," she said. "What would your parishioners say?"

A look of disdain colored his face. "To tell you the truth I don't really care. I wouldn't be in that chapel day after tedious day if it weren't for my father. He's so bloody controlling. He'd cut me off if I didn't do as he told me to."

Lily wondered what her mother would think if she could hear Richard now.

Richard crossed behind her. "There aren't many people I would say something like that to," he said, "but I've seen the way you are with your mother, and tonight I've begun to suspect that you would like nothing better than to break free of your confines, too. I'm hoping we are kindred spirits."

He discreetly brushed a finger up her arm as he came to stand before her. She was reminded of what had happened to her three years ago, when Pierre had convinced her to run off with him. She had wanted to break out of her confines then, to get away from this house. She had been desperate for attention and affection—from anyone—and she had wanted to prove to herself that she was not in love with Whitby. She'd wanted to smother the hurt and the longing she always felt, especially when she watched him flirt with other women.

She would not make that mistake again, because she had learned from it. She had learned that one could not simply distract one's self from things that hurt. Those things must be faced and dealt with.

The dance ended and she was glad. Richard escorted her off the floor, but remained at her side. A few other guests joined them.

While the conversation went on all around her, Lily found herself searching the room for Whitby. She spotted him sitting down in a corner with Lady Stanton. He had not danced all night, which was odd, Lily thought. It was not like him. He always danced at these parties—with every woman in the room.

While one part of her feared that he was purposefully trying to stay out of her path because she had made a complete fool of herself earlier, another part of her wondered again if he was not feeling well.

At that moment, he stood. He bowed to Lady Stanton who stood also and left his side to go talk to someone else. Whitby approached Sophia and James, spoke to them briefly, and headed for the door.

Lily watched all this from the opposite side of the room. She noticed James take a step forward, as if to try to convince Whitby to stay, but Sophia grabbed his arm and shook her head. James consequently did not follow.

Lily turned her attention back to the conversation around her, and tried to hide her immense disappointment over the fact that Whitby had left.

The next day while the gentlemen were out with the guns, the ladies enjoyed an extravagant lunch of soft shell crabs, tossed salad and pickles. Afterward, they all donned their cloaks and headed outside for a leisurely stroll to the lake.

Lily walked beside Miss Jennie Carrington, whose mother had played the piano the night before. As they wandered down the yew-hedged walks through the terraced garden, they paused occasionally to identify the flowers that were blooming so late in the year. The group went on ahead of them, so they had to hurry to catch up, walking around the rectangular pond.

Just then Jennie's gaze darted to the tawny figure of a man in a light brown jacket sitting on the stone bench on the other side of the water, under the oak tree. He had his back to them and was not aware of their presence. He was leaning forward with his elbows on his knees and his head down.

"Who is that?" Jennie asked. "I thought all the men were out shooting."

Lily knew at once who it was. She recognized everything about him—the color of his hair, the line of his shoulders, the manner in which he sat. The fact that he was not with the other gentlemen made her slow her pace.

"It's Lord Whitby," she said.

Jennie slowed her pace, too. "He's losing his looks, I believe. Did you see him last night? He had dark circles under his eyes. I suppose that's what happens when you lead the kind of life he does. Have you noticed how thin he is?"

"Yes." Though she didn't think it made him any less handsome.

"It's a shame he is so wild," Jennie said. "He's going to do himself in with all his drinking. That's probably why he couldn't get out of bed this morning to go with the other gentlemen."

Lily, distracted by the image of Whitby sitting out here alone when he should have been with the others, finally stopped. She could not continue on to the lake.

Jennie reached the far corner of the pond and was about to disappear around the hedge, when she realized Lily was not beside her anymore. She turned around. "Are you coming?"

Lily searched her mind for an excuse. "If you don't mind, Jennie, I think I will head back to the house. I have a bit of a headache."

Jennie studied her intently. "All right. I'll tell Sophia."

Lily waited for Jennie to disappear around the hedge, then she turned and walked back along the edge of the pond.

The wind was blowing fast, but it was a warm wind for this time of year. She glanced across the choppy, gray water to where Whitby was still sitting in the same position, his elbows on his knees, his head bowed. Lily stood for a moment, just watching the back of him. Was he asleep?

At that instant, he lifted his head. He turned on the bench as if someone had whispered to him, and looked at her from across the pond.

Lily waved. He swiveled around so he was facing her, and hesitated a moment before he waved back. Lily had the distinct feeling he didn't want to be disturbed, but it was too late now. She couldn't very well turn around and walk off.

So Lily did the only thing she could. She put one foot in front of the other and started off to join him and find out why he was sitting there alone, looking so very low.

Chapter 6

Whitby sat on the cold bench and swallowed over his sore throat while he watched Lily approach. The wind was blowing her cloak open and her dark green skirts were hugging her legs. She raised a hand to hold on to her hat.

As she came closer, he marveled at how petite she was. He could easily wrap his hands around her tiny waist. Last night, he'd noticed how tiny her wrists were, too. They were slender and delicate and he was sure he could easily wrap his thumb and forefinger around one of them if he tried.

She was most assuredly a small woman, which is probably why he'd failed to realize she had become one.

She came to a slow, hesitant stop before him. He should have stood up to greet her properly, but he couldn't. He didn't have the strength. Instead, he met her gaze and smiled rather sheepishly, and rested his elbows on his knees again.

"Good morning," she said. "Or rather, good afternoon."

He simply smiled again and nodded at her, for he didn't really need to say anything. She knew something was wrong with him. He could tell by the look in her eyes.

She sat down beside him. "You're not out with the guns. Are you all right?"

He stretched his legs out in front of him and crossed them at the ankles. "I'm fine. I just didn't feel like getting out of bed this morning."

She gazed toward the pond. "I don't believe you. I don't think you're fine. You don't *look* fine."

When he didn't reply, she turned on the bench to face him more squarely. "You must know what people are saying about you, Whitby—that your wild manner of living is catching up with you."

He shook his head and chuckled. "You too, Lily? Yesterday, James gave me a lecture on this very subject. He seems to think I'm trying to drink myself to death."

"Are you?" she asked, sounding quite decidedly horrified.

He looked her in the eye. "Of course not. I've had a sore throat, that's all. The doctor suggested brandy."

There it was again—the lie about having seen a doctor when he had not seen one. He'd only seen his solicitor. About his sister, Annabelle.

And Magnus, of course.

"Surely not bottles and bottles of it."

He gazed out at the pond again. He didn't particularly want to talk about this.

"Perhaps James could call on our family physician," Lily said. "He's very good."

But Whitby did not want to see a doctor. Not yet. He would have to in time, of course, but for now, there was no need, because he already knew what was wrong with him. It was what his father had had.

And he was not ready to hear it confirmed.

"This will pass," Whitby said. "It's nothing."

Neither of them said anything for a moment or two, then Whitby inclined his head at Lily and deliberately changed the subject. "So tell me, was Lord Richard polite last night? I saw you dancing with him."

The concern in her eyes softened, and he was glad—glad that she was not going to ask more questions about his health.

He was also perceptive of the fact that she seemed pleased he had asked her about Richard. He could tell she wanted to talk about her flirtations, and he found it endearing. Perhaps a little intriguing as well.

"You would have been surprised if you could have heard him," she said. "He was—as you put it so eloquently last night—quite shockingly *daring*. He said he hoped we were kindred spirits."

Whitby shifted on the bench. "You don't say."

"I do indeed."

"And are you?"

"Are we what?"

"Kindred spirits?"

She pondered that for a few seconds, then replied with a teasing smile. "I haven't decided yet."

Ah Lily, still playing games. Aside from last night, he hadn't seen her play games like this in many years.

He felt a sudden longing for something vague and elusive. He wasn't quite sure what it was specifically, because he'd been overwhelmed by an avalanche of different emotions lately, but whatever it was, longing for it hurt somewhere deep inside of him.

"Was Richard charming?" he asked, hoping to distract himself.

Oddly, Whitby was hoping to hear that Richard had been a buffoon. Again he chocked it up to his competitive nature and nothing else. This was *Lily*, he reminded himself. He and she should not be flirting.

"He was charming for some of the time," she said, then she turned her blue eyes toward him and licked her lips as a cool breeze blew into her face. Her dark lashes fluttered, as if she were taking pleasure in the caress of the fresh air on her skin.

He stared wordlessly at her for a moment, feeling awestruck, a little weak in the knees. Aroused.

No . . .

Dread poured through him.

He didn't want to acknowledge the arousal, but he had to, because Lily—yes, Lily—was a lush and fetching young maid, fresh as spring rain, sitting here beside him smelling like roses and delighting in physical sensation. She was bewitching, and dammit, even in his current state of health, his body was responding on cue with a fervor he wished had not awakened.

"But not quite as charming as certain *other* gentlemen of my acquaintance," she added seductively.

He sat still, immobile, completely arrested by the shock of her effect on him, and the impossible temptation she presented.

His finely tuned male instincts sparked and flared into flame, and the natural urge to reply in a most unbrotherly manner came upon him. God help him, he had discovered Lily's sexuality.

He steeled himself physically and looked away from her, when he would have instead liked to smile at her—in a way that told her he was game if she was. It was a smile he'd given many women over the years, a smile he was very good at and very comfortable with at moments like these—sexually charged moments in the country with secluded garden houses nearby . . .

But no, not today. Not now. It was not a smile he could give Lily.

"You left early last night," she said, as if she'd recognized his unease. "Were you not enjoying yourself?"

He spoke without looking at her, with a forced

coolness in his tone. "This cold got the better of me. I just wanted to go to bed."

Everything felt very awkward all of a sudden.

Lily sat beside him for a moment, saying nothing. He could feel her grow tense and ill at ease. He did not strive to fill the silence. He wanted her to understand that he did not wish to cultivate this kind of thing between them. He did not want to be attracted to her, and she should not be attracted to him.

Another awkward moment passed in silence, then she stood.

He was relieved.

"Well, I'm glad to hear that it's just a cold you have," she said. "I was a little worried."

He squinted up at her.

Lily ran her gloved hands uncomfortably over the front of her skirt. "I suppose I should get back to the house. I have a bit of a headache myself."

She started to leave, but stopped and turned back. "But I really think you should ask James to send for his doctor. He might be able to help."

Whitby continued to squint up at her against the gray sky, the clouds passing swiftly overhead. The wind blew, and she reached up to hold on to her hat again.

"If I don't feel better by tomorrow, I'll see someone," he promised, wanting only to appease her.

Her shoulders rose and fell with a sigh. "All right. But let it be known, I will check on you tomorrow to hold you to it."

"Ah, Lily, you sound just like my own sister, Annabelle. You are as dear to me as she is."

The color drained from Lily's face.

Whitby felt the color drain from his own face as well. *Jesus.* That was cruel. He had just openly rejected her. She looked humiliated.

But no, it was more than that. She looked hurt. Heartbroken.

His gut wrenched. Good God, was there more to this than he realized? Was this more than a light flirtation on her part? Did she actually fancy herself in love with him?

"Well, I should go," she said.

Whitby merely nodded.

She lowered her gaze and walked off. As soon as she was out of sight, he squeezed his eyes shut and cupped his forehead in a hand. Bloody hell.

What in God's name had caused this foolishness in her head? He hadn't done anything to inspire it, had he? He wracked his brain. No, he couldn't recall anything. Not before last night.

Had she lost her mind?

He ran a hand through his hair, wondering how in the world he was going to treat Lily gently and tactfully over the next few days. She was not like other women he could simply avoid if he needed to. She was Lily, and this was a problem because he cared for her. But not *that* way.

Well . . . He watched her in the distance, reaching the house. Maybe he did feel something, but that was only because he was a man with a heightened awareness of feminine sexuality. He picked up on it like a wolf on a scent, and his libido sometimes responded quicker than his brain. He would not let himself think it was more than that.

Either way, he did not want to flirt with Lily or lead her on in any way, and he hated the fact that he might have to hurt her or humiliate her if she did not come to understand that he was not interested. Because he was not. Nor would he ever be.

He glanced to make sure she was not going to come back, and when he saw her disappear into the house, he sighed deeply with relief, then reached into his pocket for his flask. While he unscrewed the cap, he recalled that he had promised himself he wouldn't touch it until teatime.

He paused for a moment, staring at it, then he brought it to his lips and tipped it up until it was gone.

Chapter 7

That evening, Lily sat in the green saloon with the other guests, waiting for the theatricals to begin. Lady Stanton and Sir Hatley had prepared a short play. Whitby was seated on the other side of the room, avoiding Lily again, but tonight it didn't just seem like he was. She knew he was. He had made it abundantly clear today, and had told her indirectly—yet directly—that he did not welcome her attentions.

She had cried when she'd returned to her room, and there was a lump in her throat still, as she looked at him sitting back in his chair, laughing with the other men as if he hadn't a care in the world.

"Are you all right, Lily?" Sophia asked, taking the empty seat beside her. Lily had not even noticed her approach.

"Not really."

Sophia glanced around at the others and lowered her voice. "What happened today? We lost you on the way to the lake."

Lily supposed she had to tell Sophia, even though she didn't really want to talk about it. She wanted to put it behind her.

But this was not a new desire. She had felt this way and wanted the same thing many times over the years following many similar types of encounters with Whitby—most of them revolving around his not seeing her or flirting with other women in front of her.

Today, it was ten times worse, for he had openly rejected her.

"I spoke to Whitby," she said.

"I thought you might have. I saw him sitting on the bench. What happened?"

"Well, we talked for a few minutes about Richard, and I tried to be flirtatious in the same way I was last night, but today he cooled instantly. It was mortifying. He wouldn't look at me, and when I mentioned I thought it would be a good idea if he saw James's physician—because he has a sore throat—he told me I was just like Annabelle, his sister. He was very clearly trying to tell me to stop behaving otherwise."

Sophia touched her hand. "Oh, Lily."

Lily sat up straighter in her chair, fighting to crush the urge to cry again. She could not keep doing this.

"I felt like a fool. It was dreadful. I have been devastated and embarrassed all day, and I wouldn't have come tonight except for the fact that I couldn't bear the thought of him knowing I was crying in my room like a child. I was determined to come and hold my head high and ignore him, hoping only that he might think he was mistaken about his suspicions, and I in fact have no interest in him whatsoever. Otherwise, I will never be able to face him again without feeling completely humiliated."

"At least now you know," Sophia said gently. "I'm sorry, Lily. I'm sorry I encouraged you. I should have minded my own business."

Lily shook her head. "It's not your fault. In fact, I should thank you. You're right. At least now I know, and I can get over him once and for all."

Sophia glanced over her shoulder at Whitby. "I was so sure the two of you were meant to be together. I can't explain it, except to say that you have similar souls. I still feel it. I just wish he could see it."

"I don't feel it," Lily said. "Not after today."

Just then, Lady Stanton walked to the far end of the room where they had cleared the floor and set up a small stage with an amber curtain as a backdrop.

"Attention, attention, everyone!" she said. "We are about to begin. Sir Hatley and I are going to perform the death scene from Romeo and Juliet."

Lily sighed. "Wonderful. They couldn't have chosen a comedy tonight?"

Sophia squeezed her hand.

The two began the performance, which turned out to be a comedy after all. They exaggerated the lovers' deaths, groaning with their tongues hanging out, while the guests cheered and whistled, finally rising to their feet, clapping and shouting "Bravo!" when Juliet gasped her last farcical, wheezing breath.

Lily forced herself to smile and clap, too, though inside she was still fighting tears.

When the applause died down and everyone was congratulating the actors, who were laughing hysterically, Lily stood and excused herself.

"You're sure you're all right, Lily?" Sophia asked, whispering.

"Yes. I'm fine." She just needed to be alone. She turned and left the room.

A short time later, she met Lord Richard in the long, carpeted gallery. He stepped out from behind a bust, startling her.

"I was hoping you weren't gone for the night," he said, glancing down at the neckline of her cream-colored, French silk gown. "I wanted to talk to you."

"About what?" she asked, looking around the gallery to see if there was anyone else present. There was not. They were alone.

He gave her a sidelong glance, as if to tell her she should know. When she said nothing, he shook his head at her. "Surely you're aware of the fact that we are being paired up this week."

Lily was feeling increasingly uneasy. "I suppose."

"I wasn't keen on coming to this party at first, because I knew the kinds of girls my father had selected for me in the past, and quite frankly, they've all been about as pretty as piglets."

Lily was disappointed. She had truly wanted to like Lord Richard. Life would have been so easy if she could have. But that comment did nothing to recommend him. In fact, she was liking him less and less with every word he spoke.

"But you," he said, lifting an eyebrow, "are no piglet. I almost think my father was disappointed when he saw you. Disappointed that his undeserving son was going to get such a prize for a wife."

Lily stepped back. "I have not consented to become your wife, Lord Richard."

He followed her with a forward step of his own. "Not yet. But I suspect you will."

"What makes you so sure?"

"Because you've had no other offers. Probably because of the whispers about you."

"What whispers?" she asked, caught off guard.

"The rumors. Some people seem to think you might be used goods. Though no one knows for sure. But I have to wonder why you've avoided society for the past few years, and why someone as lovely as you with such a large dowry isn't already spoken for."

He was standing very close now, but Lily would not back away. "That is all utter nonsense," she said. "And you have just severed any chance whatsoever that I might ever consider becoming your wife. You are disrespectful, sir."

She moved past him to return to the saloon, but he took hold of her arm. "Where are you going?" He looked surprised.

"Back to the party," she said tersely. "Sophia is waiting for me."

"Don't go yet."

Did he not understand she was not attracted to him in even the most minuscule way? "Let go, Richard."

"I said not yet."

Just then, someone else spoke. Whitby. Lily knew his voice like she knew her own.

"Everything all right, Lily?"

She glanced toward the door. There he was, leaning at his ease against the jamb. Richard let go of her arm.

"Yes, Lord Whitby," she replied shakily. "Thank you."

He stayed where he was for a moment—just watching them until they both began to walk toward him to return to the party. He backed up against the doorjamb to let them pass.

He said nothing. Lily glanced up at him briefly as she brushed by. The three of them walked in awkward silence back to the saloon, where they each went to different sides of the room.

Chapter 8

Later in the evening, after the second theatrical performance by Lady Stanton and Sir Hatley, Lily found herself sitting alone near the fireplace. Not for long, however. The empty chair beside her was almost immediately filled by Whitby.

"I wasn't sure," he said, going straight to the heart of things, "if I should have interrupted you when you were in the gallery. I thought perhaps you might have arranged to meet Richard there."

Lily's heart began to pound, and she cursed herself for it. After all her tears today and all her grand intentions to forget Whitby, all he had to do was say two words to her, and she melted.

She shook her head. "No, I didn't arrange it. He must have followed me when I left here earlier."

"Yes, he did, and I noticed, so I followed *him*."

"Why?"

He hesitated a moment before he answered. "Because I was worried he might not be entirely trustworthy. I just had a feeling."

She'd had a feeling, too. "Why didn't you tell James?" she asked.

"Because James would have beat him to a pulp."

She couldn't help but smile. "So you wanted to protect Richard, did you?"

"No, not Richard."

Her body began to feel warm as she sat beside him this way. Wishing he did not have such power over her, she reminded herself that he had been worried about her just as he would have been worried about Annabelle, his sister.

"Well, I'm fine," she said, which was not entirely true in every sense of the word, but she would not let him see that.

"Good. But what are you going to do about Richard? Am I right to presume you do not welcome his attentions?"

"Yes."

Whitby looked across the room at the man. "Well, you might consider telling James. You certainly wouldn't want to be pressured into marrying a worm."

Lily chuckled despite herself.

Whitby leaned a little closer to her. "I can hardly

blame the man, though. You look stunning tonight, Lily. He probably lost his head."

Lily felt her brow crease as she looked at Whitby. What was he doing? When he said things like that, he made it impossible for her to get over him. Because quite honestly, right now, she felt euphoric and hopeful again, and she wanted him more than life itself.

How little it took.

"Thank you for the compliment," she replied, but she was angry with him. Did he not realize he was playing with her feelings?

"You're most welcome." Then he walked off to go sit with Lady Stanton.

Whitby listened to Lady Stanton talk about Ascot with only half of his brain. The more thoughtful half was mulling over his conversation with Lily.

He wasn't sure why he had told her she looked stunning tonight. Well, she did look stunning in that cream-colored dress, her neck dripping with pearls, but it hadn't been necessary to tell her. Earlier in the day, he had compared her to Annabelle with the full intention of discouraging her from having any non-sisterly feelings for him—because he was not the man for her—and just now, after seeing Richard make an advance, Whitby had forgotten all that, and had said something that would likely have the opposite effect. He had paid her a compliment and he'd done so flirtatiously.

He wished he hadn't said it. He wished he could

take it back. He didn't want her to have romantic notions about him. He didn't want to stir her passions—however innocent they may be.

In truth, he wasn't entirely sure how innocent Lily was after what happened three years ago with that French nuisance of a man. She had been with him in his boardinghouse and on a boat with him overnight, and everyone had been very closed-mouthed about it afterward.

The fact that he was curious about her innocence now—after not even wondering about it over the past few years—was not lost on him.

He glanced over at her. Strangely, he could not imagine her giving herself to that scoundrel, Pierre. Or that worm, Richard. Just the thought of it offended him. It made him want to strangle the both of them.

But as he comprehended the excessiveness of his agitation, he began to realize with considerable surprise and uneasiness that he was not as disinterested in Lily as he had hoped he could be.

He reached a hand up to rub the glands at his neck, then glanced over at James, his closest, oldest friend.

Whitby's pulse began to beat erratically. This was not going well. *Nothing* about this week was going well. It seemed like everything was spiraling out of control, and there was nothing he could do to stop it.

The weather was overcast again the next day. It was unseasonably warm, however, and many of the gentlemen had removed their hunting jackets and wore only their shirts and waistcoats as they stood in the autumn field, firing shots high into the air over the lake as the ducks took flight.

James aimed his rifle and fired, bringing another bird down from the sky. Whitby stood beside him, the tip of his own rifle resting on the ground while he used it to lean upon.

"Good shot, James," he said, squeezing the handle of his gun.

A hound jumped into the lake with a resounding splash and swam out to fetch the fallen bird. Whitby watched him swim past the cattails, paddling silently into the deep.

"It was, wasn't it?" James said, grinning over his shoulder. His gaze dropped to the rifle Whitby was leaning upon. "Why aren't you shooting?"

Whitby picked up his rifle and loaded it. "Just taking a break." He waited for the beaters to send another flock into the air, then aimed and fired. A number of shots rang out from the other gentlemen standing a distance away.

"Well done," James said, while they watched a few birds fall from the sky to the water.

Whitby lowered his gun while James reloaded his.

"Tell me," Whitby said, "are you in on the plan to marry Lily off to Lord Richard?"

He hadn't intended to talk to James about this. In fact, he'd promised himself that very morning that he would stay out of it. So much for self-control.

James cocked his rifle. "No. That's Mother."

Whitby was relieved. "I'm glad to hear it."

"What makes you say that?"

More birds took flight, and James quickly aimed and fired. "Damn," he said, missing the shot.

"Well," Whitby replied, pausing while he reloaded, "I walked in on them last night in the gallery, and Richard was rather bold with his attentions."

James immediately faced Whitby. His tone took on a hard edge. "Explain if you will."

"Don't panic. It wasn't anything serious. It was just something in his manner I didn't like."

"Did he touch her?" James asked.

"He took hold of her arm to try and stop her from returning to the party when she made a move to leave. It was clear to me that Lily was uncomfortable. If I were you, I would discourage the match."

Whitby worried suddenly that he was overstepping his bounds. It wasn't his place to tell James who his sister should or should not marry. But hell, he couldn't help himself. He couldn't bear the idea of her being pressured to marry Richard, and he knew it wasn't just a brotherly protectiveness. Which was becoming very unsettling.

Or perhaps this "concern" was simply a symptom of his state of health. He'd certainly been preoccupied lately with making sure Annabelle was going to be taken care of. He'd arranged for an allowance for her, so she would not have to depend upon Magnus . . .

"You don't believe she fancies him?" James asked.

"I know she doesn't."

"How?"

"I asked her."

Three more ducks took off with a flutter, and both James and Whitby aimed and fired, bringing down two of them. They lowered their guns.

"I appreciate you telling me," James said. "To be honest, I've wanted to clobber Richard a few times myself over the past few days. He keeps boasting about his horses. But I've refrained because of the possibility that he might one day be my brother-in-law."

"He's trying to impress you," Whitby said casually.

"No doubt. It's hardly working, though. Especially after what you just told me."

The tension in Whitby's shoulders drained away while they both gazed out at the lake.

"I'm feeling rather ready for lunch," James said. "How about you?"

Whitby merely shrugged. "I could eat, I suppose."

James rested his rifle on his shoulder. "I'll go talk to Anderson and see if he's got the table laid out yet." He started off, but stopped and turned. "Help me keep an eye on Richard tonight, for caution's sake. Lily doesn't need another problem like the last one."

"Absolutely, James."

Whitby was only too happy to oblige. Far more happy than he should be.

Chapter 9

That evening, the ballroom was adorned with colorful flowers and greenery, tall potted tree ferns, and bolts of ivory crepe draped over the doorways and windows. The shiny brass chandeliers glittered in the light from the candles they held, and the whole room spun magnificently with the circular movements of the dancers swirling around the floor.

Lily wore a silk gown of mulberry, trimmed with lace flounces on the skirt, and she was laced so tight, she could barely breathe. At her neck, she wore a pearl choker that she had borrowed from Sophia, and on her feet, matching satin slippers with French heels.

She felt beautiful, more beautiful than on any other night, and she was thankful for that because the shooting party would conclude tomorrow, and she had come to the ball tonight knowing it would be the last time she would see Whitby before the long winter set in.

She was hoping for one last encounter with him—a dance perhaps, or a pleasant, friendly conversation free of flirtation.

She had tried for something more with him, and she had failed. He had communicated his feelings on the matter, and she had understood the message: He was not attracted to her. For that reason, tonight, she was going to finally lay her childish infatuation to rest. And she did not want him to feel that he must avoid her in the future because she was pining away for him. She could not imagine a worse fate. She did not want things to be awkward between them.

Lily spotted her mother approaching and walked to meet her. When she reached her side, she clicked open her plumed fan and cooled herself, for it was warm in the ballroom.

"You've had a few days to get to know Lord Richard," her mother said flatly. "What do you think of him?"

"Honestly?" Lily replied, pausing because she did not enjoy displeasing her mother. She never enjoyed it, but she knew it was necessary in this matter. She could only pray that her mother would understand. "I don't think he is the right man for me."

She could sense the frustration in her mother's long, drawn-out silence. "Lily . . ."

Lily faced her. "I know what you're thinking—that I'm too fussy, but it's not true. I just—"

"Lily, you must think of your future."

"I am thinking of it. Please understand, Mother, I don't care for Lord Richard."

Marion led Lily toward the wall to speak privately. "Lily, I'm getting tired of this. You are far too romantic. Marriage is a serious matter, and I don't think you truly understand your duty as a member of this family. You are the daughter of a duke and you are twenty-one. By the time I was that age, I had been married for two years."

"But not happily." Lily had never spoken so bluntly to her mother before. She could hardly believe she had done it.

Marion went pale, then her face clouded with anger. "How can you judge *me*, after all I endured? Do you think it was easy?"

Lily shuddered inwardly, regretting her words, wishing they had not been so stinging. It was all her mother had—her pride over the fact that she had never abandoned her post, no matter how horrendous it had been. She must have wanted to leave it, like a soldier in the trenches, but she had not, because she ranked duty above all else.

And she resented Lily because Lily was not so dutiful. Lily questioned her orders. She followed her heart and her desires, and her mother could not understand that. They were two very different people.

"I'm sorry, Mother," she said.

She was sorry for criticizing her, and she was sorry for defying and disappointing her—for all the times in the past, and all the times she would continue to do so in the future.

The orchestra began a minuet, interrupting their conversation briefly, but not for long.

"Just give me more time," Lily said, wanting desperately to appease her mother as best she could. "I do want to be dutiful. I want to please you, but I cannot marry Lord Richard. I'll be successful next Season, I promise."

Marion would not meet her gaze. She was breathing hard, angry and shaken. "Well. It's obvious I can't force you. I've learned that such tactics do nothing but cause you to rebel." She turned in the other direction. "I must go and sit down."

She walked away, leaving Lily to struggle with the ache that had existed in her heart since she was a child—the aching need for affection, or merely approval from her mother. Lily laid a hand on her chest to try and soothe it, and went outside for some fresh air.

On the other side of the ballroom, Whitby watched Lily with her mother. There was a marked intensity in their exchange, he noticed, though he tried not to stare. He wondered if they were talking about Richard.

Whitby searched the room for the man and spotted him not far from where Lily stood, probably waiting to dance with her. Whitby remembered his promise to James—that he would keep an eye on them—and decided he would do just that. Keep a very close eye.

Just then, Lady Stanton, wearing a sky-blue gown with a cluster of pearls at the bosom, arrived beside him. She touched his arm with one long, slender gloved finger. "Good evening, Whitby. I hope you intend to dance with me. It's the last night of the party and we all go home tomorrow. Yet I haven't seen nearly enough of you."

He turned to her and smiled, though tonight it felt like a pretense, for he didn't have the energy to be charming.

A waltz began and he held out his hand regardless, for he was never one to disappoint a lady. "Are you free for this one?"

"I believe my card indicates I am."

Whitby led her onto the floor and took her into his arms. They stepped into the waltz and swept smoothly around the room. They danced well together, as they had danced many times before.

"I haven't done anything to offend you, have I?" Lady Stanton asked after the first few measures.

Whitby met her troubled gaze. "What do you mean, Eleanor?"

"I had thought we might spend some time together this week. I thought you might come to my room, but I've been disappointed each night, and I've had to sleep alone."

Whitby turned her around at the far corner of the

ballroom. He recalled last year's shooting party and remembered how he and Eleanor had amused themselves. She was a delightful woman; he knew it today just as he'd known it last year. She had certainly not offended him.

Yet he'd felt no desire to spend time in her bed this week.

"I apologize, Eleanor. I've not been myself. It's nothing you've done. I've been rather unwell with a damned inconvenient sore throat."

Her body seemed to relax in his arms. "That's all it is? What a relief. I was beginning to fear you were suffering from a broken heart—that some woman had captured your interest while I wasn't looking, and jilted you."

He chuckled. "No."

"Well, thank goodness," she said with a smile.

As they continued to dance around the room, Whitby found himself feeling uncomfortably short of breath. He began to feel weak and light-headed.

"You know you're welcome to come to my room tonight," Eleanor said with an enticing tone. "My door will be unlocked for you, if you'd like some company."

Whitby swallowed hard, barely hearing what she had just said, while he labored to concentrate on the steps of the dance.

Then he saw Lily walk alone through the open doors that led out onto the veranda. His gaze perused the room for Richard, who predictably was not far behind, following her outside.

Suddenly, a wave of dizziness came over Whitby, and he was forced to stop in the middle of the floor.

"My apologies again, Eleanor. I'm afraid I can't go on." He turned to look for James.

Eleanor put her hand on his cheek. "Good heavens, Whitby, you're blazing hot. Why didn't you tell me?"

He wiped the perspiration from his brow. "It came upon me rather suddenly just now. Where is James?"

Eleanor took him by the arm and led him off the floor. He went with her, crossing the room to where James stood drinking champagne and laughing with Sophia.

"Richard just followed Lily out onto the veranda," Whitby said, wasting not a single breath on anything but that, while he struggled not to stagger sideways.

James glanced over Whitby's shoulder and went immediately to his sister.

Sophia took one look at Whitby and grabbed his arm. "Good gracious, are you all right?"

Whitby turned to ensure James was heading in the right direction—to the veranda where Lily had gone. When he witnessed James exiting the correct door, he relaxed at last. He turned to Eleanor and whispered in her ear.

"I apologize in advance for not coming to your room tonight. I believe I'll be catching up on some much needed rest." He turned to Sophia and said, "Will you call a doctor?"

Her face went pale. "Of course."

With that, he walked out of the ballroom, climbed the main staircase, and only made it as far as the door to his bedchamber before he collapsed in a heap in the corridor.

By the time the physician arrived an hour later, Whitby was slipping in and out of consciousness. Dr. Trider entered the room and set his black bag on the side of the bed. He opened it, pulled out his stethoscope and listened to Whitby's chest.

James and Sophia watched from opposite sides of the bed. "How is he?" James asked.

The doctor ignored the question for a moment while he moved the scope around, listening to Whitby's heart and lungs. He removed the earpieces and lifted Whitby's eyelids one at a time, looking at his pupils. He put his hand on Whitby's forehead. "How long has he been like this?"

"The fever came upon him rather quickly tonight," James replied. "Though he's had a sore throat all week and saw a doctor for it before he came."

Dr. Trider pressed upon both sides of Whitby's neck, just under his jaw. "His lymph nodes are swollen."

"What does that mean?" Sophia asked.

"It could be a number of things, depending on the symptoms he's had."

James raked a hand through his hair. "Well, he's lost some weight, and he's been fatigued. No appetite."

The doctor nodded. "I see." He put his stethoscope back in his bag. "Has he been in contact with anyone else who's had these symptoms?"

"I don't know. He didn't mention anything. He didn't seem overly concerned, but he has been drinking more than usual lately."

"Drinking, you say."

The doctor felt Whitby's neck again, and appeared to be concentrating very hard upon what he was feeling.

Just then Whitby opened his eyes. The doctor leaned over him. "Lord Whitby, I'm Dr. Trider. Do you know what's wrong with you? Have you been in contact with anyone who's been ill?"

"No, no contact," Whitby said, slowly shaking his head on the pillow. "What I have is not contagious."

"How do you know? Have you been diagnosed?"

"No. No need."

Whitby closed his eyes again, and the doctor gently slapped at his cheeks. "Lord Whitby, wake up. What do you think you have?"

Whitby opened his eyes and looked at James. "Did you find Lily?"

"Yes. She's with my mother."

"And Richard?"

"Richard is nursing a bloody nose and is packing his things as we speak."

Sophia's gaze darted across the bed. "A bloody nose? James!"

He shook his head at her. "I didn't give it to him.

Lily did, after he tried something he shouldn't have. And he bloody well deserved it, too."

"That's good news," Whitby said groggily, before he fell back into a feverish sleep.

James stepped forward and leaned over him. "Whitby! Wake up. The doctor needs to ask you some questions."

But Whitby did not wake.

James backed into the chair by the bed and sank into it. "What could it be, doctor?"

Dr. Trider's brow furrowed. "I can't be sure, but the swollen glands indicate a few possibilities. It could be influenza or lymphatic tuberculosis, but that doesn't usually come on this quickly. Typhoid on the other hand develops very fast, but a sore throat for more than a week . . . ?" He shook his head. "I don't believe it's typhoid. And he said it wasn't contagious, which influenza and tuberculosis both are."

The doctor appeared baffled. He took another step toward the bed and felt Whitby's glands again. "The other possibility is . . ." He glanced at James. "Have the glands been getting increasingly swollen over a long period of time?"

"I don't know."

Dr. Trider pressed upon Whitby's abdomen, through the thin nightshirt his valet had dressed him in earlier.

"His spleen is enlarged. Do you know how long he's had the sore throat? Weeks? A month? More?"

James went to the adjoining dressing room and opened the door. "Jenson, how long has Lord Whitby had the sore throat?"

The valet came out of the room. "He's had a few of them, Your Grace. The first one was about a month ago."

The doctor stepped away from the bed and pushed his spectacles up the bridge of his nose. "A few of them, you say? Is it possible it has been one continuous sore throat?"

Jenson looked uneasily at James and Sophia. "I suppose it's possible."

Dr. Trider nodded thoughtfully. "One disease that is consistent with his symptoms and is not contagious is Hodgkins. But how would he know that, if he was not diagnosed?"

"Hodgkins?" Sophia said. "What's that?"

The doctor paused a moment before he faced her and spoke with a slow, gentle voice. "It is a type of cancer, Your Grace."

James and Sophia stared at him in stunned silence. "That's what killed his father," James said.

Chapter 10

~~~OO~~~

Lily was taking part in a quadrille—still exceedingly unnerved over what had happened on the veranda with Lord Richard—when she noticed Sophia and James enter the ballroom after having been gone for quite some time. Whitby had been missing as well, and Lily was beside herself with worry. It was not like James or Sophia to leave their guests for so long. Something was wrong.

As soon as the dance ended, she thanked her partner and quickly made her way through the tight crowd to where Sophia stood. Their gazes met with a heightened intensity.

"What's going on?" Lily asked. "Where were you?"

Sophia took her aside. "Whitby is ill."

The music from the orchestra and the laughter from the crowd seemed to fade into silence, and Lily wondered if her heart had stopped beating. "Oh no."

"The doctor has just seen him, and we don't know anything for sure yet. But he has a very high fever and some swollen glands."

"Can I see him?" Lily asked.

"Yes, but he's not conscious. And I must warn you that the doctor said it could be a very serious illness."

"Is he sure?"

"No, not yet. He'll need to examine Whitby further when he wakes." Sophia led Lily out of the ballroom. "I'll take you to him, then I'll have to come back and be a better hostess. I don't want any gossip over this. I'd prefer to keep this quiet if we can. It's no one's business but ours and Whitby's."

"Of course."

They discreetly left the ballroom, and while they made their way through the corridors of the house, Sophia asked Lily about Richard.

"Did he hurt you?"

"No," Lily replied. "He just tried to kiss me and was very persistent when I resisted. He's a repulsive letch."

"James said you hit him."

"I couldn't help myself."

Sophia smiled. "Good girl."

When they reached the Van Dekker Room, the

door was closed, so Sophia knocked gently, then pushed it open.

The room was dimly lit and quiet, except for a fire crackling in the hearth. Lily followed Sophia inside, but stopped when her gaze fell upon Whitby in the huge bed.

He was drenched in sweat and his face was ashen. He wore a loose-fitting, white nightshirt open at the neck, and it was sticking to his damp skin. He looked half dead.

Lily sucked in a shaky breath, barely able to comprehend that this was her Whitby—who had always been so strong and full of life. He was silent and unresponsive. She couldn't bear to see him this way or to think that—God forbid—he might not recover.

Then her eyes drifted to Lady Stanton, who was sitting next to him with her slender hand upon his.

"Lily, you've come to see the patient," she said.

Lily merely nodded.

"I just got here a few minutes ago myself. He became feverish while we were dancing, you see. But do come and sit down." Lady Stanton vacated the chair by the bed and went to join Sophia near the door.

Lily slowly moved to the chair and sat down.

"I should return to the ballroom," Lady Stanton said to Sophia. "Will you keep me informed?"

"Of course, Eleanor. Lily will sit with him for a few minutes, while I walk you to the stairs."

Lily barely heard what they said. She only noticed the door close behind them, and felt the sudden jarring impact of being alone with Whitby here in his bedchamber, when her entire being was dissolving into dread and despair over the fact that he was so very ill, and it could be serious.

She let her gaze travel down the length of his bare forearm to his hand on top of the sheet. She reached to touch it. God in heaven, he was scorching hot. She rubbed his hand gently between her palms, then rested her head upon it and prayed tearfully for him to get better.

Raising her head, she laid her open palm on Whitby's chest where his nightshirt lay open. His heart was beating fast beneath his fiery, damp skin.

The door clicked and Lily abruptly sat back, wiping tears from her cheeks. Sophia entered and walked around the bed.

"Any change?" she asked.

"No. He hasn't moved."

"How are *you*?"

Lily considered the question for a moment, while she stared at Whitby's sleeping face. Her brain didn't seem to be working very well. "I've been better."

Sophia squeezed her shoulder.

"What is there to be done?" Lily asked. "I want to *do* something."

Sophia nodded, understanding. "The doctor had another call to make tonight, but he will return in the morning. Until then, someone needs to stay and keep Whitby cool with damp cloths." She touched Lily's forearm, her expression grave. "And the doctor said we should give him a tablespoon of brandy every six hours. But no more than that, even if he begs."

Lily understood. She had been watching him this week. She knew . . .

"Let me stay," she said. "I can do all that."

Sophia nodded. "I'll tell your mother."

"She won't like it."

"I'll talk to her," Sophia said. "I'm sure she would want to know we are doing everything we can for Whitby."

"I hope so," Lily said desolately. "Because nothing could make me leave this room tonight."

After going back to her room to change out of her ball gown into something more comfortable—a plain brown muslin day dress—Lily sat through the night with Whitby. She spent most of the time in the chair, holding his hand and watching him in the firelight, waiting and hoping he would stir. He slept very soundly, however, never moving, except occasionally when his eyelids twitched and he turned his head to the side with a moan or a sigh.

Lily was glad he did not wake and ask for brandy. She would have had a difficult time saying no to him.

The music from the ball downstairs continued until after two in the morning, at which time Sophia and James came to check on Lily before going off to bed themselves. After that, the house was deathly quiet.

She dozed off only once, very briefly, and stayed awake the rest of the night. At one point she rose to open the window and let in some fresh air, but the breeze was too strong and too cool, so she closed the window and sat back down again.

The night seemed dark and endless, and there were moments when she felt lost in a tunnel, unable to see light at the end. She was the only person awake in the household. But how could she possibly sleep? Reaching around to put a hand on her lower back, she stretched and yawned and prayed that Whitby's fever would break.

It did not break, however. Not through the night. Nor had it broken in the morning, when he finally opened his eyes.

The sun was just rising and Lily herself was waking from a nap in the chair by the window. James was sitting by the bed.

It was the sound of their voices that woke her. She sat up sleepily, but remained quiet, for she did not want to interrupt their conversation.

"We've sent a telegram to Annabelle," James said, sitting forward in the chair with his elbows on his knees and his hands laced together.

Whitby lay there motionless for a moment, then he wet his lips and whispered, "I'd like a drink, James."

James shook his head. "The doctor said no."

Whitby chuckled bitterly. "You're going to dry me out, are you? What's the point?"

"The point is you've had too much lately."

Whitby lay in silence for a moment, staring blankly at the canopy above him. "I'm dying, James."

Lily sat up straighter, a spear of dread piercing through her heart. She strained to hear James's reply.

"No," he said firmly, touching Whitby's hand. "We don't know that. It might be nothing."

"I feel like I'm dying. I've felt it for weeks."

James was momentarily staggered, which was uncharacteristic of her brother, who was always in absolute control.

"You told me it was just a sore throat," he said.

Whitby wet his lips again, and it seemed to take forever for him to find the strength to speak. "I lied. I've been getting weaker and weaker."

"You said you'd seen a doctor. What did he say about it?"

"I lied about that, too. I didn't see anyone. I wanted to put that part off for a while. I thought I had more time."

James took a moment to digest this. "Is that why you've been drinking so much?"

"I suppose. Brandy numbs the regrets."

Lily watched her brother bow his head. Her heart broke a little at the sight of him, for he himself had had a difficult life with their father, and she knew Whitby was the one person in the world James had trusted when he was young. Whitby had been his only true friend at a time when he'd had no one—not even a mother he could rely on for love.

"You have nothing to regret, Whitby."

Whitby turned his head from side to side on the pillow. "I beg to differ. I should have grown up a long time ago and gotten married like you did, but I thought I'd be young forever. And now I'm probably dying, and Annabelle will be . . ." He tried to sit up. "I need to see her. Is she coming?"

James managed to keep Whitby from getting up. "She'll be on a train today."

"Good. I must see her, James."

"I know."

"I've arranged for an allowance for her, so she won't need to depend upon Magnus, but I don't want her to live alone. I can trust you to take her in, can't I?"

"Of course you can."

Lily realized at that instant that Whitby didn't know she was in the room. She wondered if she should make her presence known. She also wondered what was causing Whitby this concern over his sister, and who Magnus was.

"If anything happens to me," he said, "promise me you'll watch out for her."

"I will. But nothing's going to happen to you."

Lily cleared her throat to announce herself. She slowly stood and smoothed out the wrinkles in her skirts as she walked to the foot of the bed. "Good morning," she said nervously.

Whitby slowly blinked as he met her gaze. She could tell he wanted to go back to sleep. "Good morning."

"Lily was here all night, Whitby," James said. "She was your devoted nurse."

Lily waited for him to say something, but all he did was stare at her for a long, agonizing moment.

She knew at once with shocking clarity that he knew she loved him. He absolutely knew.

Then she saw a spark of something else in his eyes . . .

Pity?

Was it pity, because he knew he was dying and she would be devastated? Or was it simply because he did not return her feelings? He felt sorry for her?

She lowered her gaze. It seemed the disappointments were never going to end. It would always be like this.

Or perhaps they would end soon. That thought made her lift her gaze in a sudden panic. He was still staring at her.

At last he spoke, his voice tired, his expression grim. "Thank you."

Her spirits, heavy and bleak, sank even lower. She couldn't bear this. She couldn't bear to lose him, even though he had never been hers.

"The physician will be here soon to check on you," James said. "He's top notch, Whitby. He'll find out what's wrong with you."

"Good," Whitby whispered, closing his eyes.

Then he opened them again. "You're certain a drink is out of the question?"

"Yes."

Whitby nodded and closed his eyes. "This is not going to be pleasant."

James looked up at Lily, who was still standing at the foot of the bed. She saw the concern in her brother's eyes, an almost desperate pleading. She had never seen him look that way before, not even when his children were coming into the world. He had been worried, yes, but he had not been without hope. There had been anticipation in his eyes, as if he'd somehow known everything would be all right.

He did not look that way this morning, and it left Lily feeling as if she were dying right along with Whitby.

Drifting in and out of sleep the next morning, Whitby experienced strange dreams and felt as if he were floating. He heard conversations in his mind. He thought he heard Magnus laughing . . .

But when he woke there was no one in the room but Jenson, poking about, folding shirts that had probably already been folded.

Whitby's body trembled and his teeth chattered, and no matter how hard he tried to relax and lie still, the shaking would not cease. He didn't know if it was the fever or the need for brandy, but it didn't matter. He was ill. It had been just like this for his father.

Each time the tremors took hold of him, Jenson came close and tucked the blankets up under Whitby's chin and said, "It's the fever, my lord. Try to sleep."

So Whitby would drift off again, only to feel delirious once more. Then he would wake and tremble again.

He felt Jenson tucking the sheets around him, and opened his eyes. "What day is it?"

"It's Sunday, my lord. The party is over and most of the guests have gone."

"Except for us."

"Yes, except for us. We'll leave when you recover."

Whitby wet his very dry lips. "That's wishful thinking."

His valet lowered his voice to a whisper. "I won't hear talk like that, Eddie."

Eddie. The sound of his boyhood name on Jenson's lips stirred uncomfortable memories of another time—when Whitby was not yet an earl, and his mother and father were alive. Whitby remembered his mother laughing and chasing him through the corridors of the house. He could hear her laughter now. He felt transported.

Strangely, whenever he thought of her, she was wearing her white nightgown and bare feet. Probably because the best moments he'd had with her were late at night, when she would cuddle with him in bed.

And when he went to see her when she was dying, she had been lying on her bed, again in her nightgown. Though there had been blood on it from the labor . . .

The tremors came upon him again, rather suddenly, and though he tried, he could not will them away. All he could do was endure the discomfort and hope it would quickly pass.

Chapter 11

～⌘～

Later that day, after Dr. Trider had thoroughly examined Whitby, Lily followed him through the house to James's study. When the door closed behind him, she stood for a moment staring at it, her heart pounding with a desperate need for information. Realizing that the time for shyness was over—for suddenly time seemed to be a great commodity—she knocked on the door.

Sophia opened it, took one look at Lily's face and stepped aside without question. Lily entered the room where James was sitting at his desk and the doctor was sitting on the other side of it, clutching his black leather bag on his lap.

"Lily would like to hear this as well," Sophia

said. She gestured to the chair beside the doctor.

Feeling anxious and apprehensive, her stomach rolling with sickening dread, Lily sat down. She felt James's curious eyes on her, but kept her gaze fixed on the doctor.

"Well," he said, pausing. "I still cannot tell you with total certainty what is afflicting the earl, but knowing that his father died of Hodgkins concerns me."

"Is it hereditary, doctor?" Sophia asked.

Dr. Trider rubbed his forehead, the tension visible in his eyes. "There have been cases recently where heredity was adduced as a possible cause, but we just don't know enough about the illness to say with certainty. Mind you, it's still possible the earl could be suffering from something else."

"So it's possible he's not dying," Lily said.

Sophia reached for her hand, and Lily suspected Sophia did not want her to get her hopes up.

"If it is Hodgkins," James interjected, "is there a cure? Didn't I read about an operation a few years ago?"

"There have been very few successful operations. Hodgkins is a type of lymphoma, and lymphomas are generalized, involving blood and bone marrow." The doctor shook his head. "I'm afraid the prognosis is not good—*if* it is Hodgkins. May I remind you, we don't know for sure that that is what ails the earl."

"If it is, how much time would Lord Whitby have?" James asked.

The doctor considered it. "From the cases I've seen, it can be anywhere from three months to a year or even more, in chronic cases. It depends on how rapidly the disease progresses."

"Have you told Whitby all this?" Lily asked.

Just then, another knock sounded at the door, and Sophia went to answer it. Lily turned in her chair at the same moment that Sophia spread her arms wide and said, "Annabelle, thank goodness." She embraced Whitby's sister, who held her tightly in return. "We are just getting the prognosis from the doctor. Come in."

Lily—who had of course heard of Annabelle, but had never actually met her—watched her enter the room. She had honey-colored hair like Whitby's, but the resemblance was coincidental, for Annabelle Lawson was an adopted sister. She had been the daughter of Whitby's mother's dearest friend, and had been taken in at infancy.

She wore a dark blue traveling gown and her eyes were blue, her nose tiny and slightly turned up. She possessed an uncommon beauty, though she did not seem aware of it. She did not carry herself with the confidence of a woman who knew she was beautiful. Miss Lawson seemed shy, and Lily was drawn to her immediately.

She was also very curious about why Whitby was so worried about her.

James rose and pulled a chair from the side of the room to bring it around next to Lily. "Annabelle," he said, "this is my sister, Lily."

Annabelle shook Lily's hand. "It's a pleasure to finally meet you. I've heard so much about you, and have wanted to meet you since I was a girl."

More than a little taken aback, Lily smiled at Annabelle. She had heard a lot about Lily? From whom? Whitby?

James returned to his own chair and sat down. He leaned forward and rested his hands on the desktop. "The doctor was just telling us what he thinks could be wrong with Whitby, though he can't be sure yet."

Dr. Trider repeated his prognosis for Annabelle, who raised a handkerchief to her eyes and began to cry. Lily leaned close and rubbed Annabelle's back.

"We're hoping for the best," Lily said.

Sophia took a step forward. "Yes, of course we are, Annabelle. Don't lose hope yet. He's young and strong."

She collected herself and lowered her handkerchief. "Thank you for everything you're doing. You know, James, he has always considered you his best friend in the world."

James nodded.

"When can I see him?" Annabelle asked.

"Right now," James replied. "Perhaps Lily, you could show Annabelle to the Van Dekker room."

"Of course," Lily replied, hiding the fact that she was glad to be able to see Whitby again, even if it was only for a moment.

Lily rose and led Annabelle out of the study and through the long, wide corridors of the house.

When they reached Whitby's room, they entered to find him sleeping, and Jenson was sleeping as well, his head tipped back on the chair, his mouth open, a noisy snore pulsing from his throat.

Annabelle and Lily shared a glance, then Lily walked around the bed to gently shake the older man on the shoulder.

"What, what?" he asked, startling awake. He took one look at Lily and quickly scrambled out of the chair to stand. "I do beg your pardon, my lady. I didn't hear you come in."

"It's all right, Jenson," she said with a reassuring smile. "I slept like that myself a few times through the night." She gestured toward Annabelle, who stood just inside the bedchamber door. "Look who is here."

Jenson's face relaxed. "Miss Lawson. Thank goodness. He's been asking for you."

Annabelle walked to him. "I'm so glad you've been here with him. How is he now?"

"He's seen better days," Jenson replied. "Low spirits, I'm afraid, and nursing a lot of regrets and worries. But I'm sure that doesn't surprise you."

"No, it doesn't. It's why I came."

Annabelle slowly moved to the bedside and touched Whitby's cheek. "He's still so hot. Is there nothing we can do?"

Neither Jenson nor Lily answered the question—for there was no answer. At least not anything Annabelle would want to hear.

Lily suddenly felt like she was intruding. "I

should leave you," she said, but Annabelle stopped her.

"No, don't go. Stay and tell me what happened and how he fell ill. I haven't seen him for weeks, you see, as he was in London, and I never go to London." She stroked his cheek. "He looks so thin."

Jenson backed away and retired into the dressing room, leaving them alone to talk. Annabelle sat in the chair by the bed, while Lily sat on the upholstered bench at the foot of it, facing her. She explained how Whitby had looked when he'd arrived, how he'd been fatigued and not his usual self, and how he'd been drinking more than he ever had before.

That seemed to garner a rueful look from Annabelle. Perhaps she was thinking of Whitby's father—her adoptive father—who everyone knew had drank a great deal before he died.

James had told Lily years ago that the man had wanted to numb his pain. Lily had been too young to understand it at the time, but she'd held onto it, like she held onto everything that concerned Whitby. Every memory. Every experience. Now that she was older, she understood it better. She understood that some people preferred to travel through life forgetting certain things.

"It was good of you to stay with him last night," Annabelle said, interrupting Lily's thoughts. "He always said you were a wonderful girl."

"He did?" Lily asked.

"Yes. Years ago when he and James were still in

school, Whitby would come home and tell me about the games you invented, and then he would play them with me. I admit, I was frightfully jealous that he would talk about you so much. I always thought you were smarter and more interesting than I was, and for a long time I didn't *want* to meet you."

Lily felt her brow furrow with bewilderment. "I can't believe you thought that."

Annabelle smiled at her. "I was just a child, missing my brother when he went away, and jealous of his stolen attentions. Then he grew older and stopped coming home with stories of your creative childhood games. He started his own games, I suppose. Games neither of us would likely invent."

Lily understood what Annabelle was hinting at—games that involved women and whiskey. And of course, Lily and Whitby had grown apart when she'd matured past childhood. The games had stopped then.

She was surprised however, that Whitby had spoken of her so often to Annabelle, that he had continued to keep her in his thoughts after he'd left their house each time.

Whitby stirred, and Annabelle leaned close. "I'm here, Whitby," she said. "It's Annabelle."

He opened his eyes, took one look at her, and said, "Thank God." He lay there for a moment with his eyes closed, then he opened them again. "I'm so sorry, Annabelle. I should have listened to you."

Neither Whitby nor Annabelle looked Lily's way,

so she remained where she was, sitting quietly and watching.

"You didn't know this was going to happen," Annabelle said.

"No, you're right. I always thought I was going to live forever, and that I had all the time in the world. I was wrong."

"We don't know that for sure. You may very well recover completely as soon as the fever breaks."

"Perhaps," he replied. "Even so, it does not excuse my failure to protect you and the estate, and to prevent a great injustice."

"You'll get well, Whitby. You must."

Lily found herself again listening to a conversation she did not feel a part of, as if she were hearing secrets, while she was invisible to the people telling them. But she had always been invisible to Whitby, hadn't she? Well, perhaps not always, as she had learned just now.

She made a move to stand and leave them alone, but her movement attracted Whitby's attention, and he gazed sleepily at her. "Lily, I didn't know you were here."

She gazed with longing at his handsome face, relished the sound of her name on his lips, and struggled to find some sensible words in her muddled brain. But she had not slept much the night before, and she was still fighting the wrenching heartache over his illness. It simply wouldn't give her any peace. No wonder she felt so rattled.

"I didn't mean to intrude," she said. "I should go."

He did not argue.

Part of her wished he would—that he would tell her she was welcome to stay as long as she liked, or even better, that he *wanted* her to say. But alas, she knew the measure of her importance in his life.

She gave a parting smile to Annabelle, but when she left the room, she felt worse, not better. She did not want to be on the outside of Whitby's life. Not now. She needed something more.

Lily decided at that moment to offer to watch over him again tonight.

Chapter 12

⌒⌒

"How is he?" Sophia asked, rising to her feet when Annabelle entered the drawing room later that evening.

Lily stood, too, anxious to hear any developments.

"He's sleeping now," Annabelle replied.

"And the fever?"

"Still high. He was asking for brandy."

Lily and Sophia glanced at each other with concern.

"He's very uncomfortable," Annabelle said, "but he doesn't argue when I say no."

Sophia gestured toward the chair opposite. "Come and sit down. You must be exhausted after the day you've had. I'll ring for tea."

Annabelle joined them, and they chatted about her long journey from Bedfordshire and other small matters until the tea arrived, then Annabelle's expression turned apologetic.

"You must both be wondering why Whitby was so desperate to see me. And Lily, you heard some of our conversation earlier."

Lily and Sophia did not pry. They simply waited for Annabelle to continue.

"I'm not sure if you are aware of the 'bad blood' in our family—the problems we've had with Whitby's cousin, Magnus."

Sophia leaned forward to pour the tea. "James mentioned something once about a disagreeable cousin, but gave no other details. Did you know about it, Lily?"

Lily shook her head.

"Well," Annabelle continued hesitantly, accepting a steaming cup of tea from Sophia and holding it on her lap, "Magnus's father was cut off socially and financially from the family when he was just a boy—and for very good reason. He was a hateful, jealous child, and tried on many occasions to harm his older brother, the heir."

"Good gracious, I had no idea," Sophia said.

"His son, Magnus, is just as cruel and very bitter about the feud, and he envies Whitby the same way his father envied his brother. But now, if anything happens to Whitby, Magnus will inherit the title and house."

"Is he that bad?" Lily asked.

Annabelle paused a moment before she replied. "You both know Whitby is a good man. He would not deny a family member what is due to him. But in this case, his feelings are well founded. Magnus has always coveted the title, you see, and there were suspicions that he may have caused the death of Whitby's older brother, who was earl before him. That is where Whitby's hatred comes from."

"Good heavens," Sophia said. "It all sounds positively dreadful."

"That happened many years ago, when Whitby was only ten." She raised her cup and took a sip.

Tension spread through Lily's shoulders. "Does Whitby truly believe Magnus killed his brother?"

"No one could ever prove it, and Magnus denies it of course, but he is extremely hateful."

"That is why Whitby is concerned about you?" Lily asked. "He thinks Magnus might hurt you? But why? You would have no claim over the title."

Annabelle took a long time to answer. She seemed to be considering whether or not she should even try to explain, but finally she did. She lowered her cup and saucer to her lap again.

"Magnus has done harm to me in the past, simply to hurt Whitby. As I said, hatred and vengeance run in his veins."

Sophia and Lily stared at Annabelle in stunned silence. "What did he do?"

She lowered her gaze and shook her head—again taking a long time to answer. "He seduced me five years ago, while keeping his true identity a secret. Then he abandoned me most callously, all to spite Whitby. I was young and very foolish."

Sophia touched Annabelle's knee. "I am so sorry." She glanced helplessly at Lily. "No wonder Whitby is suffering so much anxiety right now."

Annabelle nodded.

"What did Whitby do when he found out?" Lily asked, setting her tea on the table because she was too shocked and upset to drink it. "Did he confront Magnus?"

"Yes, and Magnus paid the price. What he did to me did not go unpunished." Annabelle raised her tea to take a sip, but the cup and saucer rattled with the shaking of her hands.

Neither Lily nor Sophia asked her any more questions after that. They sat in somber silence for a minute or two, then Annabelle gazed toward the window.

"If only Whitby had married someone years ago and had an heir. Then at least if he was to die, he would be able to die in peace. It's sad, how death almost inevitably brings regret."

"For things we did not do when we had the chance," Lily added, realizing suddenly that she was speaking to herself. She knew she had been drifting aimlessly in life's current for too long.

Both Sophia and Annabelle smiled sadly at her.

"Yes, exactly," Annabelle said. "That's it exactly, Lily."

* * *

That evening, Lily stood outside Whitby's bed-chamber with her ear to the door, trying to hear what the doctor was saying to Whitby and James. From what she could decipher, the doctor had found no change in Whitby's condition, and his future was still as uncertain as ever.

A short time later, the doctor left the room and headed down the dark corridor. Lily quietly followed him to the main hall and watched from the top of the stairs while he accepted his coat and hat from the butler. As soon as the butler had closed the door behind the doctor and left the hall, Lily dashed down the stairs and ran outside.

"Dr. Trider!" she called out, just as he was stepping into his carriage. She ran up to it and put her hands on the side to keep him from driving away.

"Lady Lily," he said, appearing somewhat startled by her desperate chase.

She took a few seconds to catch her breath. "I know Lord Whitby is no better today, but tell me . . ." She paused. She was nervous, but she forced herself to dig deep for the courage to be blunt. "Can a man with an illness such as he has . . . conceive a child?"

The doctor stared speechlessly down at her in the dim light from the outdoor lanterns. He pursed his lips and considered the question very carefully. "I suppose so. There is nothing afflicting his reproductive abilities. Though the fever has weakened him."

"If someone . . . *helped* him . . ."

To be honest, she didn't really know what she

was asking. She wouldn't know the first thing about *helping* Whitby do anything regarding such intimate acts. But she could certainly carry out instructions if she had them.

Good Lord, this was awkward.

The doctor hesitated again. "I suppose it would be possible."

"Would the child be healthy?" she asked.

The doctor leaned back against the seat, looking rather uncomfortable with this conversation, but he answered nevertheless. "There are never any guarantees that any child will be born healthy, my lady, but if you are asking if his illness would be passed on to the child . . . Current wisdom is that Hodgkins is not contagious, and whether it is hereditary or not is not proven either."

"But do you truly think Hodgkins is what he has, doctor? It couldn't be something else?"

He stared uneasily at her.

"Please be frank with me. What is your honest opinion?"

"I cannot say for sure, Lady Lily, not until I can do the proper test."

"Please, doctor."

He sighed heavily. "I believe, given his symptoms, that Hodgkins is the most likely malady. But again, I cannot be sure."

Lily nodded and accepted the doctor's opinion, then she stepped away from the carriage. "Thank you."

He picked up the reins and slapped them on the

horse's back, then clicked his tongue. "Move along now." The carriage lurched forward, the wheels crunching over the gravel. "Good night, Lady Lily."

"Good night, doctor."

She wasn't entirely sure he knew what she had really been asking. He would probably figure it out about a mile down the road.

She hoped he wouldn't drive his carriage into a tree.

Lily knocked softly on Whitby's door at midnight, to take over for Annabelle, who had been sitting with him all evening.

The room was lit only by the fire burning in the grate and a single candle beside the bed. Whitby lay on his side facing away from the door, and just the sight of his masculine form beneath the light sheet made Lily's heart pound with a longing to be near him.

Annabelle had been slouched back in her chair, but she sat up when Lily entered. She yawned and stretched her arms over her head. "I thought you'd never get here. He's been asleep for hours, and I'm exhausted."

Lily walked around the bed. Jenson had bathed and shaved Whitby earlier that evening, so his hair looked clean but wildly disheveled from lying in bed. He wore a fresh white linen nightshirt open at the neck, and Lily could see the hard, muscular lines of his smooth chest.

How many times had she dreamed of seeing him

sleeping? And here she was finally, gazing upon him, realizing there was something extraordinarily intimate about watching someone sleep. The bedroom at night in the near dark was surely the most private place in the world.

Though she would never have wanted her dream at this cost.

She gazed down at Annabelle, who was staring at her. Lily smiled, trying to act nonchalant when in reality she was trembling inside—for she was about to attempt the unthinkable, and surely everyone would believe she'd lost her mind.

"You care for him, don't you?" Annabelle whispered unexpectedly as she looked up at Lily.

Lily took a moment to consider how she should reply. Her first instinct was to deny it because that was her habit, but the time for denial was over. There was no point in it now. "How did you know?" she finally asked.

Annabelle took hold of her hand. "I can see it in the way you look at him."

Lily sighed. "I suppose I've given up trying to hide it. Yes, I do care for him, Annabelle. Very much."

"How long have you felt this way?"

"Forever."

Annabelle squeezed her hand. "I'm not surprised."

"You're not?"

She shook her head. "No. You've always been a presence in his life."

"A sisterly presence," Lily said.

"What makes you think that?"

Lily gazed down at him sadly. "He told me so this week—that he cared for me the same way he cares for you."

Whitby breathed deeply and rolled over onto his back. Annabelle lowered her voice. "Whitby has never known permanence in his relationships with women, Lily, except for me, and I believe that because he has known you almost all his life and cares for you deeply, he doesn't know what to make of those feelings, except to categorize them with how he feels about me. That doesn't mean he could not find you attractive as a woman."

Neither of them said anything for a moment, while Lily struggled to find a way to put her feelings and desires into words. She loved Whitby; she'd never loved any other man and could not imagine she ever could. She wanted to be a part of his life, even if it was only for a short time.

If she'd learned anything over the past few days, it was that life was too short, and you had to make the most of every day. She wanted to love Whitby, to give herself to him completely and hold nothing back, because she didn't want to someday regret what she had not been courageous enough to say or do. She knew all too well that the clock could not be turned back.

"Annabelle," Lily whispered, "there's something I want to offer, and I need to tell you what it is. Come and sit with me."

Lily led Annabelle to the upholstered bench at the foot of the bed. She folded her hands on her lap and whispered, "I spoke to the doctor this evening, and he said it would not be impossible for Whitby to . . . to conceive a child right now."

Annabelle's eyes revealed immediate understanding, but she said nothing. She sat very still, waiting for more of an explanation from Lily.

"I could try to give him an heir," she said daringly, and the words sounded unbelievable even to her own ears.

Annabelle continued to stare at her blankly in the dim, flickering firelight. Then her brows drew together with concern. "Lily, that is too much to offer, too much to give of yourself."

Lily shook her head. "I know it looks that way, but I confess, I am not just being generous or selfless by wanting to help you and Whitby—though I *do* want to help you. But the true foundation of my desire is less charitable. I *want* him, Annabelle, desperately. I've wanted him all my life and lately my feelings have grown to such enormous heights that I can't bear the thought of never touching him or kissing him or telling him that I love him. I am in hell right now, being so separate from him, when I'm afraid that I'm going to lose him forever. I want his child in my womb to have after he is gone, whether God takes him now or years from now. I love him, Annabelle."

Annabelle bowed her head. "I'm so sorry that you are in pain, Lily, and I understand. Honestly, I do. If it were up to me, I would say yes. Do it. Marry him and love him and bear his child. Don't let anything stand in your way. But it is not up to me. It is up to him, and he will never agree. He would never want to use you that way, especially if he thinks he will not live to take care of you and the child."

"He would not be using me," Lily said. "He would be giving me a beautiful gift and happiness for the rest of my life." She realized what she was saying sounded ridiculously idealistic and romantic.

Annabelle covered Lily's hand with her own. "As I said, it is not up to me. He's the one you need to convince."

Lily nodded. She knew it was true, though perhaps a deep, frightened part of her had hoped that Annabelle would think it a marvelous plan and talk Whitby into it herself, thereby sparing Lily the task of allowing herself to be so vulnerable by revealing her heart to Whitby, who had the power to break it. It was the more likely outcome, after all—that he would refuse and reject her. He had rejected her before, hadn't he, when she'd made overtures?

Perhaps she *had* lost her mind, she thought suddenly, feeling her heart sink like a stone. Maybe she should plead with Annabelle to forget they'd ever had this conversation and put the ludicrous plan out of her head.

Annabelle stood. "I must go and get some rest. I'll be able to sleep, Lily, knowing you're here with him."

Lily merely nodded. She stood and walked

Annabelle to the door, but Annabelle paused in the corridor before she left. "Talk to him tonight, Lily. What have you to lose by trying?"

"My dignity. My pride."

Annabelle shook her head. "No one can take that away from you. No matter what happens, he'll respect you for your courage and he'll treasure you for offering such a beautiful gift."

Lily imagined talking to him about this and realized that if nothing else, it was a chance to be intimate with him, and speak of honest, heartfelt things. Even if that was all that came of it, it was more than she had now. It would be something to remember.

She glanced back at him, sleeping soundly, then met Annabelle's compassionate gaze.

"I will talk to him," she said finally. "I will tell him everything, and I will try to convince him. Even if it is hopeless."

Chapter 13

Lily stood over Whitby, gazing down at his handsome face as he slept, and felt a deep, soulful love that eclipsed everything in her world—her mother's disapproval, Lily's own duty to her family, and even her fear of talking to him about her proposition. None of that mattered. All that mattered was that she desired him beyond any imagining. What she wouldn't give to climb into this bed beside him and feel his arms around her, to hold him close to her body and her heart. She would give anything for one night in his arms. She would pay any price.

Gently brushing the hair off his forehead, she laid a hand on his cheek. He did not feel as hot as he had last night, though he was still warm. She touched his forehead, too, and his neck.

Would she be brave enough to confess her deepest, private feelings? she wondered nervously, imagining what she would do if he woke right now.

She did not need to wonder long, however, because Whitby stirred and opened his eyes, wetting his dry lips.

"Lily," he whispered, his voice deep and husky, not weak. Even when he was ill, he was vigorous, and she realized that was the strength and allure of his character. He was captivating, in any state of health.

She leaned forward, drawn in. "Yes, I'm here."

"I need water."

Quickly, she turned and poured him a glass from the pitcher on a tray beside the bed. He leaned up on his elbows, and when she tried to hold the glass for him and tip it over his lips, he politely took it from her.

"I can do it, thank you," he said, taking a few sips and handing it back.

She set it on the tray. "How are you feeling?"

"Bloody awful." He lay down again. "I despise this."

"I know you do." She paused for a few seconds, then sat down. "Annabelle told me about your cousin."

He raked his fingers through his hair, combing it off his forehead. "Did she indeed? It's a filthy business, really—my tragic family. Quite the motivation to get well, wouldn't you say?"

She smiled faintly. "Yes, and I'm glad to hear you say that."

His eyes narrowed questioningly. "Why? Did you think I was just going to give up and die?"

Knowing what the doctor had said was a possibility—that Whitby could be dead in as little as three months—she tried to word her answer carefully.

"You've been very sick, that's all. But you don't feel quite as hot tonight." She put her hand on his forehead again.

He did not take his eyes off hers. He simply lay there, looking up at her.

She was shocked by the fact that his illness hadn't diminished his powerful masculinity, nor her inappropriate awareness of it—now, of all times. To be honest, she was ashamed of herself for thinking of her desires when he needed care, yet she couldn't ignore the way he made her feel when she stole a glance at his nightshirt, open at the neck, and the sheets tangled about his hips. Even now, he excited her, aroused her, by doing nothing but lying there damp with sweat, looking at her.

They were quiet for a few minutes until Lily forced herself to gather up the courage to say what she'd come here to say. "Whitby, I need to talk to you about something."

He stared at her in the dim firelight, while she could not meet his eyes, because she was fighting a swarm of butterflies in her stomach so intense it was making her sick.

She swallowed hard, fearing that her voice was going to quaver when she spoke, or that her heart was going to give out. Her body felt like a stick of dynamite about to explode.

How in God's name was she to say this?

"What is it, Lily?" he asked as the seconds and minutes ticked on.

She cleared her throat, and with her eyes lowered, realized there was no proper way to say it. He would surely laugh in her face if she did. It was such a preposterous plan. First of all, he would never agree, and even if he did, there was no guarantee that Lily would conceive, and even if she did, she could not be sure the child would be a son and solve all their problems. Good God, her pulse was galloping.

She shook her head, telling him without words that she could not say it.

"Tell me, darling," he said in a gentle voice that made her melt like butter before him. *He'd called her darling.* "Don't be afraid."

When she still could not say it, he asked, "Is it something the doctor said? Is there bad news?"

Realizing she had given him reason to worry, she looked up quickly, and before she even realized what she was doing, she had taken hold of his hand. "No, no, it's not that."

She continued to hold his warm hand in hers, running her thumb over his firm knuckles, relishing again the simple fact that she was here alone with him, gazing into his eyes. She had never felt a greater longing in all her life. She felt as if her insides were being pulled painfully from her body. She wanted so desperately to touch all of him.

He stroked her hand in return and sat up slightly, still waiting with curious eyes.

"Whitby," she whispered.

Then something in his eyes changed. He knew what she was feeling, he could see it, and apprehension passed like a cold breeze over his face.

"No, Lily," he said, and she heard a gentle warning in his voice. He was telling her not to do this. Not to express what she was about to express.

Not just that. He was telling her not to feel it.

Tears filled her eyes, and when she looked into the depths of his, she saw only his continuing warning, telling her no.

"I can't help it," she said firmly. "I've never been able to help it. I've tried. Honestly I have."

"I'm not the man for you," he said. "I'm a worthless rake."

"You're not worthless."

"Yes, I am. I've never been faithful to any one woman, I drink too much and gamble too much. I neglect my duties as a landlord—my estate is a bloody mess—and now I'm probably dying. I'm not the one for you, Lily. You deserve better."

She lowered her head to rest on his hand. "I don't want anyone else." *She couldn't believe she was saying it.*

His fingers moved over her hair. She could feel the apology in his touch.

"Why did you never tell me this?"

She lifted her head to look at him. "I couldn't. You always considered me a child, and you were always with other women and barely ever noticed my presence."

"That's not true. I've always cared for you."

"Like a sister," she said, her heart burning in her chest.

"Yes." His tone was firm.

She was breathing hard now, as if she were climbing a steep hill. But she would not give up. "Even this week? When we spoke in the drawing room? I sensed there was something more than a brotherly regard. I began to hope . . ."

"No," he replied, cutting her off.

For a long moment she sat there, trying to accept this, but she could not. She loved him.

She breathed deeply, working hard to calm the ferocity of her emotions and the violence of her need for him. She closed her eyes and laid her cheek on his hand again, realizing that love combined with sexual desire was a fierce and potent thing. It was pummeling her standards and morals. Right now, she would settle for being one of the many women he would casually bed.

But she knew he would never treat her that way.

As she sat there with her cheek on his hand, stroking his index finger with her thumb, her whole body pounded and quaked with a fiery, passionate yearning. Then she remembered what she had originally planned to say to him, but hadn't.

She had wanted to offer to give him an heir.

It seemed impossible now. And foolish. He would never agree.

Feeling all hope slip away like a flower floating downstream, she touched her lips to the back of his hand. She kissed it slowly, achingly, again and again until she heard herself make a sound—a sigh, a tiny breath of sensual pleasure. She continued to kiss his hand, making a trail to his wrist, then slowly up the firm bands of muscle on his forearm.

He did not stop her, which surprised her, so she continued to take all she could from this strange, desperate joy—from kissing him at last, after all these years dreaming of it.

"Lily," he whispered gently.

But she did not want to listen. She loved him.

Her hungry mouth reached the inside of his elbow, and she slid her hands up to push the loose cuff of his nightshirt upward and out of the way. Eyes closed, she kissed the soft skin there and felt gooseflesh beneath her fingertips on his forearm.

She waited for the word "stop" to come, and when it did, she would obey. She would put all this foolishness to rest and accept that he did not return her feelings.

Because she could not force him to love her.

But he did not say stop. He said nothing.

When the rejection did not come, she felt as if she'd been given a gift—another moment of this bliss.

Her body, feeling warm and supple, tingled all

over with a sensual delight she had known only when she was alone in her bed, dreaming of him. Dreaming of doing this and so much more.

She daringly parted her lips and tasted the inside of his arm with the tip of her tongue. She kissed and gently suckled the tendons in the juncture between his forearm and upper arm.

Then she heard him whisper: "God, Lily, you really need to stop that."

She glanced up to see his head tipped back on the headboard, his eyes closed. When he realized she'd stopped, he lifted his head, and his eyes were drowsy with desire. It was a look she had never seen before, on anyone.

Surprised, dumbfounded, she continued to stare at him, her chest heaving with her own unconquerable desire, her heart pounding with hot, fierce arousal.

They stared at each other intently for a few seconds, and Lily felt the distance between them like a canyon.

She licked her already moist lips and left them parted. His eyes fixed on them, then he sat up, and quickly but smoothly took her face in his hands and pulled her toward him, covering her lips with his own.

Chapter 14

I *shouldn't be doing this*, Whitby thought in a mindless, baffling fog as he thrust his tongue past Lily's sweet lips and devoured the hot whole of her mouth. But God, he couldn't stop himself! The feel of her lips and tongue on the inside of his arm had driven him half mad with a fierce, throbbing need.

He'd never imagined wanting to make love to Lily, but he did, dammit, he did. He'd taken one look at her big blue eyes, had seen the fierce sexual yearning pulsing in their depths, and couldn't keep himself from touching her, couldn't stop the scorching flood of need that, despite everything, was sweeping him away at this very moment.

He tilted his head from one side to the other, kissing her deeply and aggressively, feeling rejuvenated, as if he'd just beaten down this fever with a heavy iron fist.

She stood up and crawled onto the bed, moaning softly and never breaking the intimate connection of the kiss. Then she straddled him and pushed him back against the pillows, and he realized his Lily was an aggressive lover. Then he remembered their childhood games and tussles. She'd always been creative and physically domineering, even then.

He held her face in his hands while he kissed her, wondering how he could be doing this and why he wasn't trying harder to stop. But all he cared about at the moment was the feel of her soft, luscious body on top of his, and the sweet taste of her intoxicating mouth.

She sat down upon his erection beneath the sheet, and thrust her hips over it, pressing down and rubbing herself over him. He thrust his own hips, too, following her rhythm while he plunged his tongue into her mouth.

He gripped her hips to help her move, sliding her this way and that for the maximum degree of pleasure possible through the sheet.

"James would kill me if he caught us," Whitby said, when Lily broke the kiss and sucked on his neck. His erection grew harder. He was a rock down there.

He thrust his hips upward, grinding against the soft folds of her womanhood through the sheet.

"I wouldn't let him," she said, bringing her lips back to his, thrusting her tongue deep inside his mouth.

Jesus, this was out of control.

Before he knew what he was doing, he had flipped Lily onto her back and was snuggling himself tight into the valley between her thighs, tugging at the tangled sheet to get it out from between them. Soon he was kissing her deeply again, thrusting his hips and running his hand down the outside of her leg, gathering her skirts in his fist and pulling them up. He raised his hips to get her skirts and petticoats up around her waist, then propped himself up on his hands to thrust between her legs.

He wondered again if she was a virgin.

"What happened between you and Pierre?" he asked directly. Finally. "Did you give yourself to him, Lily?"

He didn't want her to say yes. He didn't want to hear that. Yet, if she had . . .

"No," she said breathlessly. "I didn't. I couldn't."

He shut his eyes and pushed hard against her, then lowered his weight down upon her. He kissed her neck and blew into her ear.

"Then you're still a virgin?" he whispered, just to be sure before he restrained himself and put the brakes on his desires.

She wrapped her arms around his shoulders and held him tightly. "Yes."

He nodded, accepting the necessary end to this all too brief and unexpected pleasure.

His body was disappointed, dissatisfied and a little perturbed that she was inexperienced. If she had not been a virgin . . .

But she was still his sweet, untouched Lily. The rest of him—his heart and his mind—was relieved.

He slowly gentled the force of his thrusts, bringing his body back under control, squeezing his eyes shut, remembering who they were and what was happening here. He was ill. He was not rational. Neither was she.

"I'm glad you didn't," he softly said. And it was the truth. He lay very still. "But we need to stop this."

"No, I don't want to stop," she replied. "I'm willing, Whitby. Please."

More than a little surprised, and still as stiff as a brick, he had to hunt for self-control and the fortitude to act responsibly. It wasn't easy. She was so soft and warm and beautiful beneath him. If she were any other woman . . .

"You don't know what you're saying," he whispered into her neck.

"Yes, I do. I love you, Whitby."

If there were ever three words more effective in curtailing the desires of a man like him, he would like to know what they were. Not even "my husband's home" had a stronger effect.

He took a deep breath and rolled off her, discreetly flipping her skirt down to cover the tops of her legs. He leaned back on the headboard, shut his eyes and tapped his head against it a few times. He needed to knock some sense into himself.

Lily inched up on the bed, too, tugging at her skirts and awkwardly clearing her throat. He raked a hand through his hair. He felt very irritable all of a sudden.

"You're angry," she said.

With his head still tipped back on the headboard, eyes still closed, he shook his head. "Not at you."

"What then? Because I can see that you're angry."

He sighed and met her gaze. "I'm angry at myself. You're James's baby sister."

"I'm a woman, Whitby."

Yes, he was more than aware of that now. And she was the kind of woman he would very much like to make love to. She was passionate, beautiful, aggressive . . .

But she was also innocent. And she was James's sister. And she loved him. *Loved* him! What a damned bloody mess this was.

Lily turned slightly toward him. "When I first came in here," she said, "I didn't intend for this to happen. I had just wanted to talk to you about something, and I never did."

"I thought we did," he said, remembering that she'd told him how she felt. Which was how all this had started.

Her face became flushed all of a sudden, as if she were nervous. He waited uneasily for her to continue.

"I wanted to talk to you about the problem you have with your cousin."

"Magnus?" he asked, more than a little perplexed. They had certainly strayed off topic if that's what she'd wanted to talk about.

"Yes. I mentioned that Annabelle told me about the situation, and I know how worried you've been since you became ill, because you have no heir."

He could feel his blood turning cool with a profound sense of dread. Where was she going with this? He didn't want to know. All he could do was stare at her with a numb and nervous anticipation, his brain incapable of sending thoughts to his tongue to form words . . .

"Whitby, I know this will sound insane, but if you are truly worried about your health and your future, I could give you an heir. The doctor said it was possible, and judging by what just happened, he was right."

Holy Mother of God.

He stared blankly at her on the bed beside him, knowing his eyes were wide, his face surely stone gray. Lily. Give him an heir? Had she lost her mind?

He swallowed hard. His stomach felt like it was made of lead. He didn't know what the hell to say to her.

He took a moment to get over the shock, and to remind himself that this had surely been difficult for her and she was probably bracing herself for a rejection.

At least he hoped she was. If she wasn't, she needed to do that straight away, because it was coming. God damn right it was coming.

"Lily," he said, striving to be calm and gentle about this when all he really wanted to do was leap out of the bed and put distance between them, as if she'd just become a hot potato in his hands. Jesus, his heart was pounding.

"Lily," he said again, "that is very kind of you to offer, but you know I can't do that."

"Why? Because I'm your best friend's sister?"

He could see in her eyes that she was determined to debate the issue and try to convince him.

He didn't want to debate it. He just wanted her to go.

"It's not just that," he replied, because he had to let her down gently. She was Lily, and she believed herself to be in love with him. "It's complicated. I would have to marry you. But I'm ill. I know you see this as an ingenious plan to solve my family problems, but what if I die? I can't marry you just to make you a widow."

"I wouldn't mind." She shook her head. "Oh, that didn't come out right. Of course I would mind if you died, but I would mind more if I could not do this for you and be close to you. And you can't tell me you didn't enjoy what just happened."

She had no idea how uncomfortable she was making him. This was madness.

"You're too young to give up your life like that, especially for a man like me. You deserve better.

You deserve to marry a decent fellow and have a whole nursery full of children and a long happy life." He waved a hand through the air. "And you're presuming I am going to die. What if I recover? Then we'll be stuck, won't we?"

She lowered her gaze. "In a loveless marriage, you mean."

"Well, yes."

"It would only be loveless for you."

God, she made him feel like such a heel. "I wouldn't want to hurt you, Lily."

Her shoulders rose and fell with a deep intake of breath. She looked defeated. "But isn't there a chance you could love me?" she asked. "I thought you seemed to enjoy what we just did."

"That was physical," he tried to explain. "What can I say? I'm a man, and I was aroused. It doesn't mean I am in love with you. I'm sorry, that sounds harsh. I care for you, Lily, you know that."

"Yes, I do, but I want more. I want to *give* you more. I could make you happy."

He was not entirely without feeling. Her words touched him. He did care for her, very deeply, and he knew it. He reached out to cup her chin in his hand.

"You're a beautiful woman," he whispered. "And you're going to make someone very happy one day. But it can't be me, Lily. I'm not the one for you, and I won't use you to solve my problems, even though it's what you want—or think you want."

She kept her gaze downcast, and he wished she

would look at him. He needed to know that she was going to be all right. "Lily," he whispered, trying to lift her chin with his finger.

Finally, her eyes lifted. They were not wet with tears as he had expected, but there was immense pain in them. He had more than disappointed her. He had broken her heart.

"I'm sorry, darling," he said, barely recognizing the tenderness in his voice. He had never spoken to a woman in this way before. But he had never felt so deeply for any woman he'd been intimate with. He'd felt sexually about them of course. With Lily, it was more than that.

She nodded, and he was glad. Glad that she was willing to accept it and not try to argue with him anymore.

"Maybe you should go," he said quietly. "I'll be fine. The fever seems to have broken, and that's good news."

Though his throat still hurt.

She nodded again and even managed to give him a sad smile that told him she was not angry with him. She was accepting this.

"I'm sorry, Lily," he said again. "I hate that I've hurt you."

"It's fine," she said. "I'll be fine. I knew it was a preposterous idea, but I had to offer. I had to try."

The tension he'd felt a few minutes ago dissipated, and he gave her a smile. "It means a lot to me that you did. I'll never forget it. No one ever wanted to give me anything so precious before."

He was still holding her chin in his hand. He hated that he had hurt her. "You'll be all right?"

"Yes." She put her hands on his face and kissed him on the lips—a gentle feather of a kiss. A sweet kiss. A kiss goodbye. It was not sexual.

Yet he felt it in his groin.

He kissed her back—another gentle feather of a kiss.

She smiled up at him, blinking her big blue eyes, then she kissed him again, this time letting her lips linger upon his for a few extra seconds.

He parted her lips with his own, cupping the back of her head in his hand, realizing too late that—*Jesus!*—he was kissing her again, even after he'd just explained that he couldn't love her this way. Yet he couldn't keep his hands and mouth off her. He was kissing her!

He pulled his lips away and rested his forehead against hers, trying to keep himself from getting another erection. It took great strength of will, but he did it.

"You'd better go, Lily," he said.

Because he didn't want to hurt her further?

No, not just that. She had to go because if she didn't, he would display a very profound lack of honor.

He was more than thankful when she nodded, got up, and walked out.

Chapter 15

⌒◝◠◞⌒

The next morning, Dr. Trider came to examine Whitby again. He was pleased to see that the fever had broken, but was concerned by the fact that Whitby's throat was still sore.

He leaned over the bed and pressed upon Whitby's neck, then upon his abdomen. He listened to Whitby's chest with the stethoscope. After instructing Whitby to breathe in and out deeply, he put the instrument back into his black leather bag. "Your heart sounds good," he said.

"But?" Whitby replied, raising a knee under the sheet and draping his arm across it.

James stood by the window, also waiting for the doctor's reply.

"The fact that your spleen and your glands are still swollen is not good news," the doctor said. "Your glands feel . . . It's difficult to explain. They are more than swollen, they are rather hard and rubbery."

Whitby glanced at James.

"Be frank, doctor," James said, stepping away from the window.

The doctor hesitated a moment before he spoke. "I've felt glands like that before. This suggests there is a greater likelihood that this could be Hodgkins."

Whitby took the news calmly and silently, though he felt as if a great weight had just descended upon his chest and was squeezing around his lungs. He had to struggle to get a full breath of air.

"But is there still a chance it could go the other way?" James asked, and Whitby was grateful that his friend had the presence of mind to think and speak for him.

"Of course, there is always hope."

"How can you determine for sure?"

The doctor picked up his bag from the foot of the bed and held it at his side. "A biopsy would tell us."

"And what would that involve?" Whitby asked, finding his voice at last.

"It would require a sample from your glands. It's not a difficult procedure, but it is a surgery and all surgeries are risky. There is always the possibility of infection. I've seen that happen, unfortunately. A patient of a colleague . . ."

"When can you do it?" Whitby asked.

The doctor shifted uneasily. "I would prefer to wait at least a few days to make sure you recover completely from the fever and get some of your strength back."

Whitby had not had his strength for more than a month. But he wanted to know. He needed to know.

"If you do this biopsy and discover it is in fact Hodgkins, will you get a better idea how much time I have left?"

"Not really," the doctor replied. "My original opinion on the matter would still hold. It could be anywhere from a month to a year. Maybe even longer if you're lucky."

"You said I'd have at least *three* months last time," Whitby said, feeling as if the clock was suddenly ticking faster than before.

The doctor gazed uncomfortably at him. "I said it depends on how quickly the disease progresses. But at the rate you've been going . . ."

Whitby simply nodded. "I understand."

The doctor reached into his bag for a bottle, which he handed to Whitby. "For now, while awaiting the biopsy, it would be prudent to take this—an iron and cod-liver oil tonic."

Whitby stared numbly at the bottle.

"And try to remember," the doctor said, "that we still don't know anything for sure. It's important that you do not give up hope. It could simply be a very tenacious infection I am not aware of."

Whitby was not convinced.

He thought of Lily suddenly—and what she had offered him. It was a chance to leave something of himself behind, for a part of him to go on living. A sudden irrational urge to go through with it came upon him, but he managed to remain calm and sensible. Getting Lily or any other woman pregnant would not save him or give him immortality. He would still die. If not next month, someday.

A knock sounded at the door. James went to answer it, and Sophia was standing out in the hall. She greeted the doctor who bowed to her and left, then she entered the room with a letter for Whitby.

"This came just now," she said, handing it to him. He turned it over in his hands, then broke the seal. It was from his agent, Mr. Gallagher.

My Lord,

All members of the household wish to express their deepest well wishes and sincere hopes that you will recover soon and return home. We all wish you to know that you are held with great esteem by everyone, and none can remember a better landlord. Please get well.

George Gallagher

Whitby folded the letter and stared at it. He could read between the lines. The note was more

than a thoughtful communication of well wishes.
First of all, Whitby was not a good landlord and
everyone knew it. He was absent too much of the
time, seeking amusements in London.

No, this was a plea, a desperate plea for Whitby
to come home and prevent a new master—a master
everyone would fear and despise—from taking
over the estate.

He laid the letter down beside him.

"What is it?" James asked.

"Just a note from Gallagher," Whitby replied,
"telling me to get well."

He and James exchanged a knowing look. James,
as always, understood. "Then you had best get to
it," he said.

Annabelle sat quietly by herself in her room,
staring at the wall. The sadness she often felt when
she was alone with nothing but her thoughts and
memories was not absent today. It was hovering
over her like a dark cloud.

Yet today, she was not thinking of herself. She
was thinking of Lily.

She sat forward and rested her elbow on the armrest and rubbed her chin. What had happened last
night? she wondered with concern, and what was
Lily doing now? Was she regretting her actions, sitting in her room, chastising herself for doing or
saying something that could not be undone?

Or perhaps she had done nothing. Perhaps she

had not found the courage to tell Whitby how she felt. If she hadn't . . .

Annabelle supposed that either way, there would be regrets.

Unless of course Whitby had said yes to her proposition. But Annabelle knew better than to speculate about that. She knew her brother too well.

Wondering if the doctor had finished his examination yet, she rose from her chair and left her room. A moment later, she knocked on Whitby's door.

"Come in," he called from inside, so she entered.

Whitby was in bed, sitting up on a pile of pillows propped up against the headboard, reading a book. Annabelle went to his side.

"Did the doctor come?"

He set the book down. "Yes." He did not elaborate, so Annabelle, wanting very much to know the situation, was forced to pry.

"What did he say?"

Whitby looked intently into her eyes. "He was not optimistic."

Annabelle felt as if a giant hand had just squeezed around her chest. She slowly lowered herself into the chair and labored to keep her voice steady. "There must be some hope," she said.

Whitby lifted an eyebrow. "There is always hope. That's what the doctor said." He held a letter on his lap, and when Annabelle glanced curiously at it, he passed it to her. "It's from Gallagher."

She read the note. "He's a good man," she said.

"Yes, and his concerns are evident. I can only imagine what's going on in the servants' wing. They are probably all scrambling for new positions of employment as we speak. At least Magnus will not have *everything* handed over to him too easily."

"Oh, Whitby, don't say that. I can't bear to think of anything happening to you, nor can I bear the thought of our family's enemy inheriting everything, not after all the insufferable things he's done. He is a devil, Whitby. You must get well. You cannot let it happen." •

She realized suddenly that she was asking him to control events that he could not control. Only God had the power to change Whitby's fate.

But no, that was not entirely true. Whitby still held some power; he still had choices.

Annabelle handed the letter back. "Lily took good care of you last night?" she casually asked.

Her brother eyed her suspiciously. "Yes. But I told her she didn't have to stay. I was fine."

Annabelle could not keep the disappointment from her tone. "You told her to leave?"

His broad shoulders rose and fell with a sigh. "I take it you know what she had intended to say to me."

"Yes."

"Good God, Annabelle," he said angrily. "You didn't put her up to it, did you?"

"No!" she blurted out. "It was wholly her idea. I was as surprised as you must have been."

"You could have at least tried to talk her out of it."

Annabelle glared at her brother. "Why should I? She's a wonderful woman. Any man would be lucky to have her as a wife. You could not ask for anyone better."

The anger in his voice intensified. "I have no doubt of that, Annabelle. You are absolutely right. But she, on the other hand, could do much better, and you forget I may be lying on my deathbed."

She gave him a look that said, *Don't be so dramatic.*

"Lily deserves better," he said regardless.

Feeling her dander rise, Annabelle leaned forward. "Who are you to decide that? She's a grown woman and can make up her own mind about what she wants. It's her life, and if she loves you, let her give you that love. If she is denied that, she will never get over it. She will always feel dissatisfied and frustrated."

Whitby looked away. She could see that he did not want to discuss it further, but Annabelle could not let it go. Not yet.

"She could give you a child, Whitby."

His gaze darted angrily at her. "Has everyone lost their minds? I could not use her that way, just to keep my title out of the hands of a man I despise."

"Why not? She *wants* to have your child. It would make her happy."

His forehead creased with both anger and confusion. "I can't quite make out your motivation in this, Annabelle. I'm not sure if you are being overly romantic, in that you want Lily to have her own 'happily ever after . . . ' Though how happy she'll be standing over my coffin, I can't quite grasp."

"Whitby," Annabelle said.

He did not let her interrupt. "Or are you thinking of yourself and the estate? Are you desperate to do whatever it takes to prevent Magnus from achieving what would surely be the greatest, most malicious satisfaction of his life?"

Annabelle gazed uncomfortably at her brother. She considered his words, and could not deny the hint of shame that sneaked through her. "Perhaps it is a little bit of both."

"You have never gotten over what he did to you, have you?"

It was not a question. Her brother was stating a fact.

"No, I have not." She had to work hard to fight the tears pooling in her eyes, but it was not easy, for what Whitby said was true. She had not gotten over the indignity of having been so foolish as to let herself be seduced by a man who did not care for her, a man who tricked her and used her like a pawn to hurt her brother, a man with nothing but hatred and vengefulness in his heart.

Regret. It was a potent thing.

"It's not too late, Whitby," she suddenly heard herself saying. "You said yourself that you wish you had married before now and had not put it off. Who knows? You could have another year. Or twenty years. Perhaps the doctor is wrong. And it's never too late for new beginnings."

He looked out the window and she knew he was thinking about everything she had said. She resigned herself to the fact that it was all she could ask of him.

Chapter 16

⌒◦◦⌒

That night, Whitby woke to find Lily at his side again, sitting quietly in the chair, but with her head resting in her arms on the side of the bed. She appeared to be asleep.

He lifted a hand and held it for a few seconds over her shiny black hair, wanting to touch her. He fought the urge, however, for he did not want to give her false hopes.

But were they so very false? he wondered.

The unnerving truth was, he had not been able to stop thinking about her all day. He had missed her, and regretted hurting her, and had yearned to tell her so. He had thought of everything they had said to each other the night before, and how satisfying it had been to lie with her on the bed when he was kissing her and holding her close. Yet not close enough.

That day, he had also ventured into the past and recalled the many conversations they'd had through the years, and the games they'd played.

He remembered tying her cape under her chin once when she was a girl, and how he had smiled at her and she had smiled back. Those smiles had always been knowing smiles, full of mischief—as if she had known with the full certainty of her soul that he knew what she was thinking and feeling.

When they were younger, he had always felt like he'd understood her and known the person she was deep inside, and he'd always known that she was aware of that knowledge. There had been an intangible connection between them, and this week, when she had looked at him that way again—with those mischievous, communicative eyes—he had felt reunited with her, and it had seemed like not a moment had passed since those days when they were close in the strange way they were—when he was a young man and she, just a girl.

He swallowed hard, resisting the urge to touch her for as long as he could, until he couldn't do it anymore.

Finally, he let his hand come down upon the back of her head, where her hair was pulled into a loose bun. He stroked the silky smooth texture of it, and at last she woke.

She lifted her head and blinked up at him sleepily. "Are you all right?"

"I'm fine," he replied. "I feel completely fine."

Except for the sore throat, which continued to plague him and make swallowing a nuisance. But at least the fever was gone.

She sat back and cleared her throat nervously.

After what had happened between them the night before, he was not surprised she was nervous. In fact, he was surprised she was here at all.

Yet, he was glad.

Which was another surprise.

"I didn't expect you to come tonight," he said, apologizing in a roundabout way for what had occurred.

"I couldn't stop myself," she said. "I needed to know how you were."

He rolled onto his side to face her. "I'm better. Are *you* all right?"

She smiled and shrugged. "A little embarrassed, unfortunately."

"Don't be."

"How can I help it? I was very foolish."

"No, you weren't."

"You're kind to try to make me feel better," she said. "But I'm afraid I'm doomed to be mortified for the rest of my life."

He chuckled. "You are always punishing yourself, Lily."

"Yes, I suppose I am. I always feel like I'm doing everything wrong."

Because her mother always told her she was, he thought to himself. But of course he did not say it.

"Give yourself a reprieve. Last night was my fault, too. You weren't alone on the bed."

She lowered her gaze. "It isn't just that. It's what I said, what I proposed. I must have been out of my mind."

"Why?"

"I offered to give you an heir! It was like something out of a bad play."

He laughed again. "I was touched. I still am."

"Are you?" she replied with a somewhat playful smile.

He felt that familiar connection again, felt the heat of their exchange, and knew they were discreetly flirting—like they had done earlier in the week.

"Yes," he replied. "I thought about you all day. I couldn't get to sleep tonight."

She stared bewildered at him, her brows pulling together. "What were you thinking about?"

He decided it was time to be open and honest with her. What was the point in playing games now, after all? There would likely be no second chances to tell the truth. "I was remembering things that happened between us years ago—conversations, secrets we shared—and I wanted to make sense of them."

"Did you succeed?" she asked, looking quite decidedly astonished.

"No, I still feel *displaced*, for lack of a better word.

And rather shaken. What you said to me last night and what you proposed came as a shock. I didn't know you felt so strongly about me. Or maybe I did, and you simply forced me to acknowledge it, to look at what we are to each other, and what we were. I had to take some time to accept the fact that you're a woman now."

She reached for his hand. "Yes, I am."

They stared at each other for a long agonizing moment. It was agonizing because he wanted to do more than just hold her hand. He was thinking about her proposition, which was not something he wanted to consider, yet here he was, doing just that—imagining pulling her up onto the bed with him again and kissing her like he'd never kissed her before. He wanted to hold her tightly, close to his body.

Now that he was looking at his life with a beginning, middle and quite possibly an end, she seemed to fit in snugly like a puzzle piece.

Or perhaps more like a set of bookends. She had been there in the beginning, bonded to him, and now if this was the end, she was here beside him again.

He experienced a bewildering desire to return to a time in his life that had been real. His youth. For when he was young, things were simple and honest. He had not been jaded—or at least he was less so than now—and he presently felt a need for a circle to be closed. Lily was the one woman in his life who had always been there, even if the dynamic had changed from nonsexual to sexual. If he were to bond with anyone in this life before he left it, Lily was surely the one, for the natural bond was already there. It was just not yet fully explored.

He was staggered. He could not have imagined considering this two weeks ago. Not even two hours ago.

She reached a hand up to brush the hair off his forehead.

"You're very caring," he whispered.

This was strange. It was not his normal behavior with women in his bedroom. He was usually much smoother than this, much more calculating and less sensitive.

But he was not himself these days, he knew. Or perhaps he was more himself; he just hadn't known who that self was.

Strange, how death had a way of turning a table upside down in an instant. It swept away all the dust that covered treasures, blew the fog from one's view, knocked away facades. He was now craving honesty and understanding about who he was and what his purpose was. And what he was meant to leave behind.

"I came also," Lily said, "to make sure you knew I wasn't angry with you. I understand that what I suggested was ridiculous, and you were right to refuse me."

He continued to gaze at her in the dim flickering

candlelight, heard the clock ticking, the fire snapping and crackling in the grate. Her lips were moist and full, her skin like ivory cream, her hair darker than midnight. She was striking. She was extraordinarily beautiful.

"And yet," he softly said, "I was questioning that refusal all day."

Lily sat back in her chair, astonished by what Whitby had just said. He had questioned his refusal?

The fact that he had been thinking of her at all was shocking on its own, but he had actually been considering her offer?

"You look surprised," he said, sitting up and inching back against the headboard. His nightshirt was open at the neck, which gave Lily a clear view of his broad shoulder as the garment slid off it. He didn't straighten it. He sat comfortably at his ease, while she had to struggle not to stare at the enticing golden skin across his collarbone.

She supposed he was used to this sort of thing— being alone with women in his bedchamber, while he was only partially dressed.

"I confess, I *am* surprised," she said. "You were very firm last night."

His lips turned up with a rakish grin, and he tilted his head slightly. Lily's body tingled with sexual awareness.

"That's not what I meant," she said with an equally rakish grin.

"No? Well, it was a fact—I was firm—just as I am

now." He raised a knee under the sheet and draped his wrist across it.

Speechless, her lips parting in disbelief, Lily shifted in her chair.

"Mind you," he said, his tone becoming serious again, "I'm still not quite ready to leap into a marriage, Lily, and start producing babies, but I didn't want you to think I wasn't tempted. I want you to know that you were persuasive, and your idea was not without some merit. Annabelle certainly thought so. She's in your camp, it appears."

"You talked to her about it?" Lily asked.

"Yes. Which leads me to my next question. Have you told anyone else about it? James? Sophia? Your mother?"

"Heavens no," Lily replied. "They would all think I'd gone mad. Especially Mother. She'd lock me up. No offense."

"None taken. I didn't think you'd told anyone, but I just thought I'd ask, in case *everyone* was in your camp and thinking me ungentlemanly for refusing you."

They sat in silence for a quivering, intense moment while their eyes never veered from each other's. Lily's heart began to race erratically with a desperate need to touch the beautiful man before her, so relaxed and potently sexual on the bed. She'd never felt such a scorching heat in her blood before—such a need for physical fulfillment and satisfaction.

Not that she really understood what went on between men and women in the bedroom. She only knew what she'd done here with Whitby the night before, and from what she had gathered, there was much more that could follow. So much more. Last night, it had ended too soon.

"I'm wanting you again," she said openly, shocking even herself with her candor. "I'm wanting to get on top of you."

She saw a flash of something in his eyes—was it surprise? Or was it the comfortable predatory instinct of a man who knew exactly what to expect from a woman in the bedroom, and how best to handle her?

His Adam's apple bobbed as he swallowed.

She had probably shocked him. She had shocked herself. But she hadn't been able to help it.

He began to breathe a little faster. She could see his chest rising and falling, so attuned to his every move was she.

They continued to gaze at each other, and she sat stiffly, tensely, waiting for something to happen. She felt panicked and shaky on the inside.

A log dropped in the hearth, and she jumped.

Whitby took a deep, slow breath and let it out completely before he spoke.

"Come and get on top of me, then," he said in a sultry voice, his knee still bent under the sheet, his wrist still draped across it.

Lily's stomach spun like a top, making her almost dizzy in her chair. She tried to steady her breathing, tried to keep herself from trembling. She took a few seconds to calm the workings of her body, then slowly rose out of the chair and lifted her skirts as she brought a knee up onto the bed.

Chapter 17

Lily kept her eyes fixed on Whitby's as she crawled over him and came to straddle him beneath the sheet. He was large and hard, and she swiveled her hips in tiny circles to rub over him.

His big hands wrapped around her hips, and he, too, shifted on the bed beneath her, moving her around, grinding against her through the sheet and the thin fabric of her drawers.

All day she had hungered for this, never believing it would happen. Yet here she was, touching him and feeling him again. It was like a dream.

She gazed drowsily into his eyes and said, "I hope you don't think I'm trying to seduce you to get what I want. Honestly, that's not what's on my mind right now. I have no strategies. All I want is to touch you and lay with you."

He thrust his hips upward. "And yet I'm worried."

She wiggled over him. "Please don't be. I'll stop when you say we should."

"What if I *don't* say we should? What if I can't?"

"Is that a possibility?"

"Quite frankly, yes."

She smiled, feeling very pleased with herself. "You mean to tell me you might not be able to resist me?"

He maneuvered her left, right, up and down, round and round. "If I were able to resist you, I would have already done it."

Lily leaned forward and pressed her lips to his, thrusting her tongue into his mouth and kissing him deeply. He tasted like heaven.

She could never have imagined the erotic delight that would tingle and surge through her body from something as basic and fundamental as a kiss. But it was the most amazing kiss. His mouth was hot and wet, and he met her tongue with instinctive skill, probing and tasting her and moaning softly with a pleasure that quickened her blood.

He cupped his hand around the side of her neck, pulling her closer and deepening the kiss, then he dragged his lips across her cheek to her ear, where he nibbled on her lobe and breathed hotly and wetly, sending a torrent of tingling gooseflesh down her whole body to her toes.

"Whitby," she whispered, nuzzling into him, still unconsciously thrusting her hips.

His lips found hers again as he slid a hand over her breast, but her corset restricted her from feeling the sensation of his thumb across her nipple. Whitby began a trail of kisses down the side of her neck, then rolled her over onto her back and leaned up on one elbow beside her, looking down at her.

"You see what a dishonorable rake I am? A true gentleman would marry you before any of this."

"You can if you wish it."

He gazed uneasily at her.

"But you don't have to," she said quickly, releasing him of any obligation. "That's not why I'm here."

"You're a very naughty girl, Lily," he said, then he sighed. "You're making me insane. I shouldn't have invited you into my bed like this. I should tell you to go back to your room like I did last night. But I can't."

She laid her open palm on his cheek. "I'm glad, because I don't want to go."

"I won't ruin you," he assured her. "I want you to have a future. There are other things we can do tonight."

"I just want to be with you. I don't care about anything else."

"But you should care. You're young. You have your whole life ahead of you."

Oh, she did not want to think of a whole lifetime without him. He was here now, and she felt as if this moment *was* her whole life. It would be the pinnacle, the hook that everything else hung upon. She would measure everything against it.

She continued to stare, blinking, into his eyes, wondering with concern if she was perhaps being overly romantic. Maybe this intensity would pass. Perhaps she was being carried away by her bodily passions and they were more powerful than she realized, and all this would fade when he was gone from her life, whether heaven took him, or he recovered and chose to avoid her after this.

She suspected she would understand it someday when her mind cleared and everything seemed normal again. But for now, she would just accept and enjoy this glorious night in his arms, for she had dreamed of it too many times to walk away now.

He pressed his mouth to hers and kissed her again, less intensely this time. He kept his eyes open and she did the same, watching him in the golden light. Then he rolled onto her and kissed her neck and down lower to the tops of her breasts, while he slowly unbuttoned her bodice.

He pressed it open and ran his hand over the surface of her corset, gracefully back and forth, then down over her hip and the top of her leg, his gaze following the movements of his hand, as if he were admiring all the places he was touching.

Lily lay quietly, watching his handsome face.

I would do anything for him right now, she thought to herself. *I would give him everything I have to give.*

His eyes met hers again, then he glanced to her breasts briefly. She saw a flirtatious spark—that familiar animal gaze that always turned her to liquid—and knew exactly what he was thinking. He wanted her corset out of the way.

She grinned and began to unhook it in the front while he watched. When the last hook came undone, she sat up and awkwardly pulled it out from under her open bodice, and tossed it to the floor. Her breasts fell free, with nothing but her thin, cotton chemise to cover them.

He tugged it up in the front and took a nipple in his mouth, suckling and flicking his tongue over it. Lily breathed faster as she weaved her fingers through his hair and cupped his head in her hand.

"Oh, Whitby," she whispered, feeling dizzy with desire. "You know what you're doing, don't you?"

"I have an idea," he replied teasingly as he continued.

She had no clue how long he pleasured her that way. It seemed like a very long time—his tongue flicking continuously, staying with one breast until she feared she might faint, then moving to the other. Dozens of pulsing bursts of delight coursed through her body while she writhed on the bed.

He began to kiss her on the mouth again, and she wrapped her arms around his neck and held him tightly. She felt his hand sliding down over her hip again and gathering her skirts into a fist . . . slowly lifting them and caressing the outside of her thigh over her drawers. A moment later, the ribbon at her waist came loose and his hand was sliding inside.

Lily gasped at the shock of feeling a man's hand

touch her curls, then venture lower. A wet, sweltering heat flooded from within her, under the skillful
stroke of his finger as he massaged in small circles,
while still devouring her mouth with his own.
There was a smooth rhythm to his movements—his
lips and tongue, his hand, his hips.

She returned his kiss with fervor, holding his
head in her hands, thrusting her own hips to match
the movements of his finger between her legs.

"I want to touch you, too," she said into his
mouth, sliding her own hand under the sheet to the
top of his hard, muscular thigh.

"Be my guest," he replied.

She pulled his nightshirt up and touched be
tween his legs, overwhelmed by what she was
feeling—his private anatomy, so hot to her touch,
soft in some places, hard in others. She wrapped
her hand around him and stroked, not sure if she
was doing it correctly, but assuming she was doing
fine when he moaned.

"Ah, Lily, you're always surprising me. You seem
to have a natural talent in certain areas."

"Do I? I have no understanding of what I'm
doing."

"You don't need to understand it. Just keep doing it."

And so she did . . .

A short time later, he tugged at her drawers,
pulling them down over her hips. She kicked them
all the way off, and he rolled on top of her and settled himself between her thighs.

Her skirts were bunched up around her waist. She still wore her bodice and chemise, though everything was open or shoved out of the way. He pulled his nightshirt off over his head and tossed it aside.

He was completely naked on top of her now, and she could only imagine what they looked like. She ran her hands up and down the glorious hard muscles on his back and buttocks.

She could feel him between her legs, poised there at her damp opening, and she wanted to rub against him. She thrust her hips.

"I knew this was going to be difficult," he whispered, leaning up on one arm to look down at her. "Yet I went ahead with it, didn't I?"

She thrust her hips again.

"Be careful," he said.

"I don't want to be careful. I just want more of you."

He rested his forehead upon hers and closed his eyes. "And I want more of you. I can't believe how badly I want you, Lily, and I'm feeling very healthy all of a sudden."

She smiled. "Maybe I'm your cure."

"You're definitely a cure for something."

She kissed him with a profound depth of feeling. "I want to feel you inside me," she whispered. "Please, Whitby, I won't ask any more than that. Just make love to me. Make me a happy woman."

She felt his desire grow; he moaned as he kissed her neck and shoulders.

"I would have to marry you," he said. "I would want to, Lily."

"You wouldn't have to, but I would, if it's what you wanted."

"But I'm ill."

She cupped his face in both her hands. "All the more reason to make the most of the time we have. Even if you have only a month to live, let's enjoy it. We could make love every day, and I . . . I know you don't love me the way I love you, but I can live with that. I just want a chance to try and make you happy."

He slid into position, pushed gently, causing her some discomfort, but she wanted it. She wanted the pain and the pleasure and whatever else came with it.

He paused. "This is insane, Lily. I've lost my mind. I'm feeling very selfish."

"I feel selfish, too."

He lay still and quiet for a long moment. Then he kissed her on the cheek. "Marry me. I want to marry you." He pushed again, not too hard, not all the way . . .

Feeling the discomfort again, Lily sucked in a breath. "Are you sure?"

"Yes. Say yes, Lily, hurry, because I'm going to make love to you."

"Yes," she replied, so overcome with desire, she could barely think.

Without another second's hesitation, he pushed slowly but firmly into her, groaning with relief while she cried out in pain.

The pain, however, turned instantly to pleasure—the most intense physical experience of her life, and with it came joy and pride. He was hers, she was his, and he *wanted* her. She would give him a child. She hoped she conceived tonight.

He made love to her gently at first, then he leaned up on one arm and looked into her eyes. "Are you all right?"

She nodded and smiled. "Oh, yes."

"I'm not hurting you?"

"No. It feels good."

He propped himself up with both hands flat on the bed on either side of her, looking down at where they were joined.

"How does this feel?" he asked, changing the way he moved, using his length to stroke the place that was the most sensitive of all, the place that made her whole body burn.

"I've never felt anything like it."

He was still looking down at what he was doing, though he had to move her skirt out of the way to see. He whispered, "What about this? Is this better?"

"Yes." She was beginning to feel almost delirious from the sensation.

When he seemed to have the position and movement mastered, he brought his mouth to hers and kissed her. He continued to pleasure her with his length, keeping a steady pace.

Before long, Lily's bones and muscles seemed to gel, and she felt like she was flying. Sensations of all kinds shot and trembled through her, and she arched her back and gasped for air, crying out into the quiet bedchamber.

Her body relaxed and she was overcome by a love so grand, it brought tears to her eyes. Whitby continued to make love to her, moving faster toward the end until he pushed one last time, with deep, pounding force.

"God!" he uttered, through gritted teeth.

Lily hugged him tightly until he relaxed his full weight upon her. He was so heavy, she could barely breathe.

"Am I too heavy?" he asked, and she wondered if he could read her mind.

"No. Yes."

He laughed and withdrew, then slowly rolled onto his back beside her. He stared up at the canopy. "Lily, you *are* a woman, and a very delightful one at that."

She reached for his hand and held it. "I thought you'd never notice."

He turned his head on the pillow. "Well, you certainly got my attention tonight."

She smiled. They gazed at each other for an easy moment, then their smiles faded and they both, at the same time, turned their eyes toward the canopy again.

They lay quiet and motionless for a long time, while their bodies returned to their normal ebb and flow, and reality settled in. Lily felt the cool air upon her bare legs. She shivered. She felt very exposed.

"That was madness," she said with a hint of humor, needing to fill the silence and the awkwardness with something—anything—as she pulled her skirts down with one hand.

He squeezed her other hand. "Indeed, it was."

They continued to lie beside each other, saying nothing.

Lily wet her lips. She breathed deeply, feeling self-conscious and uncomfortable. She didn't know what to say. What *did* a lady say to a gentleman after something like this?

Was Whitby feeling uncomfortable, too, or was he regretting what they'd done?

"You don't have to marry me," she blurted out, without really thinking. "That wasn't why I did this."

He turned his head on the pillow again, but she kept her gaze directed upward.

"I want to Lily. I must."

She closed her eyes. She yearned to believe that he truly wanted to marry her—the way she'd believed it in the seconds just before he'd taken her virginity. He had made her believe it because he *had* genuinely wanted her. He *had*.

Or was it just sex that he'd wanted? And had he lost his head because of it? She had certainly lost hers.

"I didn't mean for this to happen," she said. "I didn't want to *force* you into anything. Or trap you."

"You didn't force me. I asked *you*, remember? And you kept saying no."

"But we weren't thinking sensibly."

He let go of her hand and sat up on the edge of the bed, bowing his head. Lily looked at his broad, sweat-covered back, so smooth and muscular, and wanted to run her hand across it and massage the tension out of his shoulders. But she remained where she was, for she did not wish to influence him in any way. She'd already done quite enough of that.

"This is an unusual situation," he said. "I've never proposed to anyone before. I've considered it many times because I've always known I had to marry, but I've never actually gone ahead and done it. Something always stopped me—a sense of panic, I suppose, like I was suffocating." He turned to look at her. "But I didn't feel that way tonight, Lily. I felt no fear, and I'm still baffled by that. I think this illness has done something to me."

She finally did sit up on her knees and laid her hand on his warm, damp back. She rested her chin on his shoulder. "You're going to get better," she told him.

"You think so?"

"Yes." It was clear, however, that *he* didn't.

He stood and crossed to the window, standing naked before the closed drapes, his back to Lily. "I *will* marry you, and I won't let you convince me otherwise. I care for you, Lily, I always have, and I do possess some honor. You have given yourself to me, and for all we know, as of tonight, you could be carrying my child."

"I didn't mean to trap you," she said again.

He turned to face her. "You didn't. Or maybe you did, but only because I wanted to be trapped. I've been alone my whole life, and I've been feeling a rather powerful need lately to be . . . Well, *not* alone." He was quiet for a long moment. "I've often heard that people say they don't want to die alone."

Realizing there was more to this than she could begin to understand, Lily quickly pulled on her drawers and tied the ribbon. She crawled off the bed and went to him. "You're *not* going to die."

"Everyone dies eventually."

She couldn't argue with that.

Still wearing her skirt and bodice, though it was open in front, she put her hands on his smooth, bare chest and slid them up to the tops of his shoulders.

"You're not alone now. I'm here, and I hope I am carrying your child. Let me love you, Whitby. Let me share your bed every night. It's not important if you marry me. Nothing seems to matter right now, but you can if you want to. It would probably be best, especially if there is a child."

He put his hands around her waist. "I *will* marry you."

She smiled. "So you've said."

He gazed down at her face, then kissed her gently on the lips. "But if we're going to be husband and wife, I think we need to know each other better."

"Oh really," she said. "And where would you like to start?"

He considered it a moment. "I believe I would

like to start with your hair." He reached up and began to pull out her hairpins. "I would like to know what you look like with it down."

He loosened the bun and it fell in a single twist down onto her back. He ran his fingers through it, fluffing it into a wavy mess.

"How's that?" she asked.

"It's exquisite."

"What next would you like to know?"

His eyes glimmered in the firelight. "You're still wearing your clothes, and I must apologize for that. I was too impatient. But now that the waters have calmed, I would like to know what you look like and feel like without them."

He took her hand and led her back to the bed and helped her remove her bodice, then he pulled the chemise off over her head. A few seconds later, her skirts were dropping to the floor in a billowing heap and she was stepping out of her drawers.

"That's better," he whispered in her ear, before he eased her onto her back on the soft mattress. Their bodies were delightfully hot and sticky as they came together, nude upon the sheets. "Perhaps we can talk about hobbies and interests later . . ."

Chapter 18

～◯◯～

James,

May I request an appointment with you this morning at ten o'clock? There is a matter of utmost importance I must discuss with you.

Whitby

Though he was still extremely fatigued the next morning, Whitby managed to rise and dress in the appropriate attire for a meeting with a duke—a duke who was surely about to oppose the marriage of his beloved younger sister. For what gentleman would knowingly marry a family member off to a dying man who was also a notorious rake? And no one knew better than James the extent of Whitby's rakishness, for James had taken part in most of it, for many, many years before he'd been reformed by Sophia.

Whitby fastened the last button on his jacket and sighed heavily. This was not going to be pleasant.

He handed the letter to his valet, who saw to its delivery, then feeling almost faint, he sat down in the wing chair by the window. He wiped perspiration from his brow.

Whitby tried to decide upon an appropriate manner of expressing himself, tried to decide upon the right words, the right way to break the news to his friend that he had deflowered his sister and intended to be married to her briefly, before most likely making a widow out of her before the year was out.

He shook his head. Indeed. It was most assuredly not going to be pleasant.

Wearing her blue and white striped morning dress—because it was her mother's favorite—Lily ventured apprehensively down to the breakfast room to convey her news. Yes, she was going to marry a man her mother despised, a man widely known as an irresponsible, disreputable rake, who also happened to be on his deathbed.

She laid a hand on her belly to try and quash the nervous knots, while holding firm to her resolve. She had to be strong, no matter how bad it got. She could not back down.

When she entered the room, Annabelle and Sophia were sitting at the white-clothed table, sipping coffee across from Marion.

"Good morning, Lily," Sophia said. "Did you sleep well?"

Heart suddenly pounding, Lily served herself breakfast from the sideboard and took a seat next to her sister-in-law. "Yes, thank you. And you?"

"Like a baby."

Marion lowered the paper and glanced up. Lily met her mother's daunting gaze and experienced a raw pang of dread, but quickly suppressed it. She could not let her mother intimidate her. Not today.

She set down her fork.

"I would like to speak to all of you," she said shakily, "about something very important to me. I must prepare you for something."

Annabelle's gaze shot to her, and Lily suspected that she knew what was coming. Sophia was sitting patiently, looking curious, while her mother's brow had furrowed with concern.

"I know this may come as a shock," Lily said, "but I am ready to be married."

Her mother leaned forward. "That is not shocking, Lily. Of course you are ready."

Feeling her cheeks flush with anxiety, Lily shifted uncomfortably in her chair. "No, I mean, I have fallen in love."

Everyone fell silent, except for the footman standing behind them against the wall, who cleared his throat.

Annabelle's face warmed with a smile. Sophia's face brightened with hope. She was probably guessing what was afoot.

Lily knew they would both be supportive. Her mother, on the other hand, was beginning to exude her ominous cloud of disapproval. Lily could feel it like a thick fog descending upon the room.

"With whom?" Marion asked, her voice deep and demanding.

Lily sat up straighter. "It's someone I have loved for a very long time."

Her mother's eyes widened with shock.

Sophia interrupted with a joyful note of congratulations. "Oh, Lily," she said as she embraced her.

Marion watched the exchange with worried eyes. "Will someone tell me what's going on? It seems I'm the last to know."

Sophia and Lily sat apart. Lily gazed apprehensively at Annabelle, then faced her mother. "I am in love with Lord Whitby," she said flatly, "and he has proposed."

Both Sophia and Annabelle covered their mouths with their hands and shouted with joy. Then another heavy silence descended upon the room as they all stared worriedly at Marion, whose narrow lips had parted slightly.

Annabelle quickly moved to fill the silence. "How wonderful."

"I beg your pardon?" Marion said. "You think it's wonderful?"

Here we go . . .

"If they're in love . . ." Annabelle said hesitantly.

Marion turned her eyes toward Lily. "He has proposed to you?"

"Yes."

"When? When did he do this?"

"Last night."

The lines in her face grew even deeper and darker. She was in shock. "Last night? What in the name of heaven occurred last night? You had no cause to be in his room. His fever had broken."

"I just wanted to be with him."

Marion stood. "Just wanted to be with him! A man like Whitby? Tell me it isn't true, Lily. You could not believe yourself in love with that man."

"I am, and he's a good man, Mother."

Marion turned to Annabelle. "Forgive me, my dear, I mean no offense to *you*. But even you must acknowledge that your brother is less than an ideal husband. He is not respectable. He drinks excessively, he gambles, his estate is in disarray because he is irresponsible and neglectful of his duties as a landlord, and I daresay his reputation with women can hardly be ignored. Not to mention the fact that he is ill, and could be dead in a month!"

"Mother!" Lily burst out, rising also on the other side of the table. "Stop it. I love him and I'm going to marry him, with or without your consent."

Lily's whole body was shaking with the intensity

of her emotions, her heart beating so fast, she was certain it was going to explode. She had defied her mother many times before, but never as ardently as this, nor over anything so significant. She supposed she had always known this day would come, when they would collide head on with no compromise possible.

Lily feared suddenly the result was going to be a complete dissolution of their relationship, frail as it was to begin with.

A cold despair knotted in her stomach, and she put a hand upon it, wishing she could be undisturbed by this and not let it break her heart. Why should it matter *what* her callous, unfeeling mother thought? Lily should just tell her to bugger off!

Yet she could not. She wished she could, but she couldn't. Even now, with all her anger blasting out of her like dynamite—*still*, all she wanted from her mother was her love. Her support, at the very least. It was a lifelong wish for the impossible, a wish she had never been able to overcome. It was her weakness, her Achilles heel.

She clenched her hands into fists.

"He'll make you miserable," Marion said, her voice quivering with fury. "One way or another."

Whitby did indeed have that power, and Lily knew it, but she could not give in to that fear. Not now.

"He's what I want."

Her mother was breathing hard. She looked almost desperate. "Have you *no* respect for my wishes?"

"Have you no respect for *mine*?" Lily answered back, shouting now.

The two of them glared at each other like cats.

"Have you told James about this?" Marion asked.

"Not yet," Lily replied. "I suspect Whitby is telling him at this very moment."

Sophia stood, too. "Right now? That's what the note was about?"

"Yes."

"Good gracious," she said. "Poor Whitby."

"Poor Whitby?" Marion said. "I hope he gets what he deserves! I hope James thrashes him. No offense, Annabelle."

Sophia gazed worriedly at Lily. "He might very well do that. I can only hope Whitby has gained some of his strength back this morning."

"Well, he obviously has," Marion said bitterly, "if he was energetic enough to seduce a young girl."

"He did not seduce me!" Lily said, her head now spinning with fury. "If anything, I seduced him!"

Her mother shot her a look. "Lily!"

Lily stood firm, fighting the urge to cry. "I am in love with him, Mother. There is no one else in the world for me. I would rather die alone than marry another man. I only wish you could accept that. *Please*."

Lily could see the censure and displeasure in her mother's expression. For a long time, she stood staring at Lily, as if she were trying to figure out a way to change her mind, but in the end, she appeared to be accepting that *nothing* would change Lily's mind. Not even her own intimidating force of will. Lily was no longer a child. She was a woman, and she would make her own decisions, whether they were right or wrong. And Marion had finally given up. She was giving up all hope that Lily would ever make her proud.

"You will not have my blessing," Marion said. "Ever."

"Mother, please . . . If you could just try to be happy for me."

"Happy?" A breath puffed out of her chest, something resembling a bitter laugh.

A long, tense moment ensued until Marion stepped away from the table. "I refuse to argue about this," she said. "Go ahead and marry him, Lily. *I don't care what you do.*"

Lily felt the denunciation like a knife in her heart.

Marion glanced at Annabelle and Sophia with one last silent reproach. "I'm going to London. Don't expect me back until Lily and Whitby are gone."

She walked out, leaving Lily to fight stinging tears, wishing that for just one moment in her life, her mother could have understood her heart, even if it meant she had to watch Lily make a mistake.

And though Lily had finally stood up to her mother, her mother had nevertheless won, for Lily was stricken with grief. Today of all days—when all she wanted was to be happy.

* * *

Marion entered her room in the dowager wing and shut the door behind her. She walked to the window and drew the curtains so it was dark, then sank into the chair in front of the fireplace.

Her fingernails dug into the armrests as she squeezed them over and over. Why would her daughter not listen to reason? Why did she insist on being so insolent, and ignoring the advice of someone older and wiser than she?

Marion would never even have *considered* being so disobedient with her parents. They had chosen a husband for her and she had never questioned or resisted their wishes. It had not been easy, but she had endured her difficult marriage because it had been her duty. Her duty!

What was wrong with these young people today who would not do the responsible thing? she wondered, seething with a pent-up rage that throbbed at her temples. They all seemed to live for their passions and impulses, and ignored their obligations. Duty *had* to be fulfilled. It was a fact of life.

Taking a deep, shaky breath, she stared into the empty grate in the fireplace. She remembered suddenly a night in the early days of her marriage when her husband, the duke, had shouted and banged at her door. He had burst in smelling of another woman's perfume, and had thrown her private childhood journal into the fire. She had burned her hands trying to retrieve it, but in the end had watched it dissolve into ash.

Lily, you will be so unhappy with a man like *Whitby. . . .*

But no. Lily was defiant. If she were ever unhappy, she would leave. If she had been in Marion's shoes, Lily would have left the duke. In fact, she never would have married him in the first place.

Marion's breath caught in her throat. Could *she* have refused to marry the man her parents had chosen, like Lily was doing? Could she have?

No, no. She could not question that now. It made her heart pinch in her chest to even *consider* questioning it. She couldn't possibly live with that thought. She couldn't think about what her life would have been like if she'd made her own choice.

I married the duke because I was an obedient daughter, and I remained at his side because I was a dutiful duchess. I did not ignore my obligations. I did the right thing.

Then she broke down into a fit of sobs.

Chapter 19

Whitby entered James's study at precisely 10 A.M. James was seated at his desk, but rose to his feet and walked around to greet him. "You've gotten your color back," he said.

Whitby nodded, but the truth was, he needed to sit down before he collapsed. Just the walk down the hall had exhausted him. "The fever is gone."

"Well, that's good news." James gestured to the sofa. "How can I be of assistance?"

Whitby wished he knew the right way to tell James what was on his mind, but supposed there was no right way to say it. He would simply have to do it as directly as possible.

He sat down on the sofa, while James sat in a facing chair. "I'm afraid this will not be easy for you to hear."

James inclined his head. "It sounds serious."

"Indeed."

James probably thought it had something to do with the illness, or Whitby's last wishes. He was most definitely going to be taken aback.

Whitby leaned forward, rested his elbows on his knees, and clasped his hands together in front of him. "Are you aware, James, that Lily has had an affection for me in the past?"

James sat back. "There were occasions over the years when I sensed she might have entertained a bit of a crush."

"Yes, well, it has become more than that. She's a woman now and—"

"Has she expressed this to you?" James asked, looking concerned.

Whitby stared numbly at him. "Yes."

Raising his eyebrows, James stood and paced around the room. Whitby gave him a moment, hoping he would calmly figure things out on his own.

"Well," James said at last, "this is indeed awkward. I wonder if it had something to do with the pressure our mother was exacting upon her to marry Lord Richard. Lily can sometimes react to things by rebelling and darting as quickly as she can in another direction. And perhaps with you being so ill, a captive audience so to speak . . . I do apologize, Whitby, if this has caused you any worries. Would you like me to speak with her?"

Whitby pinched the bridge of his nose and shook his head. This was not transpiring as he had hoped it would. It was going to be difficult to explain.

"No, James. That won't be necessary. Lily and I have already discussed it, and the reason I am here is to ask for your blessing in regards to . . ." He paused, not quite able to finish. In an attempt to start again, he stood, thinking it would be easier if he could face James at eye level, but it was not easier. He had no strength. "In regards to my marrying her."

James's face pulled into a frown. "I beg your pardon. Did I hear you correctly?"

"Yes, you did."

They both stood tall, each with their hands at their sides, though it cost Whitby dearly, for he was still exceedingly weak.

"You want to marry my sister," James said.

"I do."

James's eyes narrowed with anger, or maybe it was confusion. Whitby couldn't be sure.

"Why?" James asked.

It was not a question Whitby had been prepared for, though he should have been. He supposed the correct answer was, "Because I love her," but he couldn't seem to say those words out loud. James would never believe them if he did.

In all honesty, he wasn't sure he did love Lily. He cared for her, certainly, and he was attracted to her. But love . . . That was beyond his experience as of yet, and James knew it.

"Because I care for her," he said, "and she wants to be my wife."

"Many women over the years have wanted to be your wife," James said with rancor, "but you could never bring yourself to commit to being anyone's husband. What is different now? Is it because you are ill and you are grasping at one last chance to live?"

Whitby could not lie to James. He was too good a friend, though Whitby wasn't sure how much longer he would be after this. "That's part of it."

"And the other part? You want to keep your title from passing to Magnus? You once told me the only reason you would ever give in to the shackles of marriage was for the sake of an heir."

Whitby didn't reply to that. He knew it was indeed a factor in his very complex motivations regarding his actions last night in bed with Lily. A part of him had wanted to conceive a child.

But not just because of Magnus.

"You must realize," James said icily, "that I would never allow my sister to be used and abandoned in that way. Not by anyone."

"I would never abandon her."

"It might be out of your hands."

Whitby could not argue with that. The statement seemed to bring a halt to their discussion. James took in a few deep, controlled breaths.

Whitby felt a great need to reassure him. He had to know that Whitby would never intentionally hurt Lily.

"I care for her, James. And you're right—I don't know how much time I have left. It could be a month, it could be years. I only know that I want to spend that time with your sister."

James stared at him in disbelief, then turned away and walked to the window. "You don't know what you're saying. You're not yourself right now. In a few days, you will look back on this and wonder what the hell had come over you. I know you, Whitby. You can't possibly want to marry Lily. *Lily!* My *sister!*"

"I'm sorry, James. I know this must come as a shock to you, but I *will* be marrying her."

James whirled around and glared at Whitby. "But you have never been true to any woman."

"I have not, as of yet," Whitby replied, "but there is always a first time. You of all people should know that. You have been true to Sophia."

James squared his shoulders. "Yes, I have, but Sophia is Sophia. We are talking about Lily here."

"She's not a child, James."

"And when the hell did you notice that?"

Whitby sighed. "I've been aware of it for quite some time."

Which was not entirely true, but it was what James needed to hear.

"Yet you said nothing to me."

"How could I? You would have thrashed me, like you want to thrash me now."

Whitby could see the tension building in James, for he had always been protective of his sister, especially since the Paris incident, for which he had blamed himself, and to this day had not completely forgiven himself.

"I certainly do want to thrash you—if only to knock some sense into you. You're ill, Whitby. You are in no position to propose to anyone."

Whitby knew it could not be avoided any longer. What was done could not be undone. He was going to marry Lily as quickly as it could be arranged. No one—not even James—could stop it. Whitby would not allow it.

"I'm afraid it's a little late for contemplation," he said. "The fact is, I have already proposed and Lily has accepted. I will remind you she is of age."

James stared at him for a long, hard moment. "Too late, you say."

Whitby could see in James's eyes that he was grasping the reality of the situation. Whitby hadn't really intended for James to know what had occurred between him and Lily out of wedlock. He had hoped no one would ever have to know about that. But James had a knack for seeing through things.

But if that's what it would take to get James to agree, Whitby would use it—because he didn't have time to tiptoe around James or anyone else for that matter. He needed a preacher here within the week.

A dark shadow of anger and loathing passed over James's features. "Tell me you haven't."

Whitby swallowed hard over his sore throat. "I'm

sorry, James." He saw the shock and devastation on his friend's face, and felt a violent onslaught of remorse. God, this was wretched.

He took a quick step forward. "James, I never intended . . ."

He could not go on.

James sank into a chair. "*You.* You came with me to Paris to bring her home. We had all been so worried that she'd been ravished and ruined by that despicable Frenchman, and now you—my oldest, most trusted friend—come into my home and ruin her under my own roof, knowing you could be dying."

Despite a sudden eruption of shame and regret that ripped brutally through Whitby's heart—for his friend was losing all trust in him, and for good reason—he struggled to cling to his purpose. "I'll be good to her, James. I'll make her happy."

But even as he spoke the words, a sudden onslaught of self-doubt nearly choked him. Who was he trying to fool? James was right. Whitby had ruined Lily, and he'd taken away all her chances for future happiness.

He began to feel a sharp sense of panic about what he'd done. He should have been more firm with her and told her to go back to her own bed. He shouldn't have been thinking of his own needs. He was not the kind of husband she deserved. Whitby had taken her innocence thoughtlessly and selfishly, and now it was too late to change it.

"For how long will you make her happy?" James asked tersely, echoing what Whitby already knew.

But there was no point in answering the question. It would not improve matters here.

They both remained silent for a moment while Whitby let the news sink in. He stood listening to the ominous ticking of the clock, and wished regretfully that he was not standing here having this conversation.

Then he squared his shoulders and surprised himself with the conviction of his next demand, considering how he was feeling at the moment.

"We'll need to make arrangements as quickly as possible." His only explanation for such resolve was that he knew he had nowhere to go but forward. There were no other choices. "A small wedding will do."

James glared up at Whitby with quiet abhorrence, then his shoulders rose and fell with a deep intake of breath. He leaned forward and raked a hand through his hair in defeat. "I'll never forgive you for this, Whitby—for what you have done to Lily."

Whitby sucked in a slow, difficult breath that made his chest ache. He had never felt like he was dying as much as he did at that moment, as he reflected upon James's biting words and thought of Lily—dear, sweet Lily, who only wanted his true and genuine love.

But he was a man who had never lived for anyone but himself.

Whitby swallowed hard over the pain in his throat. He did not want to disappoint Lily—*he did not*—but God help him, James was right. Whitby simply did not possess what it would take to make her truly happy, and she was surely going to suffer for it.

Chapter 20

Facing James in his study that morning had taken a great deal more strength than Whitby had possessed, so he was forced to retire immediately to his room afterward and collapse onto the bed.

Still wearing his morning jacket, he lay on his back staring upward, contemplating what he had just done and feeling as if he were existing in a tilted reality—as if this were not his life. It was another life running parallel to his own. A life he had no control over.

He had just driven a wedge into his friendship with James, and he'd committed himself to marrying Lily. *Lily*.

Last night suddenly seemed an ocean's breadth away. The woman he had made love to was surely someone else, not the little girl in braids whom he had known forever. Not his best friend's baby sister.

He closed his eyes and laid a hand on his chest, feeling as if he'd been swept away on a wave that was about to crash onto the beach and disappear into millions of tiny droplets of water, sinking into the sand. Once the wave was gone, he wouldn't be able to make sense of it. There would be nothing to make sense of.

Perhaps that's why he had gone through with all of this. He felt like his life was going to break on the shore and disappear. In that way, there was no future to fear. Even alienating James had not seemed important.

Only one thing had truly mattered to him this morning: Buried deep under all the self-doubts and regrets, like a small ember glowing within a heap of ash, he had yearned to spend every precious moment he had left with Lily. And he'd needed to make sure she would be taken care of later.

A knock sounded at his door. He managed to sit up, leaning on one arm. "Come in."

The door opened and Lily walked in. She wore a blue and white striped dress with lace at the sleeves and a high-necked collar. There were other dresses he liked more than this one. This one made her look young.

She stopped just inside the door, which she had closed behind her, and he immediately recognized her agitation. She was nervous and unsure about what would happen between them this morning, now that they had to face what they'd done.

He felt uneasy himself. This was all very strange.

"I . . . I wanted to see how you were feeling," she said.

Whitby felt an immediate need to reassure her. He might as well, since the rest of his world seemed to be falling apart. He at least had the power to fix *something*.

He gave her the smile he knew always worked with women—the teasing one, where he inclined his head.

"I suspect the real reason you came was to make sure I wasn't at this very moment packing my trunks and planning my escape."

Thankfully, she recognized the humor in his tone, and the tension drained from her face. She let out a deep breath and smiled.

He was glad he had succeeded in easing her worries, but realized he still had his own to deal with. But he would not let her see that.

He smiled in return and held out his hand. "Come here."

She relaxed even more and crossed toward him, sat on the edge of the bed and took his hand.

"Did you tell your mother?" he asked.

"Yes. She wasn't happy." Lily lowered her gaze. "She was quite miffed at me, actually."

He tried to lighten the mood. "What mother wouldn't be, knowing her daughter was dashing into the clutches of an irresponsible, reckless man like me?"

Lily's smile seemed forced. "You're not reckless."

He nodded as if to say *thank you for the sentiment*, even though they both knew it wasn't true.

"Will you be all right?" he asked, after a few seconds of heavy silence.

"Of course." She raised her chin and strengthened her tone. "I don't care what she thinks anymore. I'm through trying to please her. I can do without her. She's storming off to London in a huff today, and I'll be glad when she's gone."

He stared at her for a long moment, suspecting she was not being completely truthful with him. Then, as he ran his fingers down the side of her face and looked into her eyes, he realized it was herself she was trying to convince, not him. She was, in actuality, suffering very deeply right now.

Dear, dear Lily. He closed his eyes for a moment. She had defied and disappointed her mother, whom she had only ever wished to please, and she had done it for him.

He felt a great weight descend upon his shoulders suddenly. There would be so many expectations to fulfill for Lily, and he *did* want to fulfill them. He *did*.

He hoped with all the pain in his heart that at least this issue with her mother would work itself out in time, because there would surely be others.

"What about Sophia?" he asked. "Did you speak to her as well?"

"Yes. She was happy for me, and so was Annabelle."

"I'm pleased to hear it."

"What about James?" Lily asked. "I see you're still walking, so it couldn't have been that bad."

Still lightly brushing his fingers over her soft cheeks, he explained what had occurred in her brother's study, and what James had said.

"He had no right to treat you that way," Lily said. "He was not always perfect himself. Besides, I'm not a child anymore and he cannot control my heart. I can make my own decisions."

They sat for a moment, while Lily seemed to be thinking about everything that was happening. Then she spoke with a hint of humor, evidently feeling a need to lighten the mood or fill the silence. "I am at least relieved that he didn't break your legs this morning. It will be difficult enough as it is to get you down the aisle."

Whitby laughed. "Yes, but if my legs were in splints, at least I wouldn't be able to dash off into the countryside when the reverend asks me to say 'I do.'"

She smiled along with him, but then turned serious again. "We are jesting, I hope."

He cradled her chin in his hand. "Of course we are. Nothing could keep me from walking down the aisle to marry you, Lily, even if I had to crawl."

Yet he knew—they both knew—that there was some kernel of truth in their teasing. Marriage was not something he'd ever been comfortable with in the past—not that he was completely comfortable with it now either—but the decision was made.

"You look tired," she said.

"I am." He felt sluggish and feverish, and he needed to sleep.

Lily took his hand in hers and kissed it, then backed away from the bed. "I should let you get some rest."

"Yes."

She crossed the room, but paused at the door and spoke hesitantly. "Unless you would like some company? I could lie down with you."

He crawled toward the pillows, thinking of nothing but closing his eyes, for he was breaking into a sweat. "I don't think that would be wise," he said. "Your mother is probably keeping a close watch before she goes."

She shrugged, as if to say it didn't matter.

He eased himself into a comfortable position on his back, let out a deep breath and draped an arm over his face. "Really Lily, I'm very tired. It's been a difficult morning, and I just need to sleep."

He couldn't think anymore. He was completely drained.

Still standing by the door, she nodded and spoke quickly. "Of course. I understand. You need to rest. I won't bother you."

He loosened his neck cloth, pulled it from his shirt collar and tossed it onto the floor. Then he wondered why she wasn't gone yet, because he really wanted to close his eyes.

He glanced over at her, and recognized immediately that she was feeling insecure and uncertain and . . . *God*, her feelings were hurt.

He swallowed painfully, knowing that he was not behaving the way he wished to behave with her—he wanted to make her feel *loved*—but bloody hell, he didn't have the energy to work at it right now. He was depleted. It was too much presently, when he was feeling dizzy and nauseous. He just needed to be alone.

Nevertheless, he managed a hint of a smile. "I'll dream of our wedding night."

He hoped that would be sufficient to fix what she was feeling, because there was nothing else he could do right now outside of falling into a deep slumber.

The corner of her mouth turned up slightly. "I will, too."

As soon as the door closed behind her, Whitby immediately drifted off.

Chapter 21

Lily stood outside her brother's study for a few nervous seconds before she knocked. She had intended to come here because she could not bear to see a friendship destroyed because of her, and she'd wanted to talk to James about it.

But now as she stood with her hand upheld, about to knock, she realized the true reason she was here was because she wasn't sure she could get through the future without her brother. Or *someone*. Which was disturbing. She had been so sure that her love for Whitby would be all she'd need. But after this morning, she wasn't so sure. She had felt a bit of awkwardness between them, and she knew it was not just his illness.

Taking a deep breath, she raised her hand and knocked, and heard a disgruntled "Enter!" from inside.

A sudden dread landed like a hot brick in the pit of her stomach, for her brother could be an intimidating man when he chose to be. But she would not let it stop her from doing what she had to do—help him see that this was going to happen, whether he liked it or not.

She pushed the door open and entered. He was sitting at his desk, and when he saw her, he laid down his pen and sat back. "Well, it's about time. I've been looking for you. No one knew where you were, so I could only assume you were in Whitby's bedchamber."

Lily stared blankly at him, her heart racing beneath the intensity of his stare.

"And I was hardly about to break down the door," he continued. "I'd already done that once before, but at least in Paris, there was no one around to witness it and cause a scandal."

She had been feeling some regret about the way things had occurred over the past twenty-four hours, for she had not included her family in her decisions, and she had come here hoping to smooth out at least one of those rifts. But right now, anger was boiling up within her. This had not been an easy day; she was unsure of so many things, and this treatment was only adding to it. First her mother, now James . . .

He narrowed his gaze at her. "It pains me, Lily, that I was the last to know."

"You were *not* the last to know," she firmly told him. "You were in fact one of the first."

"But too late to have any say in the matter. From what I understand, this marriage is a necessity."

"A necessity that I desire more than anything else in the world."

James leaned forward and rested his elbows on the desk, weaving his fingers together. "So you made sure there would be no way to stop you—even though there are many issues that could be considered more than reasonable grounds to do so."

Lily shook her head in dismay. "I hadn't planned on things happening the way they did. They just did."

James stood and walked around the desk. He came to stand before her. "I'm not surprised to hear you hadn't planned it. You're young and inexperienced, and Whitby has that effect on women. He knows what he's doing. I am, however, surprised that he allowed it to happen, considering the fact that you are my sister. He should have known better. He should have exercised some self-restraint."

She slid forward in her chair. "You can't blame him. I know this may be hard for you to believe, James, because you still see me as a child, but I was the one who initiated it. I seduced *him*. I wanted it."

He was indeed surprised. She could see it in his eyes. He had not expected to hear his baby sister speak in such a way.

"You could be a widow before the year is out," he said flatly.

"I am aware of that. I am not a fool. I weighed it carefully in my decision. But I would rather have six months or even one month with Whitby, than no time at all."

"This is all very romantic, Lily—giving yourself to your dying love, but what if he lives and is an unfaithful, unloving husband? That could result in a lifetime of pain that never gives you the chance to recover and move on. You could be waking up every day for the rest of your married life attending another funeral—the funeral for your dead happiness. And there would be no burial, no closure, till death do you part."

God, she had not wanted to hear that. It made her stomach burn with apprehension.

She dropped her gaze. This was all so terrifying.

Lily took a moment to pause and gather her resolve and remind herself that she had known this was going to be difficult when she had made the decision to pursue Whitby. She knew he would not be an easy man to love.

But she did love him, and she needed to marry him, nothing could stop her, and James's disapproval was not going to help anyone. She needed his support. And to get it, she needed to prove to him that she could—and would—make her own decisions and not need to be bailed out like last time.

"Why does everyone assume Whitby will hurt me or make me unhappy?" she asked. "Does no one believe he might possess some honor deep down?"

"Whitby has many different kinds of honor. I would not be his friend otherwise. But he is a broken man, and I believe it is only this close brush with death that is making him behave out of character. It is romantic for him, too. He doesn't have to worry about the future. He can have this time with you, risk free. Risk free for *him*."

"What do you mean, 'he is a broken man'?"

James shook his head and took her by the arm. He led her to the sofa and sat down beside her. "His parents died when he was very young, and losing his mother was especially traumatic for him. After she was gone, Whitby had many nurses and a vulgar uncle who ran the estate and managed Whitby's upbringing. Poorly."

"How?"

"None of the nurses stayed very long because Whitby's uncle liked to help himself to the help, if you understand my meaning."

Lily covered her mouth with a hand.

"Whitby once told me that he made a point at a very young age not to become attached to any of the women in the household because he knew they would all leave eventually."

Lily was beginning to understand what James was trying to tell her—that Whitby was not even capable of loving someone.

"Lily, you think you weighed your decision carefully, but how could you have, when you don't really know everything there is to know about Whitby?"

Lily considered this. She *had* been very romantic about her feelings toward him, and caught up in the sweltering heat of her passions.

But no, she could not let herself be talked into the belief that there was no hope for happiness. She would never be able to survive the future if she gave into that.

She responded by forcing herself to remember how she had felt in Whitby's arms the night before, and how he had loved her with his body. Those loving emotions had been real, and she'd felt them from him. She *had!* She could not let this change her mind. She was meant to be with him. She had to believe that.

Lily brought her mind back to the things James was saying to her. She had to argue her point. She had to convince him she would be all right. "Sophia didn't know everything about you, James, but it hasn't stopped the two of you from making a good marriage. Love can heal wounds."

"You are very romantic; you always were. But it's dangerous to believe you can change someone."

"I don't want to change him. I love him the way he is."

"But you don't know who he is. You know the young man who played games with you as a child and laughed with you and chased you around the garden. You know the charm he can wield in a drawing room. There is much more to him than that. There is a darker side he rarely shows to the world. He is not a happy man."

Lily felt her brows pull together with bewilderment. "If that's true, I can help him."

"Again Lily, you are being overly romantic, thinking you can rescue him. I don't want to see you get hurt."

"I'm a woman, James. It's no longer up to you to protect me. I *will* be marrying Whitby."

He bowed his head, and she knew he was finding this all very difficult to bear. Finally he met her gaze and took her chin in his hand. "You have indeed become a woman, Lily, and I am at least pleased to discover that you have become a strong one."

She smiled faintly, wanting him to know she was grateful for this concession on his part, yet deep down in the fretful places in her soul, she did not feel particularly strong at this moment. She felt like she would crumble to dust if the breeze blew a certain way. And she felt as if all her words were a great pretense, for she was *not* entirely confident in what she was doing.

He shook his head at her. "If you love him that much, I suppose I can't stand in your way."

"Do you mean it, James?"

He nodded.

She put her arms around his neck and hugged him.

A knock sounded at the door, and Lily and James stepped apart.

"Come in," James said.

Dr. Trider entered. "Good morning, Your Grace. I've come to see the patient, and I'd like to consider doing the biopsy today."

Lily quaked with sudden panic. She wasn't sure if it was because she didn't want to know the results of the procedure, or if she was simply afraid of a possible infection from it. She supposed it was both.

James spoke matter-of-factly. "I'm afraid it can't be done yet, Dr. Trider."

"Well, if I could examine him, we might find that he is well enough to—"

"You may certainly examine him. That would be good of you. But the procedure must be postponed at least a week, as Lord Whitby and Lady Lily are to be married."

Lily gazed up at James.

There it was.

It was official, and suddenly very real. She would be Whitby's wife. Till death do them part. In sickness and in health. And she had her brother's support.

But when she looked into his eyes, she understood that that support was tenuous. James looked mournful, certain that she would, in a very short time, suffer great anguish and despair.

All of a sudden, she experienced a painful burning sensation in her chest. She couldn't look at her brother.

So she did the only thing she could. She tore her gaze away from his face—very hastily—and tried to paste on a smile as she accepted the doctor's tentative congratulations.

Chapter 22

Lily and Whitby were married in a private ceremony at Wentworth Chapel, with only James, Sophia, and Annabelle attending. They enjoyed an intimate wedding supper of cream of love apple soup, roast duck and roasted pepper sauce, tossed salad made with flowers, and wedding cake for dessert. They were inclined, however, to retire to Whitby's bedchamber immediately after dinner, for he was feeling fatigued from standing during the ceremony.

As they entered the room, the warmth of the fire caressed their faces, and with more than a little anticipation for the night ahead, Whitby closed the door gently behind him.

He watched Lily meander around, then turn to face him. She had changed out of her wedding gown for dinner and was wearing the crimson dress she had worn one of the nights during the shooting party—the first night he had noticed how beautiful she was.

She was beautiful again tonight, more beautiful than she had ever been. Her skin looked like smooth porcelain, her cheeks were flushed, and her smile was dazzling. She had worn her dark hair up in a tidy bun for the wedding ceremony, but had changed it when she'd dressed for dinner. Though it was still swept up on top of her head, there was a single wavy lock spilling down between her shoulder blades, with crimson ribbons flowing down as well. And despite his many doubts and misgivings, despite his fatigue, despite his fear that he'd just made the worst, most selfish mistake of his life—the way she looked tonight was enough to drive him mad with yearning. He simply had to have her.

Slowly he crossed the room. He looked down into her eyes and saw love in them—love and joy and anticipation. Today they had signed their names in the church register. He had put a ring on her finger. It was done. They were married.

He shook his head in disbelief, wondering how they had gotten here so quickly. He felt stupefied.

Lily—bless her adventurous little heart—distracted him from all that by stepping forward and sliding her gloved hands up his chest. She smiled enticingly while she unfastened his neck cloth.

"I almost leaped across the table at dinner to do this," she said. "That was the longest meal of my life."

"It was rather tedious," he replied, letting his hands come to rest upon her hips. "But I suspect the evening is about to take a turn for the better."

He watched her face while she unbuttoned his jacket and waistcoat, and pushed both garments off his shoulders and let them fall to the floor.

"I suspect you're right, Lord Whitby," she said. "As long as you're not too tired . . ."

"Tired? Why yes I am, but I'll do much better once I'm horizontal."

He raised his arms while she pulled his shirt off over his head, then he watched her pull off her gloves, finger by finger, and drop them onto the floor as well. She returned her eager hands to his bare chest, and he shuddered pleasurably at the feel of her warm palms upon his skin.

"Lady Whitby, you are irresistible," he said.

She closed her eyes and sighed. "Ah, *Lady Whitby*. You have no idea how many times I've dreamed of being addressed that way."

She was indeed Lady Whitby, wasn't she?

"Since you dismissed your maid," he said, "I suppose it will be up to me to undress you."

"That is most chivalrous of you, my lord."

He took her hand and led her to the bed, then turned her around to unfasten her gown in the back. She held her hair out of the way, and he couldn't resist the desire to drop open-mouthed kisses along the back of her soft, succulent neck.

"That gives me shivers," she whispered.

He slid the dress off her shoulders and let it fall to the floor. She stepped out of it, and he bent forward to pick it up. He folded it and draped it carefully over a chair, then returned his attention to the task of getting her out of her clothes.

He began to unhook her corset in the front, while he laid gentle kisses across her neckline, and when the corset came loose, he tossed it to the chair on top of the dress and pulled her chemise off over her head.

He stood for a moment, admiring her ample bare breasts in the firelight, noting with some surprise that the rash impatience to bed her was fading. Now, he wanted only to slow everything down.

Whitby laid a hand upon her breast, and gently massaged it.

Lily closed her eyes. "I love the feel of your hands on me," she whispered.

"And I love what I feel when I touch you."

It was all very strange, he thought, reflecting upon this slow, quiet foreplay. It was not his customary style. He was usually more aggressive than this. Perhaps it was his illness. Or perhaps not. He didn't know.

He unfastened the ribbons on her petticoats and drawers, and everything fell to the floor in a soft, white heap. His bride stood naked before him wearing only her stockings and dainty black heels, and he took a step back to allow his gaze free rein— to travel down the length of her beautiful body and back up again.

It pleased him to know that she belonged to him—that he was the only man who had ever made love to her. He possessed her virginity and he always would, and it felt very right.

Thinking she might be cold, he pulled back the covers on the bed to discover dozens of fresh red rose petals hidden in the sheets.

Lily looked down and laughed. "Sophia must have done this," she said, inhaling the fragrance. "She looked rather mischievous today."

Whitby watched Lily step out of her shoes and climb onto the bed—with an impressive lack of shyness, given her nudity—then he removed the rest of his own clothes and joined her, sitting back on his heels at her feet.

He proceeded to remove her stockings, stroking her delicate foot and calf, until he heard her whimper with anticipation.

His heated gaze lifted, and he caught her staring at his sizable erection. Whitby smiled knowingly.

"Perhaps I should come closer," he suggested with a husky, enticing voice as he kissed the arch of her foot.

"Yes," she replied breathlessly, clearly finding it difficult to think and speak.

He continued to lay a trail of kisses up the inside of her calf while she sighed with delight, then he lay down beside her. She turned onto her side to face him, and they stared at each other for a moment.

"When will we go to your estate?" she asked suddenly, surprising him with the question. "I would very much like to see your home. I've never been there."

He brushed her hair off her forehead. "Have you not? James has been there a hundred times. I suppose I assumed you had been there at least once."

"No, never."

"Then we shall have to remedy that. When can you be ready to go?"

She paused, her expression growing serious. "That depends. How soon after the biopsy can we leave?"

The biopsy. He had managed to forget about that over the past few days, but he knew he could not put it off forever. It would have to be dealt with.

He slid closer to her and brushed his fingertips across her flat stomach and the gentle curve of her hipbone. "Are you anxious about that?"

"Yes. Aren't you?"

He took his time before he answered. "It's a simple procedure."

She did not appear convinced, so he slid his hand slowly down to the top of her thigh. "You've given me reason to come through it, Lily."

She smiled and turned onto her side to face him. "Then I won't worry. All I'll think about tonight is how I'm going to make this the most erotic experience of your life."

With a naughty little smile, she slid her warm, open hand down the center of his chest to the coarse hair beneath his navel, then reached down and gently massaged him.

He closed his eyes and inhaled deeply, lost in the absorbing rapture of her hand as it worked its magic.

Whitby slid a finger between her thighs and grinned. "You're off to a good start."

A burst of energy came to him suddenly from somewhere, and he rolled onto the sweet, soft heat of her body, kissing her lips and neck and working his way down to her breasts and flat stomach. She sighed and wiggled irresistibly beneath him, running her fingers through his hair, spreading her legs so his chest was pressing upon the damp center between them.

"Oh, Whitby," she whispered in breathless anticipation. "I've been waiting so long for this."

He wanted, with unstoppable urgency, to taste her. So down he went, devouring the intoxicating flavor of her flesh, kissing and suckling, while she gasped first in shock, then in delight. She thrust her hips and wrapped her hands around his head, making sounds only a woman pushed over the edge of reason can make.

Lily . . . He couldn't get enough of her. He hungered greedily for everything she was.

He brought her to a swift orgasm—almost too swift—but contrary to what he expected, the climax only drove her further into a realm of sensual desires, and she grabbed for his shoulders, pulling him up to the supple heat of her lips, driving her pelvis hard against his.

"Make love to me now," she pleaded, her tongue plunging into his mouth.

"With pleasure."

So with one firm, deep thrust, he entered the glorious heaven of her body, marveling at the fact that this was so much more than just sex. The pure, unadulterated joy—*yes, joy*—flooding his senses shook him from the inside out, and he found himself believing in angels, for surely Lily had to be one. She had brought something unexpected into his life—a sense of contentment and gratitude and a dozen other things he could not begin to understand or describe.

He'd never experienced anything like it in the whole of his life. He was thrusting into her, making love to her, giving her everything he possessed as a man, and thanking God that she had fallen in love with him.

"I'm glad you're here with me," he whispered in her ear as he thrust slowly, gently, then faster and harder.

And he was *so very glad*. If this was the end of his life, he was being rewarded in a way he did not deserve. He was the luckiest man on earth, and he didn't know why.

She clutched onto him then, tightly, before her body shuddered with another climax that made her sob. He pulled back and saw a tear running down the side of her face.

He kissed it away. "Don't cry, Lily. Everything will be all right."

"I can't help it," she said. "I'm so happy."

He smiled gently and nodded. "So am I. More than you will ever know."

And more than he'd ever dreamed possible, he realized, as he thrust into his wife one final time and experienced his own powerful, trembling release.

Chapter 23

Lily and Whitby spent the first three days of their marriage in bed, but hardly because Whitby was weak or ill. He was, in fact, quite remarkably energetic when in a horizontal position, and he had even regained enough of an appetite to attend dinner each evening with James, Sophia, and Annabelle.

On the fourth day, after breakfast, he told Lily he wanted to go outside for a short walk, and she immediately called for his valet. A half hour later, they were wearing their coats, slowly making their way through the corridors and down the main staircase to the back door.

"Are you all right?" Lily asked, stopping with

concern as soon as they stepped into the clear sunlight. The air was cool and crisp.

He held up a hand to shade his eyes. "It's bright, that's all. I suppose I've been indoors too long."

She slipped her arm through his. "Come. You'll get used to it."

They slowly descended the steps on the other side of the flagstone veranda, and crossed the terraced garden to the pond, where they had to stop and rest. They sat down on the bench in the shade of the big oak tree.

They sat quietly, gazing at the water and the bright blue sky, breathing in the scent of the autumn leaves that were, at that very moment, falling to the ground all around them.

"Remember the last time you came and sat here with me?" Whitby said, taking Lily's hand in his. "I was not kind to you."

She gazed compassionately at him. "You were fine, Whitby."

"No, I wasn't. I wanted you to leave. I wanted to be left alone."

"But you were ill."

"No more than I am now. Less so, in fact." He kissed her on the forehead. "I brought it up because I wanted to apologize to you. For that and for every other time in my life when I did not see you as the woman you are. I've been blind."

She rested her head on his shoulder and closed her eyes. "It was barely more than a week ago, but it seems like a year."

"Yes, because I'm not the man I was that day."

They sat in silence listening to the leaves blowing in the breeze, watching a sparrow swoop down from the sky and fly low, close to the water's surface. To Lily, it was like a dream—a perfect, perfect moment in time. "You've made me so happy, Whitby."

Yet simmering beneath her unimaginably profound joy was a fear that would not fully relinquish its hold on her, for there was still a very real likelihood that this bliss would not last.

"And you, me," he replied. "I never believed I would ever experience anything like this. It's astounding." He cradled her chin in his hand and looked into her eyes. *"Thank you."*

While he touched his lips to hers and kissed her tenderly as the leaves blew past them, Lily managed to sweep her fears away. She did not want to spoil what she had now, here in the present.

"Jenson won't be impressed with me," he said, pulling away slightly.

"Why not?"

"He spent all that time getting me dressed, and now all I want to do is go back to bed."

Lily sat back, her brow furrowing with concern. "Did we overdo it? Are you tired?"

Her husband grinned. "We definitely overdid it, but I'm not tired."

He gave her a mischievous look, and she nodded her understanding while helping him to his feet.

*   *   *

On the fifth day, Lily woke naked in Whitby's bed, and smiled contentedly as she finally began to believe that she had won Whitby's heart—something she had never imagined she could ever do. They had spent every minute of every day together since their wedding, and had given their bodies to each other passionately and devotedly at night.

On top of that, he'd gained back some of his appetite and strength as well. Not only had they gone for a walk the day before, at dinner that night, he'd eaten some of almost every course.

He had not yet had the biopsy, however, nor had he seen the doctor all week, for he'd been determined to enjoy their brief honeymoon. But they both knew the time was drawing near. They could not avoid the truth forever.

Lily sat up in the big disheveled bed and hugged the covers to her chest. Wondering where her husband had gone so early, she looked at the clock and realized it was not so early after all. He must have left her to catch up on some sleep, as they certainly hadn't slept much during the night.

She rose from bed and called for her maid, and a short time later, made her way to the breakfast room.

She walked in and was pleased to see Whitby sipping coffee not only with Sophia and Annabelle, but also with James. He and James had not spoken amicably since the wedding day, when James had found it necessary to shake Whitby's hand. Over the past few days, however, her brother had appeared to be accepting the situation, and Lily hoped he would eventually grow to understand that their marriage had been the right decision.

Her handsome husband met her gaze just then, and gave her a look that was meant only for her—a knowing look, a look that told her he felt just as jubilant as she did this morning, and was recalling a few delightfully wicked things they had done the night before.

With a flirtatious little smile, Lily said good morning, served herself breakfast and took a seat beside Annabelle and across from Whitby.

"Have you all eaten?" she asked.

"Yes," Sophia replied, taking a sip of her coffee. "Did you sleep well, Lily?"

Lily glanced at Whitby. "Yes, very well, thank you."

He raised a skeptical eyebrow at her. What a cheeky devil he was. She grinned at him again and tried not to blush as she picked up her fork and began eating.

The conversation turned to what was in the newspaper James was reading, and they all enjoyed a leisurely time, lingering over their coffee. A moment later, the butler entered the room to announce that Dr. Trider had arrived.

Lily had not known he was coming.

Whitby stood.

"Is today the day?" she asked, setting down her coffee cup.

"Yes," Whitby replied.

An unwelcome tension pulled through her as she stared panic-stricken up at her husband. "Why didn't you tell me?"

He gave her an apologetic smile. "I spoke to the doctor only last night, darling, and I didn't want to spoil our evening."

"I see. Well." Despite her fears and anxieties, Lily resolved to be brave. She took a few deep breaths to calm her racing heart, and stood also. "Can I go with you?"

He moved to kiss her on the cheek. "It would be best if you remained here with the others. The doctor will tell you when it's over. It shouldn't take too long."

Lily struggled to smile and appear confident. "Of course."

She sat down again, though she couldn't finish her coffee. She couldn't imagine swallowing anything when dread and fear were filling her, for the doctor was going to slice her husband's skin with a scalpel. She couldn't bear to envision it.

Whitby hesitated a moment, gazing down at her one last time before he left the breakfast room.

"Let's have a look at you before we get started," Dr. Trider said cheerfully in Whitby's bedchamber. "Have a seat."

Whitby had been through this examination all too many times. He unbuttoned his waistcoat and untucked his shirt before he sat on the edge of the bed.

The doctor asked him how he'd been feeling over the past week.

"Better, in fact," Whitby replied. "My appetite has returned somewhat, and Lady Whitby and I went for a walk yesterday. I can only attribute it to the benefits of marriage." He grinned pleasantly up at the doctor.

Dr. Trider nodded his understanding and withdrew his stethoscope from his bag. He listened to Whitby's chest, looking up at the ceiling as he did so. "Yes, yes, very good."

He lowered the stethoscope and felt the glands at Whitby's neck. He pressed everywhere, his brow furrowing with what looked like concern.

It was not the look one wanted to see upon the face of a physician while in the midst of an examination. Whitby's pulse quickened slightly.

"What's wrong?" he asked.

The doctor shook his head and took his time before he answered. He continued to press upon Whitby's neck in various places. Finally he said, "Lie back, I want to check your spleen."

Whitby reclined, and the doctor felt around his abdomen. He continued to wear that unsettling expression on his face, as if he were both confused and concerned.

Finally he stepped back, and Whitby sat up, waiting uneasily for the doctor to say something. Finally, his shoulders rose and fell with a deep intake of breath. "Your glands and spleen appear to be slightly improved."

Whitby sat staring at the doctor, realizing he was now wearing a similar confused expression. "Could this mean I am getting better?

Dr. Trider spoke frankly. "I cannot say. Periods of quiescence are not uncommon with Hodgkins, you see, where the glands diminish in size unexplainably."

"So this could just be a temporary respite."

"Yes."

They both stared off into the distance for a moment or two, while Whitby tried to remember what had happened to his father in those final months. So far, everything Whitby had experienced was exactly like his father had experienced it. But had he ever had a respite?

"Will the biopsy tell us?" Whitby asked.

"It will at least confirm or rule out Hodgkins," Dr. Trider replied.

Whitby considered this carefully, then met the doctor's earnest gaze. "I would like to know for sure. Can you do it now? Do you have everything you need?"

"Yes, my lord. I came equipped."

"Then let's get started."

Whitby's blood quickened slightly as he watched the doctor remove a number of razor-sharp instruments from his bag.

Lily and the others were relieved to learn from the doctor that there had been no unexpected problems during the surgery. It had gone as well as he could have expected, but he also informed them that they would have to wait a few days for the results.

All continued to go well while they waited. There were no post-operative infections, and though Whitby's health did not improve a great deal, he did not suffer a relapse.

He wore a bandage on his neck, but it did not stop him from spending time with Lily and making the most of the hours they had together—both of them fully aware that they were enjoying a blissful state of ignorance. They did not yet know the results of the procedure, so as far as they were concerned, there was no point worrying. They talked of other things, including the future, which helped to keep Whitby's mind off the reality of his life.

On the third day, Dr. Trider returned from London with the results, having enlisted the services of the most renowned pathologist in the country. Dr. Trider rubbed his chin and walked to the window in the drawing room, while Whitby sat on the sofa, tapping his foot while he waited rather impatiently.

"I don't know what to tell you, my lord," Dr. Trider said, "except that you must have had some form of influenza or perhaps even tuberculosis." Still looking dumbfounded, he faced Whitby. "I will certainly report this case to my colleagues in London. Perhaps there have been other similar cases."

Whitby stood up. "So I'm not dying."

The doctor shook his head. "At least not of Hodgkins. Though I am most decidedly confused by this." He faced the window again and stared out at the horizon. "If it was influenza, I see no reason why you shouldn't continue to improve. Otherwise, I just don't know."

Whitby realized he was staring blankly at the doctor, and his mouth was open. He could hardly believe this news.

"But you should continue to be monitored closely," the doctor told him. "You're still very ill, my lord."

"Of course. I understand."

The doctor walked to him and patted him on the upper arm. "But this is good news. Congratulations. Lady Whitby will be overjoyed."

Still in shock, feeling almost in a daze, Whitby managed to form a reply. "Indeed she will be."

Lily's gaze flitted to the door when Whitby entered the breakfast room where she had been waiting with James, Sophia and Annabelle.

Her heart pounded suddenly with apprehension, for despite Whitby's improvements over the past week, she had been preparing herself for the worst. The doctor had said, after all, that periods of quiescence were not uncommon, so she had not quite been able to let go of the fear that Whitby's condition would worsen.

Nevertheless she steeled herself, stood up and went to him. "What did he say?"

Whitby gazed down at her with a calm and

pleasant smile on his face. "Perhaps we should sit down."

She frowned, allowing him to escort her back to her place at the table. James, Sophia and Annabelle all waited in silence for Whitby to explain, while Lily herself could barely keep still.

"Well," Whitby said at last, and Lily could tell he was endeavoring to sound casual about whatever he was about to say.

"What were the results, Whitby?" James asked.

Whitby sat forward and looked at each of them in turn. "It's good news."

"Good news?" Lily's hopes erupted within her. Was he going to live? Was her husband going to live? She was afraid to believe it.

Whitby seemed to be in a state of disbelief himself, and appeared to still be ruminating over what he'd just been told. "The pathologist concluded that whatever ailed me was *not* Hodgkins. It was something else. Dr. Trider is still trying to ascertain what."

Lily stared blankly at him for a moment, digesting this news, then her whole body shook wildly with jubilation. She sucked in a breath. Whitby was going to live! He was not going to die! She would not be a widow! He would live to see his children grow!

She only then realized that she was panting and smiling brightly from ear to ear.

Whitby, however, was only smiling faintly. Perhaps he was still in shock.

He turned toward James. "I suppose I owe all of you an apology."

"An apology!" Sophia blurted out. "Good heavens, what for?"

"For causing you unnecessary worries. I was too quick to assume the worst."

"We were all just as quick," Sophia assured him. "We heard what the doctor said. It really seemed as if there was good reason to worry, so please do not apologize, Whitby. We are all overjoyed to hear that you will live."

He glanced uneasily at Lily.

She put on her best smile, to show him that she did not blame him for the mistake, either. Of course she did not. She was thrilled that it was a mistake, positively ecstatic that he was going to live!

He looked away again, this time lowering his gaze to the tabletop.

Then strangely as she stared at him, the joy in her heart began to drain away like water seeping through a crack in a bucket. Trepidation poured in, coursing through her veins like a stream of cold river water.

Was he not happy?

She swallowed hard while James and Whitby talked casually about the mysterious illness and how Dr. Trider intended to investigate its uniqueness.

Lily felt rather displaced from her body. She was only half listening to what they were saying, because her mind was slowly digesting the idea that this meant everything was different. Everything was not what they'd thought it was.

Her eyebrows pulled together. She thought of the past week with Whitby, how it had been both terrible and wonderful at the same time. Terrible because she'd known Whitby could be dying. Wonderful because he had appeared to fall in love with her and had allowed himself to do so unreservedly. He had believed there would not be a future, so he had lived fully in the present.

The future had suddenly reappeared, yet Lily felt as if she had just been shot like a bullet back into the past, when she was simply James's baby sister, always hanging about. Except that now, there was this small matter of an impulsive marriage between them.

Was this going to make things awkward? she wondered in a panic. Would it be a problem for him?

She swallowed hard over the thick lump of anxiety rising up from her belly, and tried to sit calmly, tried to keep herself from fidgeting or turning pale. It was not so easy, however, when she felt sick to her stomach.

It was all very strange. She would not have expected this reaction from herself upon hearing that Whitby was going to live. She would have expected to feel only joy, nothing else. But she had not anticipated Whitby's response.

She had not imagined how it would feel to see him avoid her gaze.

Chapter 24

L ily woke from a brief nap when a knock sounded at her door. She sat up groggily in her bed, wondering if it was Sophia. Sophia had wanted to talk to her earlier about the good news, but Lily had wanted to be alone. She hadn't wanted to discuss the situation, for she didn't feel ready.

For one thing, she didn't fully understand what Whitby's true feelings were, and there was no point speculating about it until she could speak to him directly. All she could do at the moment was tell herself that everything was fine. Perhaps he had just been in shock at breakfast.

The knock sounded again, so she called out, "Come in!"

When the door pushed open, she sat up on the edge of the bed and felt her heart flutter at the sight of her husband.

Yes, he was still her husband, she reminded herself. The news about his illness did not change that, even though so much of what had occurred between them over the past few weeks did not seem real.

Lily watched him with apprehension as he entered the room and closed the door behind him. He did not approach the bed right away. He stood in front of the door and faced her. Lily had to force herself to keep her eyes fixed on him. She was so afraid he was going to tell her they'd made a terrible mistake.

"You disappeared from the breakfast room before we had a chance to talk," he said with a charming, jovial, heart-stopping smile.

There it was. That magic, playful appeal.

He's back, she thought instantly, feeling her heart return from its pathetic rendezvous with self-pity and despair. He was as charming as he had been every night in his bed since they were married, as charming as he was in a drawing room, surrounded by pretty ladies. Did this mean he was not uncomfortable with what they'd done?

"I knew you had to escort the doctor out," she said. "I assumed you would come to see me when he was gone."

Whitby did not need to know that she had spent a good amount of time lamenting over the certain fact that he would *not* come to see her, or that she had practically convinced herself that he would never come to see her again.

He walked to the bed where she was sitting, her hands squeezing the edge of it, her feet not quite touching the floor.

She was surprised by the compassion in his eyes as he ran a finger down the side of her cheek. For a long moment he looked at her. He pushed a fallen tendril of hair behind her ear.

Lily's heart was now racing like a wild stallion. She did not know what to expect. She was still afraid he was going to tell her they'd made a mistake.

"Don't look so worried, darling," he gently said, and all the pent-up tension in her body blew away like feathers in a breeze. "Good God, at breakfast, you almost looked disappointed that I was going to live."

Lily let out a tight breath. "No, Whitby, not at all."

He chuckled. "I'm only joking. I think I know why you were so serious, and why you're still serious now. You were afraid I was going to regret marrying you."

Lily shuddered with both joy and fear—joy because he did understand her—he *did*—and fear that he was about to tell her the truth: that yes, he did harbor some regret over their hasty marriage.

He cradled her chin in his hand and shook his head at her, looking almost amused.

"What's so funny?" she asked, slightly miffed that he could find her anxiety humorous.

"You," he replied, bending to kiss her lightly on the lips. "Why is it so impossible for you to believe that I desire you, and more than that, I care for you like I've never cared for anyone? Didn't you see that over the past week?"

Lily stared at him, quite unable to get even the smallest word past her lips.

"No woman could ever mean more to me than you do, Lily," he continued, "and I will never regret my actions when I was ill. I feel quite the opposite, in fact. I will always be thankful for that brush with death, because it forced me to finally grow up and recognize how precious and brief life is, and how none of us should waste a single minute drifting along, waiting for things to happen or feeling as if we have all the time in the world to do later what we could, and should, do today."

Lily continued to stare up at him, speechless while her heart pounded in her chest. She could hardly believe what she was hearing. He was speaking to all her fears, as if he had been able to read her mind all morning, while she was lying up here alone in her bed, imagining the worst.

"You don't regret what we've done?" she asked.

He rested his forehead upon hers. "Of course not. It was the best thing I ever did. You're my wife now, and nothing is more important to me than you and our future children."

He lifted her chin and kissed her, his tongue sweeping smoothly past her parting lips and into her eager mouth. All her womanly desires sparked instantly into red-hot flames, and she reached up to hold his head in her hands.

"Oh, Whitby," she whispered breathlessly, dragging her mouth from his and tipping her head back as he kissed her neck. "Make love to me?"

He rose from the bed, looking down at her while he removed his jacket and began to unfasten his trousers. "I had every intention of doing just that when I knocked on your door."

Then he came down upon her, heavy and warm and so much of a man.

She smiled up at him, though inside her head, she could not stop herself from doubting what was happening. *This can't be real. It can't be true. It's too wonderful. He can't possibly love me like this.*

He lowered himself upon her, coming to rest snugly between her parted legs while he devoured her mouth. He thrust his hips against her, and she cupped his muscular buttocks in her hands.

He rose up on his hands to free space between them, so she could untie the ribbon on her drawers and slide them down. Lily slid his trousers down, too, while he was still propped up on his hands.

As soon as the way was clear, he lowered his hips between her legs and positioned himself. Lily closed her eyes, as the pleasure of his entry flowed through her like wine.

He made love to her slowly and gently, and without a word as the early afternoon sunlight beamed through the window. Lily tossed her head back and gave herself up to the ecstasy of the moment.

She would *not* let herself think of his behavior in the breakfast room earlier that day, after he'd learned he would be her husband until he was an old man. She was going to forget that. She would *force* herself to forget it. And she was going to enjoy the gift she had been given—the gift of Whitby's life.

A short time later, Whitby slipped quietly out of Lily's bed while she slept. He picked up his clothes from the floor and carefully pulled them on, for he did not want to wake her. Shrugging into his jacket, he left the room, closing the door gently behind him.

As soon as he was alone in the corridor, he breathed in a deep sigh of relief at having a difficult chore fulfilled: He had reassured Lily that he had no regrets.

He leaned against the wall and tipped his head back, feeling weary and depleted. He shut his eyes and covered his forehead with a hand. *Jesus . . .*

He might have reassured her, but dammit, he had also lied to her. He *wasn't* entirely comfortable with what they'd done, and he suspected that on some level, she knew it.

His chest tightened painfully. What was wrong with him? Now that he was no longer on death's door, he felt like his feelings for Lily had changed, that the mad passion had diminished, and he felt agonizingly guilty about that.

What the devil had happened? Had he misinterpreted his feelings for her? Had he simply wanted a chance to be more than a lover to someone? To experience what it would feel like to be in love? Had he been swept away by everything, and had it all been a distorted reality?

He raked a hand through his hair. He didn't want it to be that way, because he *had* felt completely in love with Lily over the past week. He remembered his wedding night, and how he had felt impossibly happy when he'd made love to her. It had been overwhelming, the most passionate affair of his life, and he didn't want it to end. He didn't want to feel what he was feeling now.

Pressure. He was in for the long haul. She could be pregnant with his child at this very moment.

His mother had died giving birth. He still remembered the devastating sound of her screams.

Feeling a sudden wrenching pain in his gut, Whitby slid down the wall to sit on the floor, and rested his forearms on his knees, his hands joined together between them.

It suddenly dawned on him that perhaps he'd also given Lily the illness he'd had. The doctor didn't know anything about it. It could have been contagious.

A very predictable bout of dread rushed through him, and he had to force himself to suppress those thoughts. It would do him no good to worry about what he could not control. He would simply have to get through it somehow and focus on the positive: at least now he would finally have an heir, and his title would not pass to Magnus.

Whitby took a deep, cleansing breath. He *would* get through this, he told himself. He would get through everything. They were married. He was a husband, and he cared for Lily. He had allowed himself to care, so he would not let her down.

He had done his best today to reassure her, and he would do his best every day for the rest of his life. First thing tomorrow, they would leave for his ancestral home and she would begin her duties as mistress of the house. He had every confidence that she would fulfill that role admirably.

He told himself it would not be so difficult. He would simply be the man she believed him to be. He would be faithful to her and kind to her, and he would treat her with the respect and adoration she deserved. He would make love to her and he would make her *feel* loved. He would do everything in his power to never, *ever* hurt her.

He rose to his feet, took a deep, shaky breath and returned to his own bedchamber to tell Jenson to begin packing for the morrow.

Stepping out of her coach in London, Marion felt a cold raindrop hit her cheek. She lowered her head as she quickened her pace to the front door of Wentworth House.

She'd had a tiring day, for she'd been keeping busy with an ambitious number of charitable projects over the past week, far more than usual for this time of year, when she would normally be residing in the country.

But she did not wish to be in the country. Not now.

She entered Wentworth House and handed her cloak to the butler. "Have a pot of tea brought to my rooms right away," she said. "I'm chilled."

With that, she climbed the stairs and entered her boudoir. Her maid, Euphemia, a portly woman of middle age, was bending forward, placing something in the bottom drawer of Marion's wardrobe, but she straightened quickly, appearing startled.

"I want to get out from under this ridiculous hat," Marion said. She began to pull off her gloves as she crossed to her mirrored vanity.

As soon as Marion sat down, Euphemia made a move to pull out the hatpin, but Marion stopped her with a hand. "I can do it myself. Fetch me the paper. I'm going to have a cup of tea while I read it."

"The paper?"

Marion's gaze darted to Euphemia's reflection in the mirror. "What's the matter?"

"Nothing. It's just that . . ." She hesitated. "It's nothing, Your Grace. I'll go fetch it now."

Twenty minutes later, while Marion was sipping her tea at her desk and reading the society pages, she discovered the basis for Euphemia's anxiety. Marion clenched her jaw as she read the most shockingly succinct announcement.

Marriage

Lady Lily Elizabeth Langdon to
Edward Peter Wallis, Earl of Whitby.

Marion leaned back in her chair and lowered the paper onto her lap. She stared open-mouthed at the wall in front of her face. So they'd actually gone ahead and done it.

She glanced back down at the announcement. No doubt people all over London were reading this and chuckling to themselves, because her careless son-in-law had probably been in the bedchamber of some flaxen-haired tart not more than three weeks ago. And he would likely be in similar places again before too long.

Marion leaned forward and rested her forehead in a hand. For a long moment she sat there, breathing hard and squeezing her eyes shut as anger ripped along her spine.

She looked across the room at the framed picture of Lily on her bedside table. *You wouldn't listen, would you? You just went ahead and did what you wanted.*

Marion rose to her feet. She marched over to the bedside table, opened the drawer and put the picture of Lily inside it. She couldn't look at her daughter's face.

She slammed the drawer shut and sat on the edge of the bed. Then she chewed on a thumbnail while she thought about Lily and Whitby together.

Were they happy? What if they were?

She sat for a long time, and contemplated such a thing.

Chapter 25

~~~◯◯~~~

Lily sat beside Whitby in the closed coach as it clattered over a stone bridge in the forest on the way to his home, Century House, which was located in Bedfordshire, a mere three-hour train ride from London.

Annabelle sat in the seat facing them, looking out the window at the leaves on the trees, brightly colored in shades of red, orange, and yellow. Lily could smell the fresh dampness of those that had already fallen to the ground.

The carriage rolled off the bridge and Lily leaned closer to the open window to see what lay ahead.

"We're almost there," Whitby said, smiling at her as if he were enjoying her excitement.

The carriage left the shady forest and drove onto a lane that crossed a field of clipped green grass. The sun was shining as they traveled up a hill and finally over the top, where the house came into view on a facing hill overlooking a lush green valley below.

"There it is," Whitby said, leaning across in front of Lily to share the view with her.

It was an extraordinary house in the shape of a U—perfectly symmetrical in the Palladian style, with identical wings on either side. A grand triumphal arch stood in front.

As they drew closer, the dirt lane became a cobbled drive, and the horses' hooves tapped noisily upon them. Lily's heart beat fast with excitement as they passed under the arch and pulled to a slow halt at the main entrance. A liveried footman approached and lowered the steps.

Whitby climbed out of the coach and offered a hand to both Annabelle and Lily, who each stepped out and gazed up at the front of the house.

"It's so good to be home," Annabelle said. "And who would have guessed I would return not only with my brother in good health, but with a new sister-in-law as well?"

Lily kissed her on the cheek.

They made their way up the stone steps to the open doors and were greeted by Clarke, the butler, just inside the grand entry hall. Clarke presented Mrs. Harrington, the housekeeper.

The servants were lined up formally, waiting to

meet the new countess. Lily smiled warmly at the members of the staff, speaking to each one. She could sense they were pleased to meet her, and some of them seemed almost ecstatic in their relief. Perhaps they had been worried that Whitby would not recover from his illness, and because he had no heir, everything would come to a screeching halt at the estate.

No, she thought—it would not have come to a halt. It would have been passed on to Whitby's cousin, Magnus. She came to the end of the line of servants and supposed that would explain their relief. From all accounts, Magnus was not a kind man.

Mrs. Harrington informed them that their rooms had been prepared and dinner would be served at eight. As they made their way toward the stairs, however, the butler requested a private word with Whitby, who politely excused himself from Lily's company.

She watched them with evident curiosity, then accompanied Annabelle and Mrs. Harrington up the stairs.

Whitby entered his study and waited while Clarke closed the double oak doors. The butler turned to face Whitby, his expression tainted with concern, though as always, he kept his hands steady at his sides.

"What is it, Clarke?" Whitby asked. "Did something happen while I was gone?"

"Yes, my lord," Clarke replied sternly. "I feel it

necessary to inform you that Lord Magnus was here three days ago, demanding to see Miss Lawson."

Whitby felt his hackles rise. Magnus and his father had been barred from the family doors many years ago, and Magnus had no right to come here. Especially to see Annabelle.

"He must have known I wasn't here," Whitby said loathingly, "to have made such a demand. Did you let him in?"

"No, my lord."

"What did he say? Did he give any explanation for why he wanted to see her?"

"Not at first. He simply requested a meeting with her, and he seemed rather smug, a trifle too confident in my opinion, which caused me some concern. When I told him Miss Lawson was not at home, he didn't believe me, and he informed me that I was making a grave error. He told me that when the earldom was his, I would be the first to go, and if I possessed any shred of intelligence, I would be seeking other employment posthaste."

"When the earldom was *his*? He said that?"

"Yes, my lord. I am of the opinion that he knew of your illness. He clearly did not know about your marriage."

Whitby felt light-headed all of a sudden and had to sit down. He was not yet fully recovered, and sometimes, just standing for a long period of time exhausted him. This news was not helping.

"But how the devil had he learned of my illness?" Whitby asked, sinking into the chair at his desk.

"No one knew, except the members of this household and some of the duke's guests."

"I don't know, my lord. It appears he has a connection somewhere among those you mention."

Whitby clenched his jaw. "This is worrisome."

Clarke said nothing for a moment, while Whitby tapped a finger on his desk.

"Are you all right, my lord? You don't look well."

Whitby raised a hand to dismiss Clarke's fears. "I'm fine."

Clarke stared uneasily at Whitby for a moment. Whitby could feel himself breaking into a sweat. He took a few deep, calming breaths.

"Would you like me to make inquiries among the staff?" Clarke asked, returning to the issue at hand. "Perhaps Lord Magnus is offering compensation to someone."

"How?" Whitby said cynically. "The man has barely enough money to keep his horse. He couldn't offer much."

Whitby turned in the chair to look out the window at his estate. "I wonder if he knows about my marriage yet. It is likely, if he knew of the illness."

"Yes, my lord."

Whitby opened and closed a fist, striving to keep his anger under control. He reminded himself that he could not lose his calm. He could not allow Magnus to have that effect on him; those days were over.

The priority now was to protect Lily, and to protect Annabelle from any further harassment, for events lately had obviously rekindled Magnus's ambitions. And in that state of optimism in regards to his position on the hereditary chain, learning about Whitby's marriage would be a great blow. Magnus would not be pleased. He might even attempt to act upon his anger, as he had in the past with Whitby's brother, John.

Whitby loathed the idea that he would have to see Magnus again, especially in his current condition, but he needed him to know that the earldom would not be handed over to him any time in the foreseeable future.

Whitby also wanted him to know that despite appearances, he was still more than capable of protecting his wife and sister.

He opened and closed his fist again, then turned to face Clarke. "Prepare the carriage if you will."

"My lord?"

Whitby recognized his butler's curiosity, and did not wish to keep the man in suspense. "I intend to protect my family, Clarke, and finally put this feud to rest. I am going to London tonight and will see Magnus in the morning, and if luck is on my side, I will get rid of him once and for all."

Magnus Wallis lived with his mother in a one-story brick house on the dingy outskirts of London, in a neighborhood most unsuitable for the grandson of an earl.

Whitby arrived in his shiny black crested coach at ten the next morning, and did not wait for the coachman to lower the steps before he opened the door himself and climbed out. He was impatient. Perhaps it was a product of his recovery from an illness he had believed would take his life. Whitby felt suddenly compelled to deal with everything in a decisive manner, and leave nothing to sort itself out at a later date, for he had learned rather abruptly that there might not always be a later date.

"I won't be long," he told the coachman, then he crossed the front yard, passing a black goat tied to a post and mewling noisily.

The musty smell of the chicken coop around the side of the house wafted to Whitby's nostrils as he arrived at the front door, causing a gray cat to leap off a rocking chair and wander off in the other direction. The cat probably sensed the next few minutes were not going to be pleasant.

Whitby raised a fist and knocked hard upon the blue painted door. A moment later, the door opened and he found himself staring down at Carolyn, Magnus's mother. She wore a shabby brown dress with a muddy hem, and was clutching a woolen shawl around her shoulders.

She had aged since he'd seen her last, five years ago. That, too, had been an unpleasant visit.

Whitby saw the shock in her eyes, and had to shove his shiny black boot in front of the door to keep her from slamming it in his face.

"I wish to speak to your son."

"He ain't here," she said odiously. "And even if he was, I wouldn't tell the likes of you."

Whitby did not remove his boot, which was still

wedged in front of the door. He simply stared down at the woman.

She sneered up at him. "I thought you might be dead by now."

"Thought? Or hoped?" he replied.

"Hoped is more precise."

Whitby inclined his head. "Sorry to disappoint you, madam. Where is your son?"

"I told you he ain't here." She tried to push the door harder against his boot.

Whitby leaned more weight upon it. "Then kindly inform me, if you will, where I can find him."

The door unexpectedly opened all the way, and Carolyn looked over her shoulder. Behind her stood Magnus, towering over her, for he, like Whitby, was a tall man.

That, however, is where any similarity ended— for where Whitby was golden-haired, Magnus was as dark as night with jet black hair and eyes equally as black. Where Whitby knew how to smile and charm, Magnus knew only how to frown and look upon the entire world with disdain. Whitby had never in his life seen the man laugh—unless it was over a bug he had crushed under his shoe.

Whitby faced Magnus. He evaluated his cousin's hostility and attempted to discern what was going through his mind. Was he surprised to see Whitby alive and well, or had he already known he'd recovered, along with the fact that Whitby had taken a wife?

Finally Magnus stepped back and opened the door. His mother did not look pleased, but evidently her opinion had no effect on her son.

"Go to the kitchen, Mother," Magnus said, his fierce gaze never veering from Whitby's.

Carolyn obeyed and left them alone. Whitby stepped inside, and Magnus shut the door.

"The last time you came here," Magnus said, "you beat me to a pulp. I should know better than to let you in."

"You deserved it," Whitby replied, "for what you did to Annabelle."

A dark satisfaction stole through Magnus's eyes. "Contrary to what you think, Annabelle very much enjoyed what I did to her."

Before Whitby had a chance to even contemplate a reply, he punched Magnus, who took it without flinching. Magnus stood soundly where he was, cupped his jaw in a hand, and moved it from side to side to make sure it wasn't broken.

He smiled faintly at Whitby, appearing pleased that he had evoked such a reaction in him, even though it had cost Magnus a punch in the face.

But it had cost Whitby a great deal, too—for the sudden movement had made him unsteady on his feet. He had to struggle to hide the fact.

Whitby turned from his cousin and walked into the front parlor. Not much had changed in the past five years. The rug still needed to be cleaned. It was discolored with ground-in coal dust.

Whitby faced Magnus again. "You thought the

earldom would be yours, and you came to my home and asked to see Annabelle, after giving me your word you would never contact her again. What were your intentions?"

"To propose of course. When I took over the estate, I could hardly turn her out, could I?"

Whitby swallowed over his pungent ire. "You expect me to believe that?"

"It's the truth."

Whitby shook his head at him. "You seduced Annabelle five years ago only to injure me."

"Yes, I did. And it worked, didn't it? It's *still* working, I'm glad to see."

Whitby turned his back on Magnus and walked to the mantel, staring for a moment at a painting of a fisherman in a small boat on a lake. Mist floated over the calm water. The painting had a unique tranquility about it.

Whitby's eyebrows pulled together in a frown. The painting did not suit the room, for the room was not tranquil. This fine painting deserved to be elsewhere.

Whitby took a moment to gather back his calm, but glanced over his shoulder when he heard the floorboards creak under Magnus's shoes.

Magnus approached Whitby. "If I had married Annabelle, you would have rolled over in your grave, wouldn't you?"

Whitby faced his cousin. "But as you can see, I am not dead."

"No, you are not, sadly so. And from what I understand, you are a married man now."

Whitby made no reply.

"A duke's sister, no less. Well done. I hear she's pretty. I'd like to meet her."

Enough was enough. Whitby could take no more of Magnus's insinuations. He had come here to put an end to this situation, and he was going to do just that. He took a step forward to glare at his cousin, only inches away from his face. Magnus stood tall and steady. He did not back away.

"Indeed I am married," Whitby said, "and we expect a child in the nursery before a year can pass. You will soon find yourself knocked out of your position as my heir, so I ask you—as a *gentleman*—to leave my family alone and take your ambitions, for lack of a better word, elsewhere."

Magnus turned and crossed to the other side of the room. "Where would you like me to take them?"

Whitby remained calm. "Anywhere you like. For years you have been cut off financially and socially from the family, and while I will never apologize for that, I would prefer to think of the future now, rather than the past. I'd like to wipe the slate clean and provide you with an income—as would have been appropriate had your father been less of a . . . *disappointment* to our grandfather. On one condition. You leave England."

Magnus glared hotly at him. "How much?"

"Five thousand a year."

Magnus chuckled. "Not enough."

"Ten thousand," Whitby said.

Bloody Christ, he hated this. He hated negotiating with this black-hearted, conniving snake. A month ago, he would never even have considered such a thing, and he wanted to take the offer back. He wanted to walk out of here and declare open war upon his cousin.

But he could not. He could not, because of Lily. He did not want a war in her backyard. Magnus had very likely killed John; Whitby couldn't be sure the man wouldn't do something like that again.

He wanted only for Magnus to disappear.

Magnus paced around the room, rubbing his chin in an irritatingly exaggerated manner, and spoke with a mocking tone. "Ten thousand you say? My, my, that is tempting. Mother and I could see Rome."

Whitby clenched a fist again. He had to work hard to remember what he'd just said to himself—that Lily's safety was the only thing that mattered. Because right now, his loathing was about to bust out of his head.

Magnus stopped pacing and pursed his lips. "Tempting, yes, but no thank you. It's not enough."

Whitby gritted his teeth. "How much would be enough to get rid of you?"

Magnus considered it. "The five thousand a year sounded interesting, so here are my terms. *You* take the five thousand a year, and you can keep the title and house because the law says you must, but

I will manage it for you and *you* will leave England." Magnus gazed off to the side, then smiled back at Whitby. "Oh, and one last thing. I will have Annabelle."

The room seemed to turn red before Whitby's eyes as he stared enraged at his cousin. He had come here to put the past behind them. He had been willing to give back to Magnus a piece of what had been taken from him and his father years ago—their financial connection to the family, even though that connection had been severed for good reason. Magnus had heard Whitby's offer, and had all but spit in his face.

The time for gentlemanly negotiations was over. Whitby took a deep breath and let it out slowly, then he took two long strides toward his cousin and spoke with resolve.

"I came here today to put an end to the feud," he said, "but I see you don't want it to end. That is your choice. But rest assured, if you ever take one step in the direction of my wife and future heirs, I will kill you."

"And I would be grateful for the opportunity to kill *you* while defending myself."

Whitby supposed that was what separated him from his cousin. Whitby did not enjoy this antagonism; he did not enjoy the fight. But Magnus did.

Whitby turned and left the house, then strode to his coach. As soon as the door to the vehicle slammed shut behind him, he collapsed onto his back on the upholstered seat and fought a violent spinning sensation.

"God, get me home," he whispered, as he closed his eyes, feeling the coach lurch into motion. "And thank you for not letting me collapse in the yard."

Chapter 26

~~~~~~~~

Lily had vowed to walk into Century House with optimism and high hopes—and in her opinion, she had done so quite successfully. She was very proud of herself, in fact. When she had been shown to her room the day before, she told herself over and over that everything was going to be fine. When she'd dressed for dinner, she'd remembered that Whitby had assured her he did not regret marrying her, hence she had nothing to fear. They were going to be gloriously happy here together.

But when she woke on her first morning alone in her new room—in an unfamiliar bed with blankets that weren't quite warm enough—she found herself wondering uneasily what had become of her husband the night before. He had missed dinner, and she did not know why. All she and Annabelle knew was that he had gone to London regarding a personal matter.

Consequently, Lily had lain awake until past two in the morning, disappointed that he had left, for she had something to tell him. She wanted to give him the happy news that as of yesterday, her courses were three days late, and she was never late.

At the same time she did *not* let herself worry that he might have gone to London to engage in his usual nightly entertainments. She'd squashed those thoughts instantly, every time they snuck into her brain.

It was late in the afternoon when she was sitting in the drawing room waiting for Annabelle to join her for tea, when she walked to the window and sucked in a quick breath at the sight of an approaching carriage.

It was him.

Her stomach flared with both excitement and nervous apprehension, and she picked up her skirts to dash down to the main hall and greet him. She would ask him where he'd been and what he'd been doing.

No. He might find that smothering. She would simply throw her arms around his neck and kiss him a hundred times, and of course tell him her happy news.

Oh, she was far gone, she thought, as her feet

tapped down the corridor. Most women would be angry with a husband who left without a word.

She was on her way down the stairs, her feet still drumming a rapid tattoo, when she saw Clarke walk calmly to the door to greet Whitby, who handed over his coat and hat. Lily halted halfway down.

Whitby and the butler spoke quietly, then Whitby headed toward his study on the first floor, but stopped abruptly when he looked up and caught sight of Lily. He looked hesitant. A second or two later he smiled at her. "Good afternoon."

She smiled in return, though she had to force it. She felt a little afraid, for something about her husband did not seem right. His smile did not seem real. "Good afternoon."

Whitby held out his hand. "Come."

Trying to appear relaxed, she descended the stairs. When she reached him, he set his hand upon her cheek and gazed at her for a moment. He kissed her lightly on the lips.

"I missed you," she said.

They stared at each other awkwardly for a few seconds, and Lily felt suddenly as if they were strangers. It was not how she had felt when he'd made love to her at Wentworth. When they'd made love there, she'd felt as if she knew everything he wanted, and not just the wants and needs of his body. They seemed to join with each other in those wonderful moments and days, unlike now. Suddenly, they were stumbling over what to say to each other.

Lily groped for words to fill the silence. "Where were you?"

There it was—the question of a smothering wife.

He hesitated, and she regretted asking the question. "I'm sorry," she said, before he had a chance to answer. "It's none of my business."

He studied her face briefly. "Of course it's your business. You're my wife. I went to London because I had to deal with . . . a difficult thing."

Lily's eyebrows lifted. "A difficult thing? Did something happen?"

"Yes. It is rather scandalous, I'm afraid."

"I don't like the sound of that," she replied.

He shook his head. "It's not what you're thinking. I had to go and speak to my cousin, Magnus."

"To tell him about our marriage?"

"Yes, and to make sure he stays away in the future."

Lily felt a momentary panic. She hadn't realized Magnus was still such a threat. "You went to his house?"

Whitby put his hand on her shoulder in a reassuring gesture. "Yes. I went to see him because he had somehow learned of my illness and was no doubt already rearranging the furniture here in his mind. I felt it necessary to inform him that he will very soon be giving up his position in line to my title, and I wanted to ensure that he would never so much as glance in your direction."

Lily understood the basis for his concern, for she knew what Magnus had done to Whitby's brother

John, and how he had hurt Annabelle. But she did not like the idea of her husband being in the same room with such a man.

"That couldn't have been easy," she said.

A shadow moved across his face. "No, it has not been easy." He paused, his fingers playing through her hair. "I'll never forgive myself for what happened with Annabelle, and I have vowed never to let anything like that happen again."

Lily cleared her throat nervously. "Well, Magnus may be nudged out of his position as heir sooner than you think. I wanted to tell you last night . . . There is a chance, you see, that we were successful over the past few weeks."

"Successful?"

"Yes," she replied, wondering why she was so uncomfortable delivering this news. It was what he wanted after all. An heir. And Lily wanted to please him.

"My courses were due a few days ago," she said, "and I am never late. I think it is possible I am with child."

He stared at her blankly.

She felt her smile die away. "That's good news, isn't it?"

He took a moment before he replied. He'd gone pale, and looked almost shaken.

She too felt shaken. She had thought it was what he wanted, but now, she wasn't so sure, and it made her heart twinge uncomfortably.

"Indeed it is good news," he finally said. "Very good news."

He reached up and removed her hand from his cheek and gently rubbed his thumb over her knuckles. "I'm quite tired," he said. "It's been a long day and I suppose I'm not fully recovered yet. I think I will rest. Perhaps you could spend some time with Annabelle."

"All right," she replied, struggling to keep her tone light. "Of course, you must be exhausted."

But her heart did not feel light, because despite all the times her husband had tried to tell her that he did not regret marrying her, she had to acknowledge the fact that she still did not believe it. She sensed it was all a lie, and that she, too, had been lying to herself. Her desperate hopes and her burning love for him had made her blind to the truth—that he did not want to be close to her the way she wanted to be close to him. And now her heart was breaking, because she was skeptical that he even wanted to have a baby with her.

Whitby sat down in his desk chair, rested his elbows on his knees and leaned forward to drop his head into his hands. He shut his eyes.

Lily was pregnant, and all he could think about was his beautiful mother, lying on her bed with the sheet being drawn up over her pale, ghostly face.

His heart began to pound. It had all happened so fast. He'd thought he was dying. Then he'd learned he was not, and now he felt like he'd awakened from a dream to discover he was a husband—to Lily—and she was pregnant.

Of all the women in the world, why did it have to be her?

Christ, he'd barely had a chance to get used to the idea and brace himself.

He looked up toward the bright window, feeling his eyes burn with sleeplessness. He had to figure out how he was going to get through this, because he had to get through it—for Lily. He could not let himself wish that everything was the way it was before he'd become ill, when he was a man without a care in the world. For he was no longer that man. He *did* have a care—a momentous one. Which scared the devil out of him.

Chapter 27

Lily realized miserably the next day that she needed to decide how she was going to survive in this marriage.

She had almost labeled it a loveless marriage when she was out walking in the garden with Annabelle earlier, feeling sorry for herself. But that was not entirely accurate. There was a great deal of love between her and Whitby. It was just simply all on her side.

Was it possible for one person to carry a marriage? she wondered uncertainly as she walked through the house to her rooms, unbuttoning her cloak as she went. At present, she felt that she could. She would do anything for Whitby. She had told him it would be all right if he didn't love her the way she loved him. She had believed she could live with that, if it meant she could be with him.

But now that she was here, she was coming to realize that she might not be as self-sacrificing as she'd thought. Not when it came to Whitby and what she wanted and needed from him.

She thought of her mother suddenly, and how frustrating and painful their relationship had been—and still was. All her life, it had been like living with a thirst she could never quench.

Lily had not believed she would have to endure that with Whitby. She had even thought that by marrying him, she was escaping that life. So it was breaking her heart now to realize that it was the same. It was exactly the same.

What then, could she do?

Lily entered her room and removed her hat, and set it on her bed. She sat down at her desk, rested her chin on her hand and wondered what Sophia would do. Lily knew that her sister-in-law had not had an easy time with James in the early months of their marriage. James had never intended to love her and he had told her so matter-of-factly.

But Sophia had not accepted that. She had never given up on her dream of love, and she had been patient. She did not push too hard, and she eventually won James's heart. Now they were closer than two people could ever be, and that's what Lily wanted and needed with Whitby.

So she wrote the word PATIENCE on a piece of paper, folded it, and decided to use it as a bookmark, so that she would constantly be reminded that there was hope for happiness in the future if not today. She'd waited all this time for Whitby. She could wait a little longer. This was still very new, after all. They had their whole lives ahead of them, and surely the hours they did spend together would foster a deeper intimacy in time.

Consequently, Lily did her very best over the following week to be content with her new life at Century House. She enjoyed daily walks with Annabelle, who was fast becoming a dear friend. She and Lily talked about books and music, and Annabelle, who loved to paint, was teaching Lily all she knew. They painted together in the crisp autumn outdoors with two easels side by side, and Lily's attempt at a landscape was slowly turning into something—though she wasn't quite sure what.

Whitby grew stronger every day, and as soon as he was able to ride, he began traveling about the estate, becoming more involved in its management.

One particular afternoon he rode his horse to where Lily and Annabelle were painting, and had appeared genuinely impressed with Lily's first effort at becoming an artist.

She smiled at him and told him he should join the theatre.

He winked at her from high in his saddle and galloped off, and that was basically the way things were between them. He was always charming and flirtatious, and she was always happy and smiling, amusing him when she could in the day, giving him pleasure and taking pleasure for herself at night.

They never talked about anything of great consequence, however, other than reporting to each other about their separate activities during the day. On the other hand, they were very candid in bed, and they were honest about how they could please each other physically, and she was thankful for that, at least.

So Lily clung to the secret hope that giving Whitby a child would bring them closer. Surely it would.

Hence, she was quick to send for the physician when her courses did not come after another week, and she began to develop a sore throat.

Sadly, the news that Lily was expecting a child was not cause for celebration, for the doctor also delivered a second diagnosis: Lily was most likely coming down with the same mysterious illness that had afflicted Whitby at Wentworth Castle.

That night after the doctor left, Whitby sat in his study alone for a long, quiet hour, not moving from his chair by the fire. He stared into the flames, remembering Lily as a young girl. He had been protective of her then, and though certain very significant aspects of their relationship had changed, he still felt exceedingly protective. She was his wife.

Later, when the flames died down and he found himself staring at a single log that was pulsing with a hypnotizing red glow, he took a deep breath and rose purposefully from his chair. It was getting late. He had to go to her.

So he went to his wife's bedchamber as he always did, though he felt very differently when he knocked on the door—for under the present circumstances, he could not seem to overlook the fact that it had once been his mother's door. And rather than the lustful anticipation he was accustomed to feeling when he visited Lily in her bed, an agonizing dread had overtaken his senses. He did not want to make love to her tonight. He wanted only to see how she was feeling. He did not want to tire her.

"Come in," Lily said from inside, so he pushed the door open and entered.

She was in the process of sitting up in bed to lean against the headboard. He could see by the disheveled state of her hair and the chaos of the blankets that she had been sleeping. She was smiling at him, however, trying to hide the fact that he'd disturbed her.

Like an angel or a devil on his shoulder, his old jaded self urged him to be careful and protect himself, especially now that she was ill and pregnant.

He moved fully into the room and sat on the edge of the bed. "I woke you," he said.

"No, no," she replied, "I was just resting."

He took her hand. "How are you feeling tonight?"

"I've felt better."

He took a moment or two to envision what the next few weeks were going to be like. He thought of the fever, the fatigue, and he thought of Lily struggling to get well as he had done.

"Would you like me to send word to your mother?" he asked.

"No."

He recognized the lingering hostility in her voice. "Are you sure? Perhaps it would be a good opportunity to—"

"No, Whitby. I don't need to see her. I don't want to." She lowered her gaze. "Besides, I doubt she would come anyway."

He nodded, deciding to let the subject go for now, for he wasn't entirely sure Lily was wrong about that, and he did not want to hurt her with such a rejection. "How is your throat?"

She swallowed with discomfort. "It's sore. I didn't feel like eating supper."

He stroked the back of her hand with his thumb. "I remember what it was like, but do try to eat, darling, even if you don't want to. You need your strength."

"Yes." Her face warmed with a smile, and she placed her hand on her belly. "I do indeed."

Whitby gazed down at her flat stomach and found himself quite unable to comprehend the notion of a baby—*their* baby—growing in her womb. It signified a future, a life different from anything he'd ever known. It was astonishing, wonderful and frightening all at the same time.

"We were very efficient," he said with a grin.

She raised her eyebrows playfully. "I knew we

would be. We're very good at doing what it takes to make a baby."

He chuckled, and though he had not come here to make love to her, he nonetheless felt a rush of arousal brought on by the luscious intimation in her voice and the teasing glint in her eye. The fact that her nightgown was unbuttoned at the collar and he could see the gentle swell of the tops of her breasts made it all the more difficult to remember that he had not intended to be selfish or irresponsible tonight. He had wanted only to think of her well-being.

The scandalous fact of the matter was—he could not keep his hands off his wife, even when he wanted to back away from her. He wanted her with all the force and passion of a tempest, and when it hit, it hit hard and he forgot all things sensible. He forgot what frightened him, for when he made love to Lily, when he was inside her, he felt as if he'd found a safe harbor.

Which was why all this was so difficult to bear. He did not want to lose her.

He gazed into her eyes for a moment, trying to resist her allure because she was sick and he had to, and said, "It's important that you get as much rest as possible. And now that we know this illness is contagious, I probably shouldn't even be touching you. I shouldn't come to your bed for a while."

The happy playfulness in her eyes drained away, and her smile turned to a frown. "Oh."

"I just want to make sure you get well." And that was God's honest truth.

Still, he could see the hurt in her eyes. She stared at him for an uncomfortable moment. "Whitby, if we can't be together at night, I fear that we . . ."

She couldn't seem to find the right words.

"What are you trying to say, Lily?"

She lowered her gaze. "You've seemed distant since we came here. It's not like it was at Wentworth."

He swallowed hard. How could he reply to that? His first instinct was to tell her that she was being silly—of course everything was fine.

That was how he'd intended to behave in this marriage. He had wanted to do everything necessary to make her feel happy and loved, even if it wasn't real. He had wanted only to be charming for her and make her smile.

He was presently, however, feeling an incomprehensible compulsion to reveal himself to her—perhaps for the same goal—to reassure her and make her happy.

Such behavior with *any* woman was outside of his experience and normal realm, and when his reply made its way out of his mouth, he felt as if the world was spinning in a new direction.

"I thought I was dying at Wentworth, Lily. Strangely enough, knowing that I'm going to live and knowing that we will be spending the whole of our lives together makes everything more . . . *complicated*. It's been an adjustment."

Lily gazed with parted lips at him. "You have reservations about our marriage."

Yes, he did. But he did not confirm it with words or gestures because he knew it would hurt her.

Regardless of that, she knew it—as if he had said it aloud. She always seemed to know things about him, to sense things, which was somewhat disturbing. It made his plan to spend his life trying to convince her he was happy seem like a daft waste of time.

"You told me that you did not regret our marriage," she said, "but I have not been able to believe it." She looked down at her hands. "There is a part of you that wishes your life was the way it was before you traveled to Wentworth and became ill. Isn't there?"

But *did* he really wish that? he wondered suddenly as he stared into her worried eyes. A part of him did, yes, especially now that she was sick. But another part of him did not.

"No, Lily, I don't wish that."

"Because I would give you an annulment if you wanted it," she replied, as if he hadn't spoken. As if she were not carrying his child.

He saw passion in her eyes, a desire to argue with him. It was the old Lily he used to know, the little girl who demanded he chase her, even when he was not in the mood.

"I want to be your wife more than anything," she said. "I've always wanted that, but I would never want to be a burden to you, and I'm beginning to fear that I can't live here with you if you don't truly want to be with me."

He took her face in his hands. "I do want to be with you."

Her eyes did not soften. He began to see she had been suppressing some anxiety for a number of days now, and she was going to blow.

"Only in bed," she said firmly. "But we never talk about anything important. You never tell me how you feel about anything, nor does anything ever seem to bother you. But I want to know you better. I want to know about your childhood and your parents—"

"None of that has anything to do with our marriage."

"It has everything to do with it! James told me about all the nannies you had."

He gave her a fierce, warning look that chilled her blood before he turned away from her.

Lily stared at him in dismay. After a long moment, she bowed her head in defeat. "I feel like all the smiles over the past few weeks have been a charade, and I've been trying to be patient and accept it, but now I don't think I can, not if we can't be together at night. I know that's not your fault—my illness is contagious—but I need the truth out in the open, Whitby. All I've ever wanted was honesty and openness in a marriage. I'm tired of pretending that everything is fine."

He faced her again and shook his head at her.

"What truth? I don't understand what you want from me. Do you want me to say that I wish I'd never married you? *Do* you? Because I won't say that."

"Even if it's true?"

He had no answer. Whitby stood up and walked to the window.

Lily tossed the covers aside and stood up also. "We both know you wouldn't have married me if you hadn't thought you were dying. I knew it and I married you anyway, so there's no point trying to deny it. We both entered into this with our eyes open. But now I sense that you feel trapped, that you feel you're stuck with me and you have to stay here and do your duty and nurse me while I'm ill, when what you really want to do is be a free man again."

He felt his temper rising. "Where the hell is this coming from? I don't want to be a free man!"

No woman had ever pushed him so far or so hard before, and now—more than ever—he did not want to be pushed. Not when he had already given so much. Bloody hell, he had given up his freedom for her. He had spoken vows of fidelity under God, and he had put a child in her womb.

Was that not enough?

"The point is," he said, taking an angry step toward her, "that I *did* marry you, and it doesn't matter why or how. That is in the past. What matters now is that you are my wife and you are expecting my child. And *dammit*! I have done everything I can to make you happy and be the husband you want me to be. I come to your bed every night."

Lily stared at him, her frustration still evident in her fiery blue eyes. "There it is. You do all that because you think *I* want you to, not because *you* want to. All I want is for you talk to me. I want to know what you're feeling."

When he said nothing, she turned away from him and dropped her gaze to the floor. Her voice softened. "I believe we have both put ourselves in a difficult situation. You are stuck with a wife you never wanted, and I am stuck with the knowledge that I was naive and didn't know what I was getting myself into. Everyone tried to tell me that, but I wouldn't believe it. I just wanted *you*, at any price. But now, I'm not so sure."

"Not so sure?" he replied furiously. She had told him she loved him, no matter what. And contrary to what she thought, he had loved her in return. He *had*! He had loved her the only way he knew how. He'd married her, for God's sake! Now she was changing her mind?

White-hot anger coursed through his veins. He had not asked for any of this. He did not want to feel this. "You're the one who came to *me*, wanting only to give me an heir. Remember?"

She nodded. "Yes. But you were different then—the way you held me, the way you talked to me. I believed you *could* really love me. But I fell in love with a man who doesn't really exist. That man died when you found out you were going to live."

Good God, he had not deserved that. "We've been married less than a month, Lily," he said. "You expect too much. I can't change who I am overnight. I wish I could, but I can't."

"Is it me?" she asked, and he wondered if she was hearing anything he was saying. "Am I not the kind of woman you find interesting?"

God, this was a nightmare. "Of course I find you interesting. I just don't understand what you want from me. I'm giving you everything I can. I made you my countess. I make love to you every night. I'm not unkind to you. *You want too much, Lily!*"

She stood dumbfounded, her chest rising and falling with deep, panting breaths, then she sank into a chair. "Yes. I do. I *know* I do. I want more, Whitby, because something is missing. But the worst part is, I don't even know what it is, because I've never had it."

He stared at her for a long moment, laboring not to feel too surprised by this. He had known he would not be able to make her truly happy. Intimately happy. He just did not know how to love that way.

Whitby turned from her and walked to the door. "Get some sleep. You need your rest."

Speechless, she watched him. "You're leaving?"

He heard the shock in her voice, but something very intense was compelling him to leave. He couldn't fight it. The ceiling was coming down on his head. He didn't know what to say to her. He couldn't fix what was wrong. He had to leave. "There's nothing more to say."

"Yes, there is."

He stopped with his back to her, holding onto the doorknob, waiting for her to speak.

"At least when you were dying, I didn't feel like you were lying to me."

He paused for a moment, then turned to face her with one last word. "Lily, you said whatever I could give you would be enough. So it appears that I am not the only one who lied."

With that he walked out and shut the door behind him. He paused in the corridor, however, and laid a hand over an unfathomable ache inside his chest, because for the first time, he *did* regret marrying Lily. And he wanted his old life back.

Chapter 28

In the days following, Whitby gave Lily a wide berth. He increased his involvement in estate business, and found himself almost obsessively wanting to take care of things that had been too long neglected.

He spent every possible minute with George Gallagher, his steward, visiting the tenants and finally seeing for himself where the rents were coming from and who was plowing his fields. He'd insisted upon learning how the account books were kept, and went over them himself at night after Gallagher was gone, making sure everything made sense.

Whitby realized that this fixation on his duties as

landlord was a direct result of his argument with Lily, for he had developed a rather sudden awareness of his shortcomings and how he had failed those who were dependent upon him. He'd been a frightfully incompetent landlord, and he could still do with some fundamental improvements as a husband. He just didn't know how to fix that aspect of his life quite yet. Account books were easier.

He was contemplating these changes and deficiencies in himself as he arrived home chilled one afternoon after a long ride across his estate. Handing his horse over to one of the grooms, he strode across the courtyard to the back entrance of the house.

He blew into his gloved fists and rubbed his hands together, suspecting that snow was little more than a week or two away. He could smell it in the air.

Taking two steps at a time up the back veranda, he stopped when he noticed Annabelle standing alone in her hooded cloak, her back to him while she gazed out over the terraced garden.

Whitby removed his hat and approached her. "Annabelle . . ."

She turned to him with a strangely hopeful look on her face, but it disappeared when their eyes met. She lowered her hood and smiled. "You're back."

"Yes," he replied, removing his gloves. "I had a productive day."

"I'm glad to hear it." She walked toward him and they sauntered casually across the veranda together. "Everyone is very impressed with your new interest in the estate," she said. "My maid told me you've been the topic of discussion at the servants' table."

He raised his eyebrows. "Is that so? I suppose they're not accustomed to seeing me up before noon."

She laughed. "No, they are not, and neither am I. I'm very proud of you, Whitby, and happy for you. I knew there was a dedicated, responsible man in you somewhere."

He smiled faintly at her to acknowledge the compliment, then turned his gaze toward the horizon in the distance. "How is Lily?"

Annabelle shrugged. "She's as well as can be expected. She's been sleeping for the past couple of hours. Did you know she's been ill in the mornings? The doctor says it's normal."

He stared at her for a few brief seconds before replying. "No, I didn't know that."

"Well, maybe you should go and talk to her. I know the doctor said you should limit your contact with her because of her illness—but I don't think he meant you had to avoid her altogether. The only time you see her is at dinner, and you're barely within hearing range at the other end of the table."

Whitby leaned on the balustrade, cupping the rail with both hands. He crossed one ankle over the other. "I'm not sure that's such a good idea."

"What do you mean? Of course it is."

He squinted in the other direction. "Things are rather strained between Lily and me at the moment."

"It's strained because you won't talk to her. She thinks you're sorry you married her, and that you're not in love with her."

"Did she tell you that?"

"No. She's very loyal to you, Whitby. She doesn't talk about you or say anything derogatory about you behind your back, not even to me. But I can see it as plain as day. She did not marry you for position or money. She married you because she loved you, so you need to be there for her and reassure her that you're not sorry you married her, and that you do care for her."

Whitby sighed and shifted his weight on the balustrade. "I assure you, Annabelle, that's been my intention all along. And I've tried."

She narrowed her gaze at him, looking perplexed. "Then what's the problem?"

He squinted at the horizon again. "She doesn't believe me. She can bloody well see through me."

"See through you?" Annabelle's shoulders rose and fell with a disheartened sigh. "Do you mean to tell me that any reassurances are untrue? That you do regret being married? Whitby . . ."

He bowed his head. "No, Annabelle. I needed to get married. I wanted to. I was just having a hard time taking the step. So I don't regret it entirely. I'm glad it was forced upon me. I'm not sure I would have done it otherwise."

"*Forced* upon you. Good God, don't ever say that

to her. It's not the kind of thing a woman wants to hear."

He slowly blinked. "So I've learned. But regardless, it wouldn't matter if I said it or not. She knows. That's the problem with marrying someone you've known forever. They don't believe your lies."

Annabelle moved to lean next to him and rested her gloved hand on his knee. "Whitby, you're not lying to her, are you? You do care for her."

"Of course I do."

"Then why do you avoid being with her? If you are happy with her, she will see it and feel it."

"And how do you know so much about love?"

She was silent for a moment as a chilly breeze swept at her skirts. "Because I did love once—foolishly, mind you—and I have many regrets about it. I've had years to reflect upon it and imagine how my experience of love *should* have been."

Whitby recalled the day he had learned what had occured between Annabelle and Magnus . . .

He turned toward her and took her hand. "I'm surprised to hear you use the word love. You hated him."

She looked down at their entwined hands. "Yes, I did, and I hate him now, knowing the truth about him as I do. But for a brief time—before I discovered what kind of man he truly was—I loved him quite passionately, and I remember all too well how it felt."

Whitby stared with melancholy at his sister.

Annabelle stood up and turned toward the garden, resting her hands on the rail. "He did break my heart, but you do not have to fear heartbreak like that with Lily. She is a wonderful woman, completely devoted to you. Appreciate her. Appreciate what you have. You don't know how lucky you are."

Whitby thought about that for a long time before he replied. "There are many different kinds of heartbreak, Annabelle."

With a furrowed brow, she studied his eyes as if trying to decipher his true meaning. "Are you worried about her having the baby?"

He shrugged, though he knew she would not buy into the dismissing gesture.

"She's healthy and strong, Whitby."

"No, she's not."

Annabelle reluctantly nodded, conceding to Whitby's point only briefly before she picked up her argument again. "She will be when it comes time to bring the baby into the world."

"Perhaps."

"*Is* that the problem?" Annabelle asked. "Because if it is, you should tell her that. She would understand, and I believe it would ease her mind. It would let her know you truly care."

"I can't tell her that," he said harshly. "I don't want her to know I'm worried. I don't want her to spend the next nine months distressing herself about having the baby."

"She'll stress about something else if you don't,

and I believe that will be worse. Trust me in that regard."

He noted the grim expression on his sister's face. It was the look of a woman who had lived once, but was now merely coasting through an existence toward the end.

Whitby pushed himself away from the balustrade. He reached for Annabelle's gloved hand, raised it to his lips and kissed it affectionately. "Thank you for trying to help. I do understand what you have said, and I will give it some thought. Truly, I will."

Annabelle responded with only a nod and a sad smile.

There was no place setting for Lily that evening at the table, for she had informed her maid that she was not hungry. As a result, Whitby found himself eating his own dinner in heavy silence, contemplating everything Annabelle had said to him that day, while he stared at his wife's empty chair.

He realized suddenly that Annabelle was right. He needed to talk to Lily and smooth out their problems. And besides that, he missed her. He wanted to go to her bedside and apologize.

When dessert was served, he declined and excused himself from Annabelle's company. Annabelle understood, of course, and was more than happy to see him go.

He headed toward Lily's rooms, wondering if she hadn't come to dinner because she was still too angry with him. Or had she not come because she was so weak, she couldn't even rise from bed just to sit in the company of others for a short while?

The possibility that she *was* that weak sent a sickening lump of dread into his gut. He quickened his pace down the dimly lit corridor.

When he reached her rooms, he knocked, but no answer came. He did not knock a second time. He pushed the door open and walked straight in.

The room was quiet, lit only by one lantern. Lily was alone, sleeping on her side, facing the window. Whitby walked softly to her, not wanting to wake her, but when he came around the foot of the bed and saw that her face was ashen and her hair damp around her forehead, he wanted very badly to wake her—*so* badly that his breath caught in his throat.

He went to her side and shook her. "Lily . . ."

When she did not stir, he placed a hand on her cheek to check her temperature. The heat from her clammy skin nearly scorched him.

"Lily," he said again, shaking her harder, but still, she did not move.

He charged from the room and dashed down the corridor and stairs, through the main part of the house to the servants' wing. He ran to Clarke's sitting room.

"We need the doctor," he said quickly to the man, who was sitting at his desk with a pen in his hand. "Send a groom on the fastest horse . . . Tell him to take Steamer. Lady Whitby has come down with a fever."

Clarke stood immediately and made haste to see that his master's firm instructions were carried out, while Whitby turned from the room to go and fetch Annabelle. He hurried back to the dining room where she was sitting by herself, quietly eating her dessert. She turned in her chair when she heard the commotion of his intrusion.

"Come quickly," Whitby said. "It's Lily."

Annabelle stood and dropped her napkin onto the table. She picked up her skirts and ran to follow him upstairs.

Time slowed to a plodding, sluggish pace after that, while they waited in Lily's bedchamber for Dr. Benjamin to arrive. Annabelle busied herself by putting cool, damp cloths on Lily's head and chest, while Whitby moved from the chair at her bedside to the window to watch for the doctor, then back to Lily's bedside again.

Finally after an hour or so, the doctor's carriage arrived. Whitby greeted the man at the door and led him upstairs to the room where Lily lay motionless on the bed.

He remembered his own mother lying motionless on that very bed, twenty-six years ago. She'd lost her baby, and Whitby, only seven, had been called in to see her before God came to take her.

The doctor was quick and thorough with his examination, and his diagnosis held nothing that could be considered a surprise. Lily's illness was progressing, and there was nothing to be done but wait and keep her comfortable and pray that her case would not be worse than Whitby's.

"What about the baby?" Whitby asked directly.

"She is young and strong, my lord," the doctor replied, not meeting Whitby's gaze as he put his instruments back in his bag and closed it. "I see no reason why she and the baby shouldn't pull through this."

But he was guessing. Whitby could hear it in his voice. He didn't know the first thing about this illness. He was as baffled as Dr. Trider had been.

Whitby forgave the doctor, however, for he knew there was no other reply. It was what must be said to all those with sick loved ones in times such as these, and it no doubt comforted most who heard it. But Whitby did not possess the optimistic hope of the common man. Whitby had suffered too much loss to believe that all would work out.

The doctor walked to Whitby and squeezed his shoulder. "I recommend that you go back to your own room tonight, my lord. You must get your rest. Consider also that this disease is contagious."

Whitby did consider that. He had thought about it very carefully, in fact. He had also realized that no one but Lily had caught it from him, even though others had tended him, so he couldn't help but suspect it was not something passed on through casual contact.

The doctor stayed for a short while and gave them instructions to continue keeping Lily cool with damp cloths. He promised to return in the morning to check on her.

After seeing Dr. Benjamin to the door, Whitby returned to Lily's room and told Annabelle that he would stay all night, and he would prefer it if she went to bed and got her rest, so she would be able to help in the morning.

He was genuinely sincere in the fact that he did not want Annabelle to become overtired, but the true basis for his request was a powerful need to be alone with Lily tonight, to be the person caring for her.

A short time later Annabelle left, and Whitby sat at Lily's bedside. As the clock ticked slowly in its case on the mantel indicating each hour as it passed, he rose only to change the cloth on his wife's forehead, or to add another log to the fire.

He spent the night leaning forward in the chair, touching Lily's hot, damp cheek with the back of his hand, pushing her hair off her face, but never kissing her.

He prayed. He prayed all night long, perching his elbows on the bed and resting his head on clasped hands. He asked God to watch over her and help her get well. He apologized for all his sins. He made promises of all sorts and sizes.

He also spent a great deal of time staring at the wall, remembering the pains of his childhood. He remembered the midwife wiping blood off the floor when he'd been taken in to see his mother; he remembered the long line of carriages accompanying his mother's coffin to the family tomb, and not long after, his father's coffin and then his brother's.

Though others had wept, Whitby had not shed a tear. He'd been too numb to feel anything. He still felt numb like that much of the time now, though he was experiencing more than a little sensation tonight—the disturbing, choking feeling of fear, the familiar dread of grief in the offing.

He did not enjoy it. He did not want to feel it again. And somewhere within the dizzying realm of his consciousness, he felt something inside himself wanting to take a step back, to retreat from all this.

When dawn finally broke and light found its way into the dark bedchamber, Whitby clasped Lily's hand. Feeling weary both physically and mentally, he rubbed his stubbled jaw and bowed his head. He wanted to kiss her hand, but resisted.

Just then, he felt the miracle of her body stirring, and heard the sweet murmur of her voice. He lifted his head and stood quickly, leaning over her. "Lily, darling, I'm here."

Her eyes fluttered open and she looked up at him, disoriented. "Was I ill?" she asked groggily.

He smiled down at her. "Yes, but you're better now. The doctor will be here to see you very soon."

She glanced around and tried to sit up, and Whitby helped move her pillows. "I'm thirsty," she said.

He poured some water and helped her hold the glass. She took a few sips, then lay back down again and closed her eyes. Whitby felt her forehead. She was not so hot now. The fever had broken.

Just then, Annabelle knocked and entered. She walked to the side of the bed. "How is she?"

Whitby could not speak. He swallowed hard over the aching knot of relief in his throat, taking a moment to gather words in his mind . . .

Lily opened her eyes again. "I'm fine," she said, then turned onto her side, facing away from them. "I just need to rest a little longer."

Annabelle touched her forehead, then gazed up at Whitby with a happy glow in her eyes. "She's much better."

"Yes, she's better," he replied. "Perhaps you can stay with her now. I'll go and get some sleep."

"Yes, you should, Whitby. You look exhausted."

He had no doubt that he did look like death himself. He'd been up all night, after all.

He thanked Annabelle for coming so early, told Lily he would be back later to see her, then went to his own private bedchamber and wept.

Chapter 29

Three months later

Lily stood at the drawing room window with a cup and saucer in her hand, staring absently out at the overcast morning. There was no color in the distant forest, only the grayness of dormant trees with a white dusting of snow on the ground. Winter had finally descended upon them.

She took a sip of tea and looked up at the low cloud cover, expecting snow to fall again today.

She laid a hand on her belly and wondered when she would feel the baby kick. Soon, she hoped. She was four months along. At least the morning sickness was gone now, and she was fully recovered from her illness. She had her appetite back, though she was still fatigued. The doctor assured her that fatigue was a normal part of her pregnancy, however, so she felt little concern when she took long naps in the afternoons.

Though life was far from perfect, she had grown comfortable in the house during her long recovery. She wrote frequent letters to Sophia and James, though she never expressed her unhappiness. Perhaps it was her pride. She had fought so hard against her brother and mother to let her do as she wished.

She also received many letters—though never any from her mother. She tried not to let it matter, but it did, because she hated this animosity between them, this silent punishment. If only her mother would bend just a little, Lily would be willing to bend a little, too.

But she knew that would never happen. Her mother did not bend. Not when it came to her precious duty. So Lily swept that hope as far away as she could.

On a happier note, Annabelle had become invaluable as a friend and sister, taking over Lily's duties while she was ill and making sure everything ran smoothly in the household. Lily had come to depend upon her, and they enjoyed each other's company, whether they were discussing the tedious details of the dinner menu, or the titillating chapters of a scandalous novel.

And Whitby had come regularly to visit her each

afternoon when she'd been ill. He had read to her from a book or played cards with her. The dynamic between them had become rather . . . *relaxed*. They had become friends. They never discussed the argument they'd had. She had known he had not wanted to upset her, and to be honest, she had not wanted to upset herself.

The illness, she knew, had taken the wind out of her sails. She'd grown tired of fighting for what had been forever elusive in her life, and she had begun to believe that she would find happiness if only she could accept life the way it was, and let go of her stubborn and perhaps greedy desire for something more—something she didn't really understand anyway, because she'd never had it.

And life was not so bad.

As a result, Lily had managed to ease into a comfortable routine, spending all her time waiting—waiting for spring, waiting to have her baby, waiting for the awkward gap between herself and her husband to disappear. For it was certainly awkward in one respect: they had not made love since she'd been ill.

Even after she'd regained her strength, her husband had not reclaimed his place in her bed. They had become mere companions, seeing each other only in the drawing room in the evenings, while he read a book, and she and Annabelle sat together on the sofa reading or taking turns at the piano.

Lately, however, her body was remembering the pleasures they'd given each other in the early days of their marriage. She felt hungry for the physical act of sex, and she wondered if it was the pregnancy causing it.

She felt especially hungry for sex now.

She took a shaky breath and wondered where her husband was. He usually went off with Gallagher in the mornings, or he was in his study, taking care of estate business. It was chilly this morning. Perhaps that's where he was.

She raised the cup to her lips and discovered that her tea was cold. Setting it back down with a clink onto the saucer, Lily wet her lips and put it on the tea cart.

Feeling exceedingly restless, she left the drawing room and went to Whitby's study, knocked firmly on the door and heard his voice from the other side. "Enter."

Lily pushed the door open. Her husband was seated at his desk with his gaze downcast, writing something. He raised a finger to say "one moment," then finished what he was writing before he looked up.

Their eyes met, and he was surprised to see her, which was no great shock, considering she had not allowed herself to seek him out like this since before that horrible night when they'd argued. Her pride had made her wait for him to come to her.

But today, she could wait no longer. Her body needed him, and nothing else seemed to matter—not her pride or her loneliness.

Lily walked in and closed the door behind her,

while she simply looked at him. He stared at her for a moment, then set down his pen. He pushed his chair back and stood.

Lily inched along the wall, her hands clasped behind her back. She said nothing, asked for nothing.

As he moved out from behind his desk, his eyes glimmered with a clear awareness of what she had come for—how did he know?—and the absolute confidence that he could satisfy her in that regard at least.

He sauntered toward her without a word, only the heated intensity of their locked gazes, the subtle yet bold connection of their sexuality. Breath held, Lily watched him approach, her heart pounding like a hammer in her chest. Never taking his eyes off hers, he walked to the door and locked it, then came to stand before her.

"Good morning," he said in a quiet, husky voice.

Ah, this is what she wanted—a piece of the connection they had once shared—and the pleasure of knowing he still wanted her in this way at least.

His unsmiling gaze roamed over her face, and she felt as if she hadn't seen him *once* in the past three months, even though she had.

She experienced a sudden urge to ask him why he had not come to her bed yet to make love to her, but resisted it. She was in the mood for sex, not conversation, and she could see in his eyes that he wanted the same thing.

Lily slid along the wall, tilting her head. Her husband let her go almost out of reach, then took hold of her wrist and smoothly dragged her back to her spot in the shadow of his large frame. His expression was dark and stern.

He leaned into her, pressing his rock hard erection up against her pelvis. She could feel the heat of his breath on her face.

He bent at the knees and swept his body down to kiss her, while she wrapped her arms around his neck. He thrust his hips in a slow, tantalizing rhythm that promised to satisfy all the erotic longings that had been assaulting her lately like a madness.

She wanted sex—raw, unbridled sex with him. That was what she had come for, yet still, at the back of her mind, no matter how hard she tried to resist it, she wanted so much more and could not keep herself from hoping that these wild moments of rampant pleasure would lead them in that direction.

He slid his hand down her leg and gathered her skirts in his fist, lifting them. Lily could feel the heat of his fingertips on her thigh, and yearned to feel them probing between her legs. She reached down to take hold of her skirts herself and hold them bunched up around her waist, while he tugged her drawers down. He kissed her again while she stepped out of them, then he kissed down the front of her gown to kneel before her.

Oh, yes, Lily's mind whispered, as she tipped her head back against the wall and closed her eyes. She wanted Whitby with the unstoppable fury of an inferno . . . here . . . now . . . She wanted to feel the tingling rapture of his mouth upon her, working its incomparable magic.

Shamelessly she wrapped her hands around the back of his head and pulled him close, crying out when he pushed her thighs apart, and his lips and tongue found the core of her desire.

She raised a leg up over his shoulder and brought one hand back to grope for the chair rail on the wall to steady herself.

Orgasmic sensation quenched all conscious thoughts in her brain. The room brightened to a white glow—only desire existed for her—and soon, she was overcome by a powerful climax that shot through her body in a trembling blast of release, and she cried out in breathless delight.

She lowered her leg and reached for him, pulling him to his feet. "Make love to me," she whispered against his cheek as he kissed the side of her neck.

Answering to her impatient need for immediate action, he quickly unfastened his trousers with swift, expert hands, bent slightly at the knees, and entered her in one smooth, steady thrust, proving to her that he had all his glorious strength back, and more.

He groaned and held her close in his arms, thrusting her firmly but gently up against the wall. Lily closed her eyes and reveled in the exquisite friction between her legs, and the incomprehensible pleasure of the rhythm of their bodies in sync—

the wicked allure of being thumped up against the wall, though he was never rough.

He drove into her again and again, until she was panting with each slick, surging penetration. Another climax came upon her and she threw her hands back against the chair rail, trying to hold onto something while he thrust harder and deeper, finally throbbing inside her and spilling his seed into her. Then his body relaxed and he buried his face into the crook of her neck.

"Ah, Lily, I missed you," he whispered.

The sweet sentiment, uttered so softly and sincerely after such a violent assault on her senses, sang in Lily's ears like a heavenly choir of angels. She wanted to shout out loud.

"Did you really?" she asked, hugging him tight.

He nodded, his lips still touching the side of her neck. "Yes. The past few months were like death for me."

Oh, this had to be a dream. He had missed her and he had told her so. Was this all she'd needed to do? Go to him and offer her body to him?

Lily sighed. She reminded herself that what he'd just said to her was not a declaration of his undying love, and she must not forget her instinctive need to be cautious and realistic where her husband was concerned. He had broken her heart once already, and he had told her that he had no understanding of what she wanted.

"I missed you, too," she said nevertheless. "I've

missed this." Not just the sex, but being held by him. "And I'm sorry."

He met her gaze, looking surprised. "Sorry for what?"

"For what I said to you before I got sick. When I said I liked you better when you were dying."

He kissed her again, then withdrew and fastened his trousers. She let her wrinkled skirts drop from around her waist to the floor.

She was surprised when he took her hand and led her to his desk chair, sat down and pulled her onto his lap, because she thought he might want to get back to his work.

But he held her face in his hands and kissed her a few more times. "I'm sorry, too," he said. "And I'm glad you're feeling better."

"I'll try not to get sick again."

Whitby looked into Lily's striking blue eyes and tried to comprehend the intensity of his emotions just now when she'd apologized to him so sweetly, after he'd made love to her wildly up against a hard, plaster wall.

He had made love in that fashion many times over the years with numerous beautiful women whose names he did not recall. This type of swift sexual encounter was almost always about sex for sex alone.

He had felt at first that this encounter with Lily was a similar thing. He had recognized the heated look in her eyes and had understood what she'd wanted, and he'd wanted to give her the pleasure she yearned for—for a lady's pleasure was always a foremost concern for Whitby. It was part of the allure of making love.

But today had been nothing like those casual encounters in the back rooms of country teahouses. Today he had been astonished by the roar of his emotions and the pure, unmitigated joy over the fact that his wife had come back to him. That she had forgotten some of her disappointment in him. And she was well and strong.

But then he recalled weeping for her three months ago on that nightmarish morning when he had prepared himself for the certain loss of her. He had consciously become a widower in his mind that day. He had given up the idea of making any effort to love his wife. More than ever, he had *not* wanted to love her—this fragrant flower of a woman who had blossomed so beautifully into womanhood over the long, sterile years of his existence.

And he was still afraid—because in five or so months, she would be crying out in pain on the birthing bed, at the mercy of God or fate or whatever one wished to call it.

Lily smiled warmly at him and ran her fingers through his hair. He leaned forward and kissed her neck, holding her tight against him.

"Lily, I. . . ."

When he did not finish, she took his face in her hands. "Yes, Whitby? What is it?"

He stared intently at her, remembering the conversation he'd had with Annabelle a few months ago.

"I worry about you," he said at last. "I worry about you having this baby."

Lily's lips parted. "There's nothing to worry about," she told him. "I'll be fine. It will all go well, you'll see."

But he did not see.

He *could* not see.

"You know that my mother died in childbirth," he reminded her.

"I know. But mine didn't." She smiled reassuringly. "Babies are born healthy every day, Whitby. You must remember that. You mustn't worry."

He nodded because he had to. He couldn't disagree with her. He didn't want to make her anxious.

"Come to my room tonight?" she asked tentatively.

He sat back and ran his hand over her thigh. "Yes," he replied, more than ready to make love to her again, for he had always been able to separate sex from love, and he would continue to do so. He simply had to. "We have some catching up to do, don't we?"

She smiled enticingly. "Yes, I believe we do."

With that, she kissed him on the mouth and left him to finish his work.

Chapter 30

~~~⌒⌒~~~

Almost immediately, Lily and Whitby rekindled their sexual relationship, and all was well between the sheets of Lady Whitby's bed. But whenever Lily brought up what her husband had said to her in his study—regarding his worries about the upcoming birth—he told her he didn't want to talk about it, nor did he wish to discuss his mother. He would either change the subject, as if there was something much more interesting he wished to talk about, or he would express annoyance.

Consequently, Lily ceased mentioning it, because she did not want to lose him again.

But as a result of those awkward, uncomfortable conversations, she had begun to accept the possibility that she was not the true mate of her husband's soul, for there was still some distant part of him she could not reach.

Many times she had felt sad for him—to think that he had never found the great love of his life and that he had married her because he'd believed he was out of time and he'd needed a wife and heir.

Other times she worried that if *she* was not the great love of his life, somewhere out there, another woman was. Perhaps there was someone else he would be able to talk to about things that caused him pain. And perhaps one day he would find that woman and need to be with her, and Lily would have to quietly stand back like other wives did when their husbands took mistresses.

She was not sure she could do that. It would devastate her.

Yet despite everything, she loved him deeply and hopelessly, and for her, there would never be another. She had no choice but to cling to the dream that after the baby was born—after he saw that childbirth was not always tragic—he would let go of some of his worries and let himself love her.

She was sitting in her room pondering all these things while she sealed a letter to Sophia and James, when a knock sounded at her door. "Come in!" she called out.

The door opened and her husband entered. He wore a white shirt and chocolate-brown waistcoat, and she found herself staring at him, speechless, caught in the glorious splendor of his masculine good looks.

He smiled questioningly at her, then closed the door behind him, locked it, and sauntered in. He leaned a shoulder against the solid oak bedpost and said, "Busy?"

She smiled knowingly in return, set the letter on a tray to go out with the rest of the mail, and rose from her chair. She walked to where her husband stood and began to unbutton his waistcoat. "It's the middle of the day, Lord Whitby. Don't you have work to do?"

"I do indeed have a number of things I wish to do this afternoon . . . to you." He slid a hand around the back of her neck and pulled her close for a deep, wet kiss.

When he finally let her go, she felt wonderfully woozy, and a hot ache was skulking through her body.

Lily realized her eyes were still closed, her face upturned. She struggled to lift her heavy lids. "You are most welcome to do everything you wish to do to me today, as long as you promise to help me get my shoes back on afterward. I can no longer seem to see my feet."

Whitby chuckled and unbuttoned her bodice for her, then led her around the bed and eased her onto her back. "Soon I won't be able to be on top anymore."

"We'll have to do it one of the other ways," she casually replied.

"I suppose it won't be so difficult." He slid a warm hand up under her chemise and across her swollen belly. His touch was featherlike over her skin. "We've certainly been rehearsing lots of alternatives lately."

He kissed her again, parting her lips with his own and touching his tongue to hers.

"You are so good at that," she whispered breathlessly as he laid a trail of kisses down her neck.

"Let me show you what else I'm good at."

Lily laughed out loud when he tossed her skirts up over her face and took his mouth on a trip in a southerly direction.

A short time later, she was sighing with the unparalleled satisfaction of a perfect climax—a most intense and long lasting one—and her husband was easing his splendidly stiff self into her. He made love to her very gently that afternoon, and she began to believe she was the luckiest woman in the world. She might not have everything, but she certainly had more than she'd ever had before.

And later, when their bodies were sated and they were both pleasurably drained of strength and energy, Lily reveled in his arms while he held her close on the bed.

"I should let you finish your letters," he said, kissing her on the forehead.

"No, don't go yet. Besides, I'm already finished. I wrote a long letter to Sophia and James and told them about the new painting I'm starting with Annabelle."

He was quiet for a moment. "Have you written to your mother at all?"

Lily ran her fingertips along his smooth, bare chest. "No, but she hasn't written to me, either."

"Do you think you should? Now that the baby is coming?"

She leaned up on one elbow, gazing into his eyes. She shook her head. "It doesn't matter anymore. I've started a new life. I don't need her approval, and perhaps I've finally realized that she never earned *mine*. I don't feel hurt anymore. I don't feel anything about her."

And it was all true. All of it. "I'm not sure why I feel this way," she added. "I hadn't thought it would ever be possible."

He pushed a lock of hair behind her ear. "You're stronger now. You defied her and you survived, and it has all worked out. At least I hope it has."

He was searching for something, she realized. He wanted to know that everything she had said that horrible night when they'd argued was no longer true. He wanted to know if she was happy.

"Yes, it has worked out," she replied, keeping her lingering reservations to herself, for this moment was the best they'd had yet in their strange, brief marriage. Whitby had spoken to her of something important. Something personal. She dared not spoil it.

With her son, Liam, resting on her hip, Sophia entered the drawing room at Wentworth Castle.

Marion—who was sitting across from James by the fire keeping warm—looked up from her needlepoint.

Sophia set Liam down, and he dashed off to the window, climbing up onto an upholstered chair to look outside. "It's snowing, Mum!" he said, touching his chubby finger to the frosty pane.

"Why look at that!" Sophia replied, watching him with a beaming smile. "You're right, Liam!" Then she turned to James and handed over a letter. "It's from Lily." She glanced at Marion. "She says all is well, and she and Annabelle have each started a new painting."

"Ah, my sister the *artiste*." James smiled as he accepted the letter and began reading.

Marion felt Sophia watching her, and she knew her daughter-in-law was hoping she would ask to read it, too, but of course she would not. Though she did wonder if Lily was still suffering from her morning illness. Marion remembered what it was like. She'd been very ill with James.

She returned her full attention to her needlepoint, but was startled by a loud *bang* that made her heart leap to her throat.

"Liam!" Sophia cried, and she and James were both darting across the room before Marion had even comprehended what had occurred—that Liam had climbed up onto the back of the chair and it had tipped over.

Marion rose from her chair, dropping her needlepoint to the floor. She felt rooted to the ground, locked in the panic of a memory—James doing the same thing in this very room, when he was not much older than Liam. His tooth had gone through his lip.

Marion remembered it as if it were happening now—her husband hearing the crash and crossing the room to pick James up and stand him on his little feet. As soon as he saw the blood, he'd slapped him across the face.

Marion sucked in a shuddering, stinging breath. She watched James go to Liam and pick him up and stand him on his feet. She swallowed anxiously, her body clenching with dread. Liam was screaming.

"Are you all right?" James shouted, staring into his son's distraught face.

"I fell over!" Liam wailed.

James pulled his son into his arms, and held him tight.

Marion felt shaken. Relieved, but nauseous.

A sudden rush of scattered memories flooded her thoughts, and she remembered a multitude of moments just like this one, when her husband had been cruel to both her and their children.

She had married him because her parents had told her to.

Her parents. Where were *they* now? she wondered. They were gone, and she had no memory of them. They had never held her like that. What did her duty to *them* matter now?

She put a hand on her chest, and for the first time

in her life, uttered the words, *"I made a mistake. I made a terrible mistake."*

The shock of the admission held her immobile as she stared blankly down at the floor. Then her gaze lifted, and she found herself looking at Lily's letter on the chair in front of her. A letter from her brave daughter, who only wanted happiness with the man she believed she loved, despite all his flaws.

A raw and primitive grief beset Marion, as she slowly bent forward and reached for the letter.

Chapter 31

It was quite surprising when Lily realized that contrary to how she had felt early on in her marriage—when she'd believed she could not live without Whitby's full devotion—she was not unhappy in the months leading up to her delivery.

She had taught herself to focus on the bright side. Though her husband never spoke of things that comprised his own heart, he treated Lily with kindness, generosity and respect. He never uttered a cruel word to her, nor did he criticize her running of the household or anything else she did. He complimented her on the way she looked, laughed at her jokes, listened with interest to whatever she wanted to talk about, and he was a magnificent, tireless lover. He made love to her whenever she wanted it—he had an uncanny ability to recognize when she did—and he was sensitive to the times she did not.

They had, as a result, learned to take each day as it came, not spending a great deal of time together, for he had transformed into a very dedicated landlord and spent most of his days making improvements to the estate, both large and small. He had earned the respect of the tenants and the household staff, and for that, Lily was proud of him.

All in all, it was a comfortable life. They were compatible and polite to each other, and though it wasn't perfect, it was a great deal better than what her mother had endured in her marriage. Lily endeavored to remember that.

Annabelle, too, seemed happier these days. She and Lily were still painting together, and though Lily knew she would never possess Annabelle's natural evocative talent, she had become quite proficient, having completed some landscapes and a number of works with fruit or flowers.

Lily had also managed to convince Annabelle to consider the attentions of Mr. MacIntosh, a most agreeable gentleman who had rented a small manor house on the other side of the village. He was an older man with three grown children, and he'd lost his wife to an illness a few years earlier. He was financially well off and was considered by all who knew him to be a man of honor and integrity. Though he was not the most handsome man in England, he possessed an attractive, masculine appeal, and he had striking pale blue eyes.

Annabelle was flattered by his attentions and even seemed willing to believe that a happily-ever-after might be possible for her. She liked Mr. MacIntosh very much.

And so spring arrived, bringing with it rain and blossoms and colorful, fragrant life, as Lily neared the end of her confinement.

With only a few weeks before the baby was due to arrive, she had taken it upon herself to redecorate the nursery, for nothing in the room had been changed since Whitby was a baby, and for all she knew, the rugs and wall coverings had been there since the dark ages.

Thus she began the joyful undertaking with an almost obsessive determination she could not explain. When she had an idea, she wanted it put into action that very instant.

Whitby seemed amused by her single-mindedness, and informed her that the doctor had warned him she might display such behavior, but not to worry, as it was considered normal for women in the late stages of pregnancy. Some called it "feathering the nest."

It was a sunny afternoon in late May when Lily felt positively desperate to escape the confines of her home, and went out to gather some proverbial feathers in the form of fabric samples for the new cradle she'd had built by one of the finest woodworkers in England.

She and her maid, Aline, traveled privately by closed coach into the village to meet with Madame Dubois, the local dressmaker, who had ordered a number of unusual bolts for Lily to peruse.

She was on her way out the back door of the shop afterward and about to step up into the coach when someone called out her name. "Lady Whitby!"

She stopped and turned. A man was leaning against the outside wall of the shop, and when their eyes met, he pushed himself away from the wall and took a few tentative steps toward her.

She paused uncertainly for a brief second before she replied or invited him to speak to her, for she was sure she did not know him, and for that reason, it was entirely improper for him to call out to her in such a familiar way, especially in her condition. She was not sure of his intentions, and she needed a moment to make a superficial judgment of his character.

She noted his face first—the dark hair and dark brown eyes—and found his expression largely nonthreatening. He looked more hopeful than confrontational. He wore a black coat and hat, which looked rather shabby after seeing all of Madame Dubois' fine fabrics and ready-made garments. Lily surmised he was not a man of great means.

In the end, it was her instincts she listened to. They led her to believe he did not mean her any harm. So she nodded at her footman, who stood ready at her side, to express that she was willing to speak to the man.

"Good afternoon," she said politely, yet with re-
serve, taking a step forward.

He approached and removed his hat. He stopped
before her, looking carefully at her face as if he, too,
needed to make a superficial judgment about *her*
character. She allowed him the freedom to do so,
but was unnerved when his gaze dropped briefly to
her swollen belly.

She reacted by clutching her reticule tightly with
both hands in front of her stomach, and feared she
might have been wrong to assume he was harmless.

Lily raised her chin. "What is it, sir? I'm in a
hurry."

He looked her in the eye, then said matter-of-
factly, "I am your husband's cousin."

Lily stared blankly at him. "Magnus?"

"Yes."

Lily wet her lips and gathered her composure,
making a conscious effort to stand up straight and
hold her head high. She did not want him to think
she was frightened or intimidated—though she
most decidedly was.

Yet, she was angry, too, for she knew what he had
done to Whitby's family, and Annabelle in particular. Magnus had taken away her trust in men, and
quite frankly ruined her life.

"You have audacity, sir, speaking to me like this. I
know all about you, you see, and I know my husband asked you to stay away."

A dark shadow of loathing passed over his eyes.
He said nothing and glanced up the street as if con-

templating something, and for a long moment, Lily wondered if he was just going to put his hat back on and walk away.

He did not do that, however. Rather, he lowered his head.

Surprised, Lily waited for him to look up and say what he wished to say.

Finally he spoke. "Your husband recently made an offer to me for compensation in return for my departure from England. I turned him down, but I've had time to reconsider, and I would be obliged if you could inform him of that."

Lily squeezed her reticule in her hands. "Why are you asking me to tell him? Why not tell him yourself?"

"Because I wanted to get a look at *you*."

Lily felt herself cowering under the disarming intensity of his assessing eyes. He was judging her.

"And now that you have," she said bitterly, "I hope you have satisfied your curiosity."

He considered that. "I suppose I have. But now I feel only pity for you."

Lily clenched her teeth together in umbrage. "Why, may I ask?"

"Because you married my cousin." He backed away and gave a slight bow. "You can tell him I will be at the King's Arms Tavern this afternoon. Thank you for your time, Lady Whitby."

Lily stood dumbfounded by his effrontery and shaken by his almost tangible resentment.

She turned to climb into the waiting coach, but he called out to her again. "Lady Whitby."

Lily froze. She thought about ignoring him, but something made her turn back. Curiosity perhaps.

"Say hello to Annabelle," he said.

They were taunting words. Later, when she repeated them to her husband, he would blow a gasket.

But strangely, as Lily stood there and looked into Magnus's eyes, she wondered if he was simply being sincere, and was not shooting a poisoned arrow.

She stared at him for a moment, not sure if she was being taken in, or if she was being too forgiving.

"I'll tell her," she said at last, realizing she was again being guided by her instincts. She took a moment to ponder that before she stepped back into her coach.

Later, when Lily was on her way home, replaying her conversation with Magnus over and over in her head and wondering how she was going to explain it to Whitby, the coach hit a bump in the road and she lifted clear off the seat. Aline, across from her, grabbed at the side to steady herself.

A second later, the vehicle swayed ominously and swerved on the road. Bouncing and rattling until it finally lurched, the back end dropped violently onto the road with a clamorous crash that Lily felt all the way up her spine.

Her heart dropped too, as blazing panic surged into her blood and she was tossed like a doll to the side. Her head smacked the window. Aline was screaming with terror.

The world shook and quaked in front of Lily's eyes as the vehicle tilted and was pulled jostling along the road at a dangerous angle. The coachman's deep voice hollered at the horses outside, then the world spun in circles as the vehicle flipped, and Lily was knocked unconscious.

As it turned out, they were not far from the house when the coach overturned. When Lily opened her eyes, she was staring up into the face of her husband, who was slapping gently at her cheek.

She blinked up at him a few times, struggling to gather her wits, for she wasn't quite sure where she was or why he looked so concerned.

Then she remembered the coach swerving and tipping, and realized she was still in it, and it was on its side.

"The baby!" she cried, touching her belly. "Is he all right?"

Whitby knelt on one knee. "I need you to stay calm, Lily. The doctor's on his way. Are *you* all right?"

She tried with difficulty to sit up, her belly heavy as she pushed up with one arm. Whitby helped support her, waiting for her reply.

"I think so," she said. "I don't feel any pain anywhere." She put a hand on her forehead. "What happened?"

"The coach lost a wheel."

Lily looked around the interior. The curtains were hanging at a bizarre angle. "Where's Aline? Is she hurt?"

"She's fine. She's the one who ran for help. It's you I'm worried about. You're sure you're not hurt?"

Lily shifted and sat up straighter, her hand still resting protectively on her belly. "I'm fine, I think."

He helped her stand, and she realized that the only way out was through the door over her head.

"Thompson!" Whitby called. "Come and lend a hand!"

Within seconds, there was a thumping on the outside of the coach and a footman's face appeared against the blue sky overhead. He reached down to Lily.

Whitby made a stirrup with his hands. "Put your foot here, and I'll boost you up."

"Boost me up? I weigh a ton," Lily replied, self-consciously.

"Don't worry. I'm prepared to put my back out." He gave her a small grin, though she could see the concern still lingering in his eyes.

Feeling more than a little concern herself, for she had not felt the baby kick since she'd opened her eyes, Lily did as he instructed, and with a few grunts and groans and the use of muscles she didn't know she possessed, she was soon on her hands and knees on top of the overturned vehicle, rising up to her feet. The team of horses, harness and all, was long gone, taken back to the house, she presumed.

"How long was I out?" she asked, as soon as Whitby—with the help of the footman—was up through the door and rising to his feet beside her.

"About twenty minutes," he said. "You have a bump on your head." He touched the tender side, just above her temple.

Lily jerked back. "Ouch!"

"My apologies. We need to get you home."

He hopped down to the ground and reached up. "Down you come, darling." She fell into her husband's waiting arms with the full trust that he would see her safely to the ground, and soon they were traveling by open carriage back to the house.

It was only then that Lily remembered her conversation with Magnus, and knowing what others had told her about his vindictive, malicious character, she balked at the coincidence of her coach losing a wheel within an hour of meeting him.

She touched Whitby's leg.

Startled, he looked at her. "What's wrong?"

"I met Magnus today," she replied, feeling half in a daze.

Her husband's heavy lashes flew up, as his eyes filled with hostile realization. His shock turned quickly to fury and he leaned forward. Elbows on knees, he cupped his head in his hands.

For a long, tense moment, he sat there in silence, then he turned to her and said, "Tell me what happened."

Chapter 32

A fter the doctor finished examining Lily and assured her and Whitby that the baby was fine, Lily watched from the drawing room window as her husband stepped into the carriage and drove off.

She was worried. He was going to the village to meet Magnus, and she was afraid of what would occur when he did.

He'd assured her he intended only to discuss the offer he had given Magnus months ago—the offer that Magnus was allegedly now reconsidering—but she feared there would be more to the gentlemen's conversation than that agreement, for her husband suspected Magnus of engineering the accident, and Lily knew he was wrestling quite violently with his wrath.

Lily heard someone enter the room, and turned away from the window. It was Annabelle, looking concerned.

"What did the doctor say?"

Lily crossed to her and took hold of both her hands. "Everything is fine. The baby is kicking again, and this bump on my head will be gone in a week."

Annabelle's shoulders heaved with a sigh of relief. "Thank goodness. I'm so glad you weren't seriously hurt. It makes me wary of ever going anywhere by coach again."

Lily nodded distractedly.

"What's the matter?" Annabelle asked, for she had grown very attuned to Lily's moods.

Lily gazed despondently into Annabelle's eyes. "Perhaps we should sit down."

Annabelle joined her on the sofa. Lily continued to hold her hand. "I must tell you what happened today, Annabelle, and explain where Whitby has gone."

Annabelle's expression revealed a sudden unease. "This sounds serious."

"I believe it is. You see, I met someone in the village today. It was Magnus."

Annabelle slowly pulled her hand away from Lily's. "That couldn't have been pleasant."

Lily studied Annabelle's eyes, trying to decipher how she felt about Magnus being so close by, and hoping Annabelle would be able to shed some light on all this.

"It wasn't so terrible, until the coach overturned."

Annabelle raised an eyebrow with a knowing cynicism. "You think he did it, don't you? Knowing him, he probably did." Then she covered her mouth with a hand. "Is that why Whitby left in such a hurry? To find him?"

"Yes. He's gone to the village."

Annabelle stood up. "They'll kill each other!"

Lily felt a surge of alarm at Annabelle's suggestion, but she had to keep her head. "No, Whitby's gone to talk to him about something else. When I spoke to Magnus today, he said the reason he was here was to ask me to tell Whitby that he'd changed his mind about the offer."

"What offer?"

Lily knew she must tell Annabelle everything. She needed Annabelle's wisdom—for Annabelle probably knew better than anyone what Magnus was capable of. "As soon as Whitby and I arrived here after we were married, Whitby offered Magnus a monthly income if he would agree to leave the country."

Annabelle exhaled a deep breath. "He wanted to protect you. But Magnus turned him down?"

"Yes."

"But why would he change his mind now?"

"That's what I'm trying to figure out. Perhaps because he knows that in a few short weeks he may no longer be heir to Whitby's title? Do you think that could be true?"

Annabelle sat down again, ruminating over the question for a long moment. "I suppose it could."

Lily squeezed Annabelle's hand. "Do you think he will leave England now? After what happened today, I'm worried about the baby."

Annabelle shook her head as tears filled her eyes. "I don't know. His hatred for this family has always been the driving force of his life. All he's ever wanted to do was hurt Whitby. What if he did this just to provoke him and draw him out?"

Lily heard the trepidation in Annabelle's voice, and began to feel that same fear herself. What if it were true? What if Magnus knew Whitby would leave here with no intention of negotiating a financial settlement? What if he knew Whitby would attempt to end the feud, one way or another, and that is what he really wanted? A full-blown battle?

"But why does Magnus hold such hatred for the family? Does he not know that his father was dangerous? Does he not understand that they had good reason to send him away?"

"Magnus only sees the world from his vantage point, and I expect his father pushed his own hatred into Magnus's head from a very young age. He thinks *we* are the villains."

"Can't we tell him otherwise? Can he not see reason?"

"Many have tried. He never sees reason. He only casts blame."

Lily stood and walked anxiously to the window. She replayed her conversation with Magnus in her head, remembering the look in his eyes and the way he had carried himself. She had not feared him, not completely. She'd been wary of him because of what she knew, but something about him had been nonthreatening.

She faced Annabelle. "I hope Magnus does not provoke Whitby. I hope he really wants that settlement."

"But Whitby has already been provoked. You and the baby could have been killed today."

Lily returned to sit beside Annabelle. "I'm trying so hard to believe this is not what it seems."

"I don't see how you can."

With a shake of her head, Lily reached for Annabelle's hand again. "Perhaps I should tell you," she said, "that when Magnus was leaving, he asked me to say hello to you."

Annabelle looked as if someone had put a knife in her heart. She bowed her head. "He is truly a vindictive man."

"No, it wasn't like that," Lily said, not quite sure why she was defending him, but she needed to tell Annabelle how it really was. "He seemed almost sincere. I would even go so far as to say there was a hint of . . ." She stopped, not quite sure she knew the right word to use to describe the look in Magnus's eyes, and not even sure she was correct about it.

"A hint of what?"

Lily thought about it for another few seconds. "A hint of remorse. He was not ridiculing you, I'm sure of that."

Annabelle leaned back against the sofa. "Remorse." She sounded doubtful.

"Yes. And that is what is giving me hope that everything will work out today."

Annabelle stared off in the other direction, then she rose slowly to her feet and walked to the window. The light illuminated her face as she gazed toward the horizon. "I understand that you need hope, Lily. But be careful not to let those hopes be too unrealistic. Magnus is a hateful man."

Lily took a deep breath, feeling all too anxious, for she knew that she had never been much of a realist where her hopes were concerned.

Whitby walked into the King's Arms Tavern and spotted Magnus at a table in the shadows of the back corner, with a half-empty mug of ale before him. His head was tipped back against the wall, his eyes closed.

Whitby took a minute to breathe deeply and slow the blood that was raging through his veins, then he slowly approached his cousin.

He stood for a moment in front of the table, waiting for Magnus to open his eyes, but the man continued to sit in oblivious silence. Whitby was surprised. He had expected Magnus to be prepared for a confrontation, but he was completely open to attack.

Whitby leaned forward, picked up Magnus's mug and smacked it down on the table to announce his presence. The beer sloshed over the brim and splashed onto the table.

Magnus did not startle awake. He calmly opened his eyes and stared at Whitby, then sat forward and gestured to the chair opposite.

Whitby sat down.

"Drink?" Magnus asked.

"No," Whitby replied.

Magnus picked up his mug and downed what was left in it, then set it on the table and raised an arm to signal for another one.

Whitby drummed his fingers on the table while he waited for the server to deliver another mug full of ale. The woman approached, and Whitby waved a hand to decline the extra mug of ale she had brought for him.

As soon as she was gone, Whitby glared at his cousin. "My wife informed me of your conversation." He stared intently at Magnus's face.

"It was my hope that she would."

"She told me you changed your mind about my offer of an allowance."

"I have," Magnus replied, wiping a hand across his mouth.

He was drunk, Whitby realized, which was making it difficult to have this conversation. Whitby wanted Magnus to be sober, so nothing would be misconstrued.

"There's only one problem," Whitby said icily. "I'm having a hard time resolving to give you money, the very day you tried to kill my wife and heir."

Magnus's face contorted into a shocked grimace. "Kill your wife? I had a conversation with her!"

Whitby scowled at him. "This is disturbingly familiar."

"How, may I ask, is it familiar?"

But Whitby could see in Magnus's eyes that he already knew the answer to that. He just wanted to hear Whitby say it.

"You denied being my brother's murderer, too."

Magnus shook his head in apparent disgust. "We're back to that, are we? Good God, you're out of your mind. I didn't murder your brother and I certainly didn't try to kill your wife. I've been sitting here all afternoon staring at the wall and drinking myself into oblivion."

Whitby sat very still, his eyes narrow. "You expect me to believe it was a coincidence?"

"*What* was a coincidence?"

Whitby cocked his head to one side. "How did you know Lady Whitby would be in the village when she was?"

Magnus tapped a finger on the scarred table. "It's not that difficult to ask questions of the right people. Look, I didn't try to kill her. I don't even know what happened to her." He took another drink, then tipped his head back against the wall again, looking blasé. "What *did* happen?"

Perhaps Whitby *was* out of his mind, because he

found himself answering the question. "Her coach lost a wheel and overturned on the way home."

"Is she all right?"

Did he hope otherwise? Whitby wondered, studying his cousin's expression with narrowed eyes. "Yes, she's fine."

Magnus took another swig of ale.

Whitby honestly couldn't say for sure whether or not he believed that Magnus had tampered with the wheel. But there was something unusual about Magnus's behavior today. Whitby felt no aggression from him.

He leaned back in his chair, still studying his cousin. Either way, only one thing mattered to him now, and that was making sure there would be no similar events in the future, and that Lily and Annabelle would be safe.

"Let's talk about the offer," Whitby said at last.

Magnus set down his mug. "I want to go to America. Ten thousand a year, and I'm gone."

"Why now?" Whitby asked.

"Not that it's any of your business, but there was a time I believed I would inherit the earldom. I'd watched you drink your life away and refuse to take a wife and I truly believed that you would end up in an early grave, like your father and John."

Whitby clenched his hands into fists.

"But now you have a lovely wife," Magnus continued, "who is expecting a child any day now by the look of things, and in case you hadn't heard, my mother passed away two weeks ago. Hence, my ties to England are no more."

Whitby's anger diminished suddenly at the mention of Carolyn's death. Though he had no affection for the woman, death was death.

"I'm sorry to hear that," he said. "She was very devoted to you." It was the only thing he could think of to say.

Magnus kept his gaze downcast as he took another drink. He did not even acknowledge Whitby's condolence.

"Was she ill?" Whitby asked.

"Her heart."

"I'm sorry," Whitby said again.

Magnus glared at him. "So. The money. If you agree to provide me with an allowance that would have been mine had my father not been cut off from the family, I will leave England and you'll finally be rid of me."

This was something Whitby had wanted for a long time—to be rid of Magnus and the threat he posed. Yet while he sat here staring across the table at the man he had despised all his life, he did not feel the satisfaction he would have expected. He looked at Magnus now and saw only a bitter man who knew no joy. He had nothing but the drink in front of him.

But Whitby shook himself out of that and remembered all the reprehensible things his cousin had done throughout their lives, like the time he had attacked John and broken his nose outside their London house, and of course, what he had done to Annabelle. If he was bitter, he had brought it upon himself.

Whitby pushed his chair back and stood. "Done. I will arrange a monthly payment, the first to be dispersed immediately. I will have it in writing however, signed by you, that if you ever return to England, the payments will stop."

Magnus glared up at him. "Fair enough. But you don't need it in writing. I won't be coming back."

"Regardless, I'll have it on paper."

Whitby studied his cousin's dark eyes for a moment before turning and walking out.

When Whitby returned to the house, he stepped out of the coach to discover Clarke dashing quickly down the front steps to meet him. A jolt of apprehension shook Whitby, for Clarke never came running outside to meet anyone. He always waited at the door.

"What is it?" Whitby asked, removing his hat as he met his butler at the bottom of the steps.

"It's Lady Whitby, my lord," he replied. "She's in labor."

Chapter 33

⁓◦◦⁓

Whitby stood outside the closed door of his wife's bedchamber, pausing a moment before he knocked, realizing that he had to do it again: knock and enter and see a woman he loved—yes, loved—in labor on that bed. He could imagine Lily now, pale-faced and exhausted.

He raised his fist and rapped on the door.

"Come in!" Lily called from inside.

Whitby was surprised by the cheerful note in her voice. He reached for the knob and pushed the door open.

The room was bright with the curtains wide open to let in the sun, and Lily was walking toward him with her hands outstretched, looking happy and glowing with anticipation. She wore a colorful pink dressing gown.

"Thank goodness you're back," she said, clasping both his hands in hers and rising up on her toes to kiss him on the cheek. "I've been so worried. What happened with Magnus?"

His brow furrowed with disbelief. "How can you even be thinking of that now?"

She smiled. "I know. It's happening. Isn't it wonderful?"

She dropped her heels back down and he found himself in awe looking at her pretty face—her blue eyes and dark lashes, her creamy white skin and raspberry lips. She'd never looked more lovely to him, nor more vibrant and alive. Perhaps there was nothing to worry about. Perhaps this would all go smoothly, without complications.

"You surprise me," he told her. "I didn't expect to find you on your feet, smiling cheerfully at me. I was under the impression childbirth was painful."

She smiled at his meager attempt at humor. "It has been a little. About every five or ten minutes, my belly aches and nothing can distract me from it, but it lasts only a brief time and then the pain goes away and I feel fine, like right now."

Just then, her face changed and she put a hand on her belly. She looked away from him and bent forward slightly. "Oh, here it comes . . ."

She closed her eyes and breathed deep and slow, and Whitby's stomach dropped like a stone. He instinctively reached for her, thinking she was going to have the baby right now, right here on the carpet.

"Should you lie down?" he asked.

She quickly shook her head, almost frantically, and did not speak or move or look up at him. She focused on a spot on the floor, then squeezed her eyes shut.

Whitby did not speak again. He just stood there until her smile returned and she lifted her gaze.

"There, it's gone. See? Nothing to it."

He dropped his hand to his side and exhaled a long breath he hadn't realized he'd been holding. "But are you sure you shouldn't lie down?" he asked again.

Lily shook her head. "Mrs. Hanson, the midwife, said it's best for me to keep moving, and that walking will help speed things up."

"I see." He glanced around the room. "Where *is* the midwife? Shouldn't she be here?"

"She just went to fetch something from the kitchen. The doctor has been sent for, but was away on another call. He should be here soon, though. Would you walk with me? We won't go far. Just down the hall and back. You still haven't told me what happened with Magnus."

Still feeling exceedingly tense, he offered his arm, and they proceeded out the door and down the corridor. Whitby told Lily everything—how Magnus had not been his usual self, and that his mother had died. Lily was sorry to hear that, but nevertheless relieved to hear that Magnus had agreed to leave England.

"So this is one burden you will no longer have to bear," she said, looking up at him questioningly.

"Yes," he replied. Though there were other, much heavier burdens today, but he did not speak of them.

They walked up and down the hall many times over the next hour, while Mrs. Hanson stood by in Lily's boudoir, waiting patiently. Every so often, Lily would stop and rest a hand on her belly, breathe deeply and stare at the floor, then they would start walking again. They talked about baby names and dates for the christening, and what university the child would go to when the time came. Whitby thought they were putting the cart before the horse—they had to get through today, after all—but he obliged his wife and let her talk about whatever she wished.

Lily's feet soon tired, and she decided she would like to lie down for a while. "Would you come back in an hour?" she asked, stopping in the corridor. "Assuming I haven't had the baby by then."

"Of course, darling." He kissed her on the cheek and escorted her back to her room. The midwife, who had been sitting in the rocking chair, rose to her feet and took Lily's other arm to help her onto the bed.

"I'm not an invalid," Lily said to both of them, smirking as she awkwardly maneuvered herself into a comfortable position. "I just happen to move like a whale."

Whitby chuckled at his wife's sense of humor,

pleased and impressed by the fact that she still had one, considering her discomfort. He gave her another kiss on the cheek. "I'll return in an hour."

"I'll look forward to it," she replied, gazing up at him happily.

Lily. Brave Lily. He left the room and stopped outside the door with his hand still on the knob, suddenly wanting more than anything in the world to hold his wife and their child in his arms and devote himself completely to them. It came upon him like a great, surging wave, like nothing he'd ever experienced, and it almost knocked the wind out of him.

He supposed he'd never imagined he would consciously admit to such a momentous hope. He'd been afraid to, because he was afraid he would lose Lily.

But he had not lost her yet. He'd come close. Twice. She'd been very ill. Her carriage had just overturned. But she had survived both those things, and so had he.

He returned to his room, sat down on his bed and looked at the clock, hoping this hour away from her would pass swiftly.

As promised, Whitby returned to Lily's bedchamber an hour later, and he and Lily paced up and down the hall again until her feet grew sore, and they decided to return to her room.

He asked the midwife to give them some privacy, then Whitby helped Lily into an upholstered armchair, sat on the ottoman before her and lifted her foot onto his lap. He removed her slipper, and for half an hour, massaged her feet and calves.

"How many children do you want?" she asked him, leaning back in the chair between labor pains and sounding dreamy.

At the moment, he wanted only this *one*, delivered safely. But he knew that was not the answer she wanted.

He stroked her arch with his thumb. "Ten."

"And how many of those would be girls?"

He lifted an eyebrow flirtatiously. "If they were anything like their mother, I would like them all to be girls." He tilted his head and reconsidered that. "But then I would have to fight off all the young pups in London who would want to steal my daughters away, wouldn't I? So perhaps boys would be better."

"You need at least one boy," she said, being practical.

He set down her foot and picked up the other. "Yes, I suppose I do."

"I hope this is a son."

He stopped rubbing for a moment and spoke with conviction. "I would love a daughter just as much."

The words came out of his mouth before he had even the slightest inclination to think about what he was saying, and he was surprised. He'd used the word love.

Lily was surprised too. She didn't say she was,

but he could see it in her eyes, in the way she was staring speechlessly at him.

He began to rub her foot again. They sat in silence after that, and excepting the moments when Lily experienced pain, it was not an uncomfortable silence.

Dr. Benjamin arrived late that evening and entered Lily's bedchamber with a pleasant expression on his face and a jolly tone in his voice. "I understand there's a baby ready to announce that today is his birthday."

Lily, sitting up in bed, smiled at the doctor as he approached. Whitby closed the book he had been reading to her and stood. "Indeed you're right, but he seems to be taking his time."

"Is that so?" The doctor set his leather bag on the bed and dug into it for his stethoscope. "Then we shall see what's keeping him."

"Or her," Lily said.

The doctor grinned as he put the earpieces in place. "Or her," he repeated.

He listened to Lily's swollen belly, moving the scope around to different positions, then he pulled out the earpieces and let the instrument dangle around his neck. "Everything sounds fine."

Whitby exhaled with relief.

"When did the pains begin?" the doctor asked, pressing upon Lily's belly.

"Around one o'clock," she replied. She explained that they had been coming steadily every five or ten minutes.

"Have the pains become more intense?" he asked.

"Not really. They've been about the same all day."

"Ah. Well, I should have a look at you." He turned to Whitby. "Will you excuse us, my lord?"

"Yes, of course," Whitby replied, kissing Lily on the forehead, then bowing slightly before he left. "I shall await your news."

About twenty minutes later, the doctor found Whitby and Annabelle in the drawing room, sitting before the fire. Whitby immediately stood and gestured to the chair facing him. "Doctor, come in. Please sit down."

The doctor set down his bag and took a seat.

"How is she?" Whitby asked.

"She appears to be fine. She's certainly in good spirits, though that might change in the coming hours when the labor pains worsen."

"I suppose that's to be expected," Whitby replied hesitantly. "But I must confess, I am surprised with how easy this has been so far. It's not what I had thought it would be."

The doctor leaned forward and clasped his hands together in front of him, his elbows on the armrests. "I must be frank with you, my lord. It's been easy because there has been very little progress."

A cold knot tightened in Whitby's stomach. "What do you mean?"

The doctor leaned back again. "Lady Whitby explained to me that her water had broken earlier today, but when I examined her, she was not dilated."

"Dilated? Be clear with me, doctor, if you please."

The doctor paused. "The cervix, which is the door to the womb so to speak, must open well enough to let the child through. Hers is still closed."

"But will it open eventually?"

The doctor paused for a moment before answering. "These things are rarely predictable. It's her first child and she might simply be a trifle slow. On the other hand, I am concerned that the accident today might have caused the water to break prematurely, which might have upset the natural progression of things. But for all we know, it could be happening now. I could go back to her room in five minutes and the baby could be coming."

"What if the womb doesn't open?"

The doctor was direct. "There are ways I can intervene to help things along."

"If that doesn't work?"

Dr. Benjamin didn't answer the question right away. He put a hand up to halt the discussion. "As I said before, this conversation is premature—"

"If it doesn't work, doctor," Whitby repeated, more firmly this time. Though he already knew all too well what would happen. That's how his mother had died—under the doctor's knife, in a last attempt to save the child.

Dr. Benjamin's Adam's apple bobbed as he swallowed. "Then you and Lady Whitby would have to consider your options. The fact is, my lord, that once the water has broken, the child must come out, or the child's survival will be at risk."

Whitby stirred uneasily in the chair. "What about the mother's survival?"

"Hers, too, of course. But truly, you mustn't concern yourself at this stage. All could very well be fine."

Whitby leaned forward with his elbows on his knees and raked both hands through his hair. "*Christ.*"

The doctor put a hand on Whitby's shoulder. "My lord, in all likelihood, Lady Whitby will deliver the baby safely in her own good time."

Whitby nodded and sat back. The doctor was right. It was Lily's first child, and she could simply be taking her time. Worrying would get him nowhere. He had to be hopeful.

But hope was not easy for a man like him, who had lost so many people in his life. He was jaded. He couldn't help but expect the worst.

Chapter 34

~~~~~~~~ ∽◯◯∾ ~~~~~~~~

By mid-morning the next day, Lily was no longer cheerful, and Whitby did not know what to say to her, for he, too, was out of his mind with worry. She had not yet made any progress.

She was growing weary of the pain and it had been a long, grueling night. The midwife had given Lily a warm bath to try and encourage the baby to come, but it had produced no effect. She hadn't been able to sleep either, not with the labor pains coming every five minutes. Whitby had dozed off a few times in the chair because Lily had encouraged him to do so, and she was very quiet when she experienced her pain, unlike his mother. Lily had told him to go to bed at least a dozen times—for a birthing room was no place for a husband, she had said—but he'd refused to leave. He would go when the baby was ready to come, he had told her.

He wished it would happen, but still, as the morning wore on, it did not.

That afternoon, the doctor began his methods of intervention. He administered three doses of chloral, which increased Lily's pain but did not produce the desired effect he had hoped. He tried manual pressure over her abdomen. When that didn't work, he gave her quinine, which he said was a general stimulant and was frequently employed in lingering labors such as these with marked benefits. Whitby sensed the doctor was getting desperate at that point.

By nightfall, there were still no changes when the doctor examined her, and his distress began to show.

"It's been more than thirty hours, my lord," he said to Whitby quietly in the privacy of the drawing room, "and Lady Whitby is exhausted. I do not want to be the forecaster of doom, but if she does not dilate soon . . . I would prefer to take steps sooner rather than later."

"Steps?" Whitby said.

"Yes, my lord."

"Surgery."

The doctor stared wordlessly at him.

"That's how my mother died," Whitby told him.

Dr. Benjamin's chest rose and fell with a compassion-filled sigh. "I am aware of that, Lord

Whitby. I read the reports. But I believe the physician attending her waited too long."

Whitby swallowed over the lump of dread rising up in his throat, while he struggled to keep a clear head. "Have you said this to my wife? Does she know what this means?"

"I've said nothing yet because anxiety can sometimes exacerbate the problem. I've only told you. And Mrs. Hanson of course knows from experience."

Whitby turned away from the doctor and poured a glass of brandy from the side table. He had not touched a drink in nine months. He walked to the other side of the room to sip it, hoping it would numb the strain upon his nerves, but in the end, all he could do was stare down at it. He realized with unnerving melancholy that he did not want to be numb. Not today. Not ever again.

Eventually, he set it down on a table and walked away from it. He faced the doctor. "Can we wait a little longer? I'm not ready to make this decision."

"Yes. But she can't go on like this forever."

"Is there nothing else you can do?"

"If the pain becomes unbearable, I can give her chloroform. It's safe, if managed properly. But again, if surgery becomes a necessity, the sooner you make the decision, the greater the chances of success."

Whitby pinched the bridge of his nose. Would he be forced to make a decision that could kill Lily and the baby? And if he acted sooner rather than later as the doctor was saying, and they did *not* survive, would Whitby always wonder what would have happened if he'd waited? Would Lily have given birth safely on her own?

He would never know the answer to that, and if anything happened to her, he would drive himself mad, because he would assume the worst—that yes, she would have been fine if he'd waited just one more hour . . .

He cupped his forehead in his hand and realized frantically that if Lily did not deliver that baby soon, he *was* going to have to make that choice. And God help him, he did not want to.

Later that evening, Whitby woke in the chair next to Lily's bed with his forehead on her hand. She was weeping.

Instantly awake and alert, he stood and leaned over her. Mrs. Hanson, who was sleeping on a cot in the dressing room, came running in.

"It's the pain," Lily said with a gut-wrenching sob. "I've been trying so hard to be brave, but I can't take it anymore! It's been almost two days. Why won't the baby come?"

Mrs. Hanson stood at the foot of the bed. "Is the pain worse, Lady Whitby?"

Lily shook her head. "No. Yes. I don't know. Maybe it feels worse because I have no tolerance left. I can't do this anymore!"

Whitby bent forward and kissed her cheeks and her nose and eyes. "Can't you *do* something!" he shouted at the midwife.

"Perhaps I should examine her," Mrs. Hanson said shakily, appearing flustered. "Perhaps she is progressing."

Lily sat up and let out a guttural cry. It was the first time Whitby had heard that sound come out of her—that familiar, nightmarish sound . . .

"If you will give me a moment, Lord Whitby," Mrs. Hanson said, quickly moving around the other side of the bed in a panic, and pulling the covers off Lily.

He kissed Lily's small hand, but she was unaware. She was panting, her face contorted in a tight grimace. Whitby met Mrs. Hanson's gaze and saw the concern in her eyes. A tense silence enveloped the room. He swallowed with difficulty.

This was hell. He'd gone straight to the depths of fiery hell.

Making haste to leave the room, hoping Mrs. Hanson would discover that the baby was ready to come, Whitby left and closed the door behind him. He tipped his head back against the wall and squeezed his eyes shut, waiting. His heart was pounding erratically. He'd never felt like this—so desperate and powerless.

Everything was quiet on the other side of the door for a brief moment, then he heard Lily cry out, "No!"

Feeling as if his heart was about to explode from

his chest, Whitby opened the door and burst back in. "What is it?"

Mrs. Hanson was covering Lily again, and Lily was crying. He felt nauseous. He wanted to give up his own life for her. If that would make the baby come, he would do it here and now.

Mrs. Hanson shook her head. "Still no progress, my lord. The cervix is closed."

Lily was writhing on the bed with another contraction, and Whitby couldn't stand it another moment. "Fetch Dr. Benjamin," he said. "He's in my study. He mentioned chloroform to numb the pain. Tell him to bring some."

"Chloroform?" Lily asked, as the pain subsided. "Are you sure? It won't hurt the baby?"

"The queen has used it, darling," Whitby said. "It will help you."

She lay back on the pillows and closed her eyes, falling almost immediately to sleep, but startling awake a moment later. She grabbed Whitby's forearm. "Perhaps you should send word to my mother," she said with desperation. "She's in London."

Whitby knew with bitter cold despair that if Lily wanted to communicate with her mother, she was anticipating the worst.

He strove to prepare himself for what lay ahead, but could not. All he could do was let her squeeze his arm as another labor pain seized her.

Marion arrived by train at noon the next day. Lily was still in the same state, suffering the pains of labor with no dilation of the cervix, but the chloroform had at least given her some reprieve. The doctor had strongly recommended the surgery, and Lily had agreed to it. She knew the risks to her own life, but she wanted to save the baby.

Whitby was devastated. He could not eat. He could barely speak.

He walked in somber silence as he escorted Marion to Lily's bedchamber. He paused outside the door, however, before he opened it.

"I know you've never approved of me," he said flatly, "and probably for good reason. But I do love her, more than my own life, more than I've ever loved anyone. I would die for her if I could. Right now."

He'd never imagined he would say those words, but there they were. It was the truth. He loved her, and he could no longer fight it or deny it.

His mother-in-law stared at him for a long moment with unreadable eyes, probably blaming him for inflicting this death sentence upon her daughter. He knew what she thought of him. He had taken both James and Lily out of her control, and now the worst was about to happen.

But there was nothing he could do to change that. He knew all too well it was out of his hands now.

Marion, however, did not reproach him. She laid a hand on his arm and nodded to acknowledge what he'd said, while he gazed down at her with both surprise and despair.

A brief second later, she turned toward the door,

so he showed her into the room, then went straight to his own room to be alone.

He sat down in the chair by the window to prepare himself, but he couldn't. He couldn't do anything. All he could do was sit perfectly still, elbows on knees, hands laced together in front of him, his head bent forward.

He did not weep. He could not. He was in shock. He thought *he* should be dead. He was the one with no life, no rewards due to him. He had not loved the one woman who had given him her heart, body and soul—not the way he should have. He had kept his soul away from her.

He would have expected that under these circumstances he would be glad he had held back so much of himself. But he was not glad. All he felt was regret for all the love he had wasted, all the joy he had missed. Now it was too late. He could not have the past back.

He had denied Lily so much.

And he had denied himself even more.

Holding onto a mask she placed over her face when the pain became unbearable, Lily lay in bed, feeling as if she were floating. The chloroform did not suppress the pain completely, but it relaxed her and helped her fall asleep occasionally, dozing through certain sporadic moments.

She had no idea how long she'd been dozing when she opened her eyes and was struck by the sight of her mother sitting by the bed.

Was she dreaming?

"Hello," Marion said, leaning forward.

Lily's mouth was dry. She stared sleepily at her mother and felt the return of all the heartbreak and anger she'd felt the last time they'd spoken. She had thought she was over it, but she had not forgotten . . .

Lily tried to keep her voice cool and reserved, though she felt nothing of the sort. "I'm surprised. I didn't think you'd come."

Another painful spasm gripped Lily, and she sat up and squeezed her eyes shut. Her mother stood, as if needing to do something, but there was of course nothing she could do.

When it was over, Lily lay back down. "I need you to know, Mother, that I hold no ill will against you. I understand why you did not want me to marry Whitby, and I accept that."

Marion said nothing.

"And I'm sorry that I've always disappointed you. I never wanted to, but I had to live my own life."

Lily had never seen her mother's face look the way it did now. The lines on her forehead were creasing in unusual directions. "I didn't come here to hear you apologize."

Lily turned her face away. "Then why *did* you come? To remind me that you were right and I was wrong, and I should have listened to you? I hope that's not the case, Mother. Not now."

Marion paused a minute before answering. "No. I came to see if there was anything I could do."

Lily stared coolly at her. Another pain gripped her, but she did not reach for the mask. She weathered it.

When it was over, Marion sat down again. For a long moment she said nothing, then she shook her head and sat forward. She spoke hesitantly, as if it was very difficult to get the words out.

"Lily, if anyone should be sorry . . ." She stopped and cleared her throat. "If anyone should be sorry, it is I."

Lily gazed with surprise at her mother.

Marion slowly blinked. "I should have let you do what you felt you must. I should have listened. I was stubborn and I just wanted you to *obey* me."

Lily pushed her damp hair away from her face. The chloroform was making her confused. She wasn't quite sure what her mother was trying to say to her. *Obey me* . . . Was she scolding her again?

"I tried to listen to you, Mother, but you never listened to me."

"No, I didn't, because if you could do what *you* wanted, it meant that maybe I could have, too. But I never did because I wasn't strong enough."

Lily held onto her belly when the pain came again. "Not strong enough," she said through gritted teeth. "Of course you were. All my life I feared you."

Marion bowed her head. "Lily, since you left, I've been forced to think about what my life might have been like if I had been more like you—if I had defied my parents and not married your father. Perhaps if I had been brave enough, I could have been happy . . . like you."

"Do I look happy now?" Lily ground out, cupping an arm around her belly.

Marion touched Lily's forehead and gently brushed the hair off her face. It was not something she'd ever done before—*touch* Lily that way.

Lily was momentarily taken aback and overcome with a strange, most unfamiliar contentment. Her mother's hand was warm. It was soothing, and a cry of relief broke from her lips.

With it came another spasm.

Lily breathed hard, staring up at her mother with desperation.

"Is it worse?" Marion asked.

Lily nodded.

"The doctor wants to intervene. I don't believe he should."

"I want to save the baby."

"It's too dangerous, Lily."

"I've made my decision." Lily reached for the mask and breathed deeply. "I love him, and I want to give him a child. I don't want to leave him with nothing."

"You haven't. You've given him your love."

Lily had never heard her mother say anything like that before. It made all of this seem unreal and illusory.

She breathed from the mask again, shaking her head. "But he never gave me his."

"Yes, he did, Lily. He loves you. He told me so."

Lily tried to make sense of what her mother was saying, but she felt the pull of sleep. She needed to drift off . . .

"I wanted to give him children," she said breathlessly, knowing she was not thinking clearly. She could not seem to focus on anything beyond the frustration over not being able to do what she had wanted to do. She'd wanted to give this child to Whitby. She'd wanted to see his happiness. "Please don't blame him," she said.

"For what? For this?"

"He's a good man, Mother. I can't let the doctor in here until I know you believe that. I need to know that you understand why I married him, and that you and I forgive each other."

"I understand. But there is nothing to forgive. Not for me."

"I wanted to give him a son," Lily said again, feeling bemused and incoherent.

Just then, a knock sounded at the door, and Whitby walked in. "The doctor is waiting," he said. "He wants to begin."

Lily heard her husband's voice, but could not seem to comprehend what he was saying.

A second later, she opened her eyes briefly and he was sitting beside her and her mother was gone.

Had her mother even been here? Or had Lily dreamed it?

"I'm so sorry," Whitby said, but Lily's eyes closed again. She couldn't open them. She could only feel her husband's lips and breath upon her hand.

"I can't live without you, Lily," he said. "Please don't die . . ."

She felt his tears on her wrist, and knew he was saying other things, but she was drifting in and out.

She let go of the mask she was clutching in her other hand and heard it drop.

"Lily?"

Lily felt another pain in her belly, then tossed her head from side to side on the pillow. She knew she was moaning. She could hear herself as if from a great distance away. Were they taking the baby out?

Then she was faintly aware of her husband rising up from the chair and running from the room.

Everything went black.

She woke to the feel of the covers being ripped almost violently from her body, and the sound of feet rushing around, people in the room, voices yelling . . . the doctor?

Then he shouted at her: *"Push, Lady Whitby! Push!"*

Chapter 35

I t was a miracle—one of God's own miracles.

Whitby sat in the chair beside his wife, holding in his arms *a son.*

A beautiful son. A perfect son with the face of an angel. Whitby had tears in his eyes over this precious, wonderful life he and Lily had created.

He looked across at her, his beautiful wife, exhausted and weary—but alive!—and could not stop the tears. He felt joy and love, astonishing, overwhelming love like an ocean wave beneath him, sweeping him up and away. He could barely breathe, he was so happy. And Lily—she was alive. Worn out, yes, but alive.

Covered in perspiration, she was smiling at him.

She touched his shoulder. "Everything's all right now," she said.

He gathered his composure and managed to speak at last. He sat forward in the chair and turned so that Lily could see the baby's face. "Look what you made, Lady Whitby."

Lily chuckled softly and laid a weak hand on the sweet infant's head. "Look what *we* made. He's beautiful, isn't he?"

"Almost as beautiful as his mother."

"Not handsome like his father?"

Whitby stood and bent forward to kiss Lily on the forehead. "All life's beauty comes from you. I would know none of it without you."

She stared up at him for a moment, looking surprised. Unsure. "All I did was marry you," she said. "Anyone could have done that. Many have certainly wanted to."

He knew she was teasing him. Even now, after a two-day labor, she still had the spirit to be playful. But he also knew there was something else beneath that surface lightheartedness. She still had her worries. She looked both curious and guarded.

"Not just anyone," he said. "I would never have married another. It's only ever been you."

Her eyes grew serious all of a sudden. "And you for me."

"You've made that very clear, Lily. But I never made it clear to you, and for that I am so very sorry. I couldn't bring myself to give in to it, or admit it."

"Admit what?"

"That I loved you. Desperately."

The weary expression on his wife's face softened with the pull of tears and the marked relief of finally hearing what she had waited so long to hear. She smiled tenderly at him, as a rosy color seeped into her cheeks and a tear fell from her eye. "That's the first time you've ever said that to me."

"No, I said it to you here today, but you were . . ." He shook his head. "It doesn't matter. I should have said it a long time ago. I should have known it."

Lily stared at him without blinking, as if she couldn't dare to believe the words he'd just spoken so sincerely from his heart. But she had to believe them because they were true, and no one deserved to hear them more than she did.

"You know it now?" she asked. "Truly?"

"I've known it a long time, I believe. Forever perhaps. But I was so afraid of losing you, like I lost everyone else."

"Your mother," she said.

"Yes, and my father, my brother. My whole family."

She laid a caring hand on his arm. "You have a new family now."

He looked down at their child, this beautiful child they had created together out of their love during those magical nights when he had been ill and he'd let himself love Lily unreservedly.

He loved her that way now. He had been to hell and back when he thought she was dying, but he had survived, and so had she. And dear God in heaven, he would survive every day for the rest of his life because of her. He would hold nothing back, because Lily had helped him see that he could—that no matter what happened, he *could*.

"Maybe you could tell me more about your mother sometime," she said. "And the nannies you remember. I want to know all of it. I want to know everything about you."

"You asked me about that once before, and I wouldn't talk to you. I won't do that again, Lily. I'll never turn away." He climbed onto the bed beside her and placed their child between them. "I'll tell you everything. You have my word. And I want to know everything about you, too. But for now, all you need to know is that I love you more than life itself, and I promise I will spend every day for the rest of my life showing you just how much."

Lily listened to the words her husband was saying to her, and felt the most glorious joy she'd ever known filling the deepest realms of her heart. It was what she had yearned for all her life, and for the first time, she understood it and believed it. He loved her. Deeply and passionately. He truly did. Her Whitby. She wiped another tear from her eye.

"But what about the future?" she said shakily. "This labor was very difficult. You won't worry about having more children?"

"Of course I'll worry," he replied. "I'll fear it and dread it, and every birth will be another hellish experience for me, but I won't let it stop me from giving you everything. I faced death, Lily—yours and mine both—and because of that, I now understand how beautiful *life* is, even with all its pain."

They both looked down at their son, and Whitby touched his sweet chubby cheeks with the tip of his finger. Lily was too tired to giggle and coo the way she wanted to, but she knew there would be plenty of time for that in the days to come. The important thing was for her to recover.

"And Dr. Benjamin said it went exceedingly well once the baby started coming," Whitby said. "That is something to be hopeful about. Perhaps next time will not be so bad."

Lily chuckled. "I thought *I* was the hopeful one in this family."

"Your hope must be contagious," he replied with a smile.

Lily sighed and closed her eyes for a moment beside her husband and son, then she turned her head on the pillow to face him more directly. "Is my mother here?"

"Yes. And you should know that while you were delivering, she was with me outside your door the whole time. She wept for you, Lily. She wept for a long time on my shoulder." Whitby gazed intently into her eyes, as if to make sure she understood what he was telling her.

More tears filled Lily's eyes and she began to cry, but they were tears of joy.

"Would you like me to ask her to come in?" Whitby asked.

Lily wiped the tears away and shook her head.

"No. I do want to see her very soon. But right now, I'm so tired. I just want to be with *you*. You're all I need."

He nodded and put his arm around her. He pulled her close and kissed the top of her head, and together, the three of them let their heavy eyelids fall closed as they snuggled on the warm, cozy bed.

"I've never been so happy," he whispered.

Then Lord and Lady Whitby rested quietly in the knowledge that there would be scores of other blissful moments just like this one—for many, many years to come.

Epilogue

Summer 1887

"**T**wo sons in two years. Very impressive, Lady Whitby."

Lily sat up on the plaid picnic blanket and raised a shoulder, batting her eyelashes at her husband. "What can I say? I have a gift."

Laughing, Whitby reached out and pulled her down for a kiss. He cupped the back of her head in his big hand, easing her down onto the blanket beneath him. "You do indeed."

Lily gave in as she always did to the erotic allure of her husband's lips—but only for a second that afternoon, for they had to keep their eyes on little Eddie, who was sitting in the grass not far away, playing with his toy train. Their newest son, James, only eight months old, was sleeping in his pram beside the blanket.

"You're an animal," she said to Whitby with a grin, playfully slapping him on the arm and pushing him off her. "We'll have three sons before long, if you keep that up."

She sat up again, and Whitby rolled over onto his back, crossing his long legs at the ankles and locking both hands together behind his head. "You like to make me wait, don't you?" he said teasingly.

"I'm just giving you something to look forward to."

"And I *will* look forward to it. Every delicious minute of it."

Lily kissed him again, then dug into the basket for the shortbread cookies, but looked up when Eddie rose to his feet and took off running.

Both Lily and Whitby scrambled to their feet.

"Come back here, you little monkey!" Whitby called out, catching up with Eddie and scooping him into his arms, swinging him high over his head.

Eddie screeched with delight while Lily looked on, laughing.

"Hide-seek!" Eddie shouted.

Whitby set him back down. "All right. I'll count. You and your mother go hide."

Lily took Eddie's tiny hand in hers and led him toward a tree, where they crouched down, facing each other behind the wide trunk. She knew Whitby would be able to see them plain as day, for her skirts were trailing out behind her.

Eddie giggled.

"Shh," she whispered, holding her finger to her lips. "He'll hear us."

Eddie crouched down into a ball, his tiny hand gripping her skirts, while Whitby hunted around in the clearing.

"Where could they be?" he said, loud enough for them to hear. "They must be over here."

She and Eddie giggled.

"Or perhaps they're over here behind the pram."

Eddie shook his head, giggling harder.

A moment later, Whitby jumped into view and said, "Found you!" startling Eddie, who screeched again and took off, laughing as he ran.

Lily stood up and brushed the leaves and grass from her skirt while she watched her husband catch Eddie and tickle him.

A gentle breeze blew from the south. She closed her eyes and tipped her face up toward the sky, basking in a calm, tranquil feeling of euphoria. She marvelled at the fact that she was so blessed with countless joys in her life. She had love, passion, and laughter, after living the greater part of her life without any of those things. Thank God she had found the courage to seek them, and had not given up.

A moment later, Eddie was running back to his toy train and Whitby was sauntering toward her, handsome and dishevelled in the afternoon sunlight, and marvelously seductive. She leaned back against the tree, anticipating his approach, yearning for his touch.

He reached her and rested both hands on her hips, then peered around the side of the tree trunk to see if Eddie was watching.

"He's playing with his train again," Whitby whispered. "Perhaps I'll steal a kiss from his mother while he's not looking?"

Lily smiled and took her husband's face in her hands. "You don't have to steal anything from me, Whitby. I'm yours, after all."

"And I will always be grateful for that," he replied in a soft voice, gazing with deep love and affection into her eyes, before he leaned down and touched his lips to hers.

Author's Note

The mysterious illness that afflicted Whitby and Lily was mononucleosis, also known as "the kissing disease," and it is easy to diagnose today with a simple blood test.

This was not the case in 1884. Though the illness has likely been around for centuries, it was not given its name "infectious mononucleosis" until 1920. Prior to that, the earliest description of a syndrome that might represent mono occurred in 1885, when a Russian pediatrician, N.F. Filatov, described an unusual case that characterized those symptoms. In 1889, a German physician, Emil Pfeiffer, described other similar cases that he called "glandular fever," and that term is still occasionally used to describe mono today.

At the time this story takes place, physicians would likely have included mono in a broad category of infections such as influenza or tuberculosis. Even today, it is estimated that only 20 percent of what we label the flu is actually the true influenza virus.

It's no surprise that mono was difficult to explain in earlier centuries, as its symptoms are somewhat dodgy.

First of all, the incubation period—which can last anywhere from a few weeks to a few months—made it difficult to determine when and how it was contracted.

Secondly, different people can experience different degrees of the illness, ranging from a mere sore throat that lasts a few days, to a more serious infection like Whitby and Lily had, which can linger for three to six months or even longer. With such a vast range of different symptoms for different people, it's no wonder it was a challenge to pinpoint and name the disease prior to the advent of more modern research methods.

Unfortunately for Whitby, the symptoms of mono greatly mimic those of Hodgkins disease, which had first been described by the British physician Thomas Hodgkin in 1832. In the late Victorian period, hereditary factors had in fact been considered a possible cause, though in most cases there was no explanation for its onset, as is the case today.

Biopsies were being performed, as there had been revolutionary developments in microbiology and laboratory investigation during the second half of the century, but there were unfortunately no effective treatments for Hodgkins. [Although in William Osler's book, *Principles and Practice of Medicine* (London, 1892), the author recommends removal of the glands when they are small and localized; he also suggests arsenic in increasing doses until "unpleasant effects are manifested."]

Though biopsies are considered minor procedures today, there was an ever-present risk of infection in 1884, although such risks had significantly declined by that time, thanks to the work of the British physician, Joseph Lister, who introduced disinfection to the hospital where he worked in Glasgow in the 1860s. He insisted that his wards and instruments be meticulously clean, and he used a variety of antiseptics, including carbolic acid. It's shocking to think that not long before that, doctors were performing autopsies on diseased corpses in hospitals, then delivering babies without washing their hands. (The fatality rate for hospital deliveries was far greater than that of home births with midwives, who of course did not attend autopsies before deliveries. Hence, women were constantly warned to avoid hospital deliveries whenever possible.)

Lister published his findings in 1867, and his methods were adapted all over the world. These developments were furthered when an American doctor, W.S. Halsted, initiated the use of sterile rubber gloves during operations in 1890.

In 1897, Lister was rewarded for his discoveries with a peerage, and he became the first doctor to sit in the House of Lords.

Regarding obstetrics, Lily's use of chloroform was true to the period, as Queen Victoria had used it for the delivery of two of her children. It was at that time that anesthesia became "fashionable" during labor.

Cesarian sections were also being performed in the nineteenth century, though they were considered a hopeless last resort, as English statistics collected between 1868 and 1879 revealed that only 18 percent of women who underwent the surgery actually survived. But in his book *Science and Practice of Midwifery* (London, 1884), physician W.S. Playfair suggested that those statistics were not reliable, as most of the operations included in the study had been performed when the patient was near death. He believed that if the cesarean section were performed sooner rather than later—before the patient became exhausted or impaired by a long and fruitless labor—its success rate would increase.

I based most of Dr. Benjamin's medical opinions on the writings of Dr. Playfair, who was, among other things, a professor of obstetric medicine at Kings College in England, and physician to the Duchess of Edinburgh.

I hope you enjoyed Whitby's and Lily's story, and

will visit my website at *www.juliannemaclean.com* for more information about Annabelle's book, which will be coming in 2006. Magnus will figure prominently in the story, and both he and Annabelle will finally face the issues that have affected both their lives.

Don't forget to stock up on these "school supplies" coming this September from Avon Romance...

Taming the Barbarian by Lois Greiman
An Avon Romantic Treasure

Fleurette Eddings, Lady Glendowne, craves adventure and passion. But she never dreamed she'd find it in the arms of a warrior from centuries past. Fleurette finds it hard to resist this sexy flesh and blood man, but she's been keeping a dark secret. Is Sir Hiltsglen there to seduce her—or to betray her?

Wanted: One Sexy Night by Judi McCoy
An Avon Contemporary Romance

Lucas Diamond is supposed to keep his eyes on the stars . . . not on the sensuous, impossibly perfect woman next door. Little does he know that Mira has an important mission to accomplish, one that will throw Lucas's whole universe out of whack. Because Mira is definitely out of this world—and Lucas is about to learn just how far out!

Still in My Heart by Kathryn Smith
An Avon Romance

Brahm Ryland, the most scandalous of the Ryland brothers, lost the one woman he truly loved, Lady Eleanor Durbane, to an idiotic mistake years ago. But when he receives an invitation to a shooting party at her home, he knows his opportunity to make amends has come at last. If only Eleanor will give him that second chance he's always dreamed of . . .

A Match Made in Scandal by Melody Thomas
An Avon Romance

Wealthy and successful Ryan Donally thought he'd gotten over his boyhood love for beautiful Rachel Bailey. But then one moment of unrestrained passion forces them into a marriage neither can afford—nor bear to give up . . .

Don't miss the next book by your favorite author.
Sign up now for AuthorTracker by visiting
www.AuthorTracker.com

REL 0805